MIDNIGHT SHADOWS

It happened so suddenly . . . the shadow of movement behind me and the hands at my back, pushing me brutally out onto the small balcony. I grabbed the wide stone balustrade which stood at waist level. As I turned to look back at the door, it slammed shut.

"No!" I stepped to the door. It was locked! I pressed my face against the glass, but the heavy curtains inside made it impossible to see the interior of the house.

The rain slashed across the house and balcony in heavy sheets. Within seconds I was soaked to the skin. The heavy drops were ice cold, propelled by the violent wind.

It was well after midnight and I was hopelessly locked outside in the raging storm with only the sheer walls of the house above and below me. . . .

CLARA WIMBERLY

MOONWATCH

ZEBRA BOOKS
KENSINGTON PUBLISHING CORP.

ZEBRA BOOKS

are published by

Kensington Publishing Corp.
475 Park Avenue South
New York, NY 10016

First printing: October, 1990

Printed in the United States of America

This book is dedicated with love and gratitude to my good friend Jeanne Turner for her never-ending encouragement, advice and support.

A special thanks to my own personal "family" of writers—the Byliners. And to Jan Powell and the members of the East Tennessee Romance Writers. All of you mean so much to me.

Prologue

The night winds from the Atlantic howled violently, like a thousand sirens crying from the sea. Sand stung the rider's face and neck as he rode swiftly from the dark outline of the house. He turned once to look behind him, certain he heard someone following him. But there was nothing there except the flapping of his coat and the long shadows cast by the lighthouse.

He could not rest until he was away from here, away from the guilt he felt for the deed he had done this night.

For a moment he felt a pang of shame and remorse when he thought of his daughter. His beautiful Victoria was safe and secure, sheltered by the respectability of Salem's fine school for young women. He had made the right choice by sending her away, he was certain of it now.

He had once hoped Victoria might come here, to Cape Fear, and the magnificent house known as Moonwatch, and even hoped she might marry Nicholas, his partner's son. But after tonight that would be an impossibility.

As Moonwatch fell away in the distance behind him, Anthony Ancona thought of how he would tell his daughter about all that had transpired in this house, all the anger and resentment that would now be turned against her.

He must warn her, lest the day ever come when he would be gone, unable to protect her. She must never come to this place, never be a part of the Hayne family. There were too many secrets here.

But even the picture of his beautiful daughter could not hold his thoughts for long. What he wanted now, more than anything, was to return to Ashford Place, to the woman he loved.

And when he would tell her what he had accomplished tonight, she would smile at him and open her soft arms to welcome him. Soon they would be far away where the Hayne family would never find them.

As the horse's hooves drummed across the sands toward the ferry landing, Anthony Ancona threw back his head and laughed, the sound rising across the mist-covered land eerily, as if a specter had just passed.

Chapter I

October, 1870
Cape Fear, North Carolina

My first glimpse of the house called Moonwatch occurred not by the light of a full moon, but through dense and swirling mists that rolled in from the ocean. So it was not a romantic vision bathed and flattered by moonlight that I saw, but a dark craggy structure moving in and out of focus as thick gray fog blew past it.

There was no train here from Wilmington and the carriage I had hired was slow and uncomfortable. By the time we crossed the ferry and made our way to this small jut of land that projected into the Atlantic Ocean, darkness was almost upon us. The driver stopped at the bottom of the sloping, sandy hill leading up to the house. We both looked silently at the structure above us. It sat like some giant bird, still and watchful upon its wind-ravaged perch. The man turned to me, his face grim as he peered through the window.

"You sure this be the place, miss?"

I pointed to a weathered sign beside the road. It swung in the stiff breeze, its rusty hinges protesting loudly in the cold October air.

"Moonwatch, it says. Yes, this must be the place," I told him.

I clasped my wool cloak more closely about me as I looked up toward our destination. I felt no eagerness at finally arriving, only sadness and a small twinge of fear.

Years ago, Father had written to me at school of this house and its occupants. He spoke with affection and trust. Recently, though, his letters held a certain trepidation, as if he wanted to warn me about something. Nothing definite had ever been said, leaving me to ponder his meaning. And now he was gone, killed in a tragic fire that swept suddenly through our home in Wilmington. I was alone now and here of all places, at Cape Fear and the house of which he had written—the house called Moonwatch.

It was hard to believe that only a few days ago I had been a carefree student, graduating from Salem's College for Young Women. As I thought of myself before receiving the message of my father's death, it was as if I were seeing a stranger.

I had been sent to Salem after my mother's death five years ago. I was fourteen then, and completely devastated by her sudden illness and death. The years at Salem had been good ones though, pleasant beyond my expectations. The school had become a home, comforting to me during my father's persistent absences.

Even now I was still childishly slim and had grown tall—taller than was fashionable. My thick curling dark brown hair was not as wiry and unmanageable as it had been when I was a girl, and I was aware that its gold highlights favorably accentuated my olive complexion. I had never considered myself an attractive young woman, wishing more than once for the petite blonde looks some of my friends possessed which always seemed popular with the young men. The few men who did notice me seemed intrigued mostly by my eyes which were gray and slanted catlike at the corners—like my mother's I had often been told when I was young. I could still remember Father teasing us both about our exotic feline eyes.

But even though I had not found a serious beau in sunny, bustling Salem, I had attained a certain comfort and security. There was no hint then, nor even a thought that I was about to enter into a world for which I was totally unprepared.

I don't think I shall ever forget the day Lawyer Jacobsen came to Salem to tell me about my father. It had been years since I'd seen him and he had hardly recognized me.

"Forgive me, Victoria—Miss Ancona, but you've grown into a lovely young lady." He was frowning as he lowered his eyes from my eager face.

"Is Father with you, Mr. Jacobsen?" I asked.

Recalling that day brought tears to my eyes. How I longed for the time prior to that, those precious moments before my existence was shattered once again and happiness seemingly expelled from my life forever.

"There's been a fire at Ashford Place . . . at your home in Wilmington. My dear, I'm afraid there's no easy way to tell you this—"

"What, Mr. Jacobsen? Tell me what?" My hands were cold as I reached out to clutch at his sleeves.

"Your father's dead, Miss Ancona."

The carriage jolted to a stop before the large stone house. The driver lifted down my trunk and handed me a large traveling bag. His expression made it clear that he was eager to deposit me and be on his way.

The slate gray walls of Moonwatch rose above me.

There, on the hill overlooking the sea, it seemed much higher than its three stories. It looked dark, vacant, and as the driver drove the carriage hastily down the hill, I felt frighteningly alone.

The letter from Captain Hayne's widow had been cordial. She had invited me to stay with them until my financial situation could be determined and I could, under calmer circumstances, decide what I would do and where I would live. Considering her kind invitation, I was puzzled that there was no one about to greet me upon my arrival.

It wasn't as if the Hayne family were strangers to me, not exactly. Although I had never actually met them, Captain Hayne was my father's business partner in the shipping trade. After the Captain's death in the War Between the States, his widow, Denise Hayne, inherited the business and continued the partnership. There was a son, Nicholas, of whom I knew little. I possessed no more information about them. Father had often told me that if he himself should die before my coming of age or my marriage, that arrangements had been made with the Haynes for my welfare.

I could not help but wonder as I stood alone before the foreboding building exactly what my father had in mind. His letters had always been formal, sometimes vague, but of late they rambled strangely and obliquely warned me of the Hayne family and the house at Cape Fear. When I wrote asking him to be more specific, my queries went unanswered—he either forgot or ignored my questions.

The mist-filled wind whistled about the house. Normally, it would have enlivened me, filled me with joy, for I loved being out in the fresh salt air. But tonight its sound only added to my apprehension.

I shook myself and lifted my skirts to step up the wide stone steps to the huge iron-hinged door.

Immediately there was a rustling in the bushes beside the stoop as a figure emerged in the gathering darkness to stand beside me. I could not help but gasp with surprise. I relaxed somewhat when I saw it was just a small boy, perhaps ten years of age, who stood looking at me.

"Who are you?" he demanded as he positioned himself before me, his hands defiantly on his hips.

The smile on his face irritated me for it was plain that he had intended to frighten me and had succeeded. I quickly determined he would not have that pleasure for long.

"I'm Victoria Ancona, and who are you?"

"My mother said you should not come here. She doesn't want you to marry Uncle Nick and neither do I!" His voice was hostile and as I looked more closely at him I could see his words held a genuine malice.

I stared at him in the flickering haze of the gaslight beside the doorway. His face was pale beneath a shock of dark curly hair. He was dressed plainly, not as one would expect a child of so wealthy a household as this. His dark eyes were rebellious, yet for all his defiance and rudeness there was something about him that touched me, made me want to comfort him and quiet his anger. I wondered why he seemed such an unhappy child.

"I do not know your Uncle Nicholas, so I can assure you I certainly have no intention of marrying him. Now, don't you think we should go inside?"

"You won't like it here, I promise you!" he yelled. Before I could stop him he grasped my cloak in his fist and jerked it cruelly as he ran past me. Only the tie at the neck of the garment kept it from being pulled from my shoulders. My throat stung where the silver clasp dug into my flesh and I cried out in pain and surprise. Never had I encountered such an angry and fractious child!

"What a very pleasant welcome," I said, watching him disappear into the darkening mist. I turned to the bleak, unfriendly door and rapped loudly.

As I waited at the entrance to the cold gray house I felt a strange uneasiness envelop me and I wanted to turn and run. But of course, I told myself, I could not do that . . . where would I go? I was only beginning to realize how little prepared I was for this. I had expected a warm welcome, but had the feeling I was entering a dark, frightening world of dreams.

The door opened and the unexpected brightness of the hallway blinded me for a moment. I could see three people before me. The light was behind them, though, and I could not clearly make out their faces. I entered the hall.

A woman stepped from behind the others. She held a lit glass lamp slightly above her as if to examine me. She was much shorter than I and dark, with large dark eyes. I estimated her age to be around thirty. Her hair was prematurely streaked with gray and dressed in a plain, almost severe fashion, pulled back tightly from her face.

I smiled and moved forward to greet her, but the look on her face stopped me. She was not an unattractive woman, but the hatred which masked her features made her appear ugly. The lamp flickered as a gust of wind blew into the hallway.

"Come in, please, and close the door," she said.

I reached behind me to shut the door as she had commanded. I did not take my eyes from her, though, studying her profile as she turned to set the lamp on a table. This had to be the boy's mother, the one who did not want me here. Who was she exactly? And why had she greeted me so rudely?

I focused then on the other two people there. One

was a tall man hidden partially in the shadows so that I could not fully see his face. The other, a rather attractive young woman, looked to be in her mid-twenties, though it was hard to tell her age. In the hallway the dim light gleamed upon hair that was a light brown. Although I could not make out the color of her eyes, I thought I saw there a glint of sympathy as her gaze held my own.

The cool greeting had left me speechless and I stood awkwardly, waiting for someone to speak. The man stepped forward into the light of the lamp. His smile and the sound of his deep voice instantly warmed me, making me feel as though sunshine had just broken through mist and fog.

"Victoria, welcome to our home. I'm Nicholas Hayne. I'm sorry for the circumstances that have brought you to us, but happy nonetheless that you are here."

He took my hand and I was completely spellbound by him. So compelling were his eyes that I could not stop looking at his face. I had surmised before he spoke that he must be Captain Hayne's son and heir, but never in my imaginings did I expect him to be as he was.

He was tall, much taller even than I, and his broad shoulders indicated that he was a man of athletic prowess, a man of action. He was dressed casually with a white shirt tucked into tan riding pants that clung snugly to his long muscular thighs. I caught a glimpse of burnished riding boots reaching almost to his knees.

I looked up into his dark eyes and the gaze that held my own was amused, almost challenging. I was glad that the poorly lit hallway hid my features, for my face stung with embarrassment. Without realizing it I had looked him over like some prized racehorse, from the top of his jet black hair to the tip of his shining boots. I was shocked at my boldness.

I pulled my hand from his. "Thank you. It was good of you to invite me."

As if he read my thoughts and felt my discomfort, he smiled, creating deep grooves in his face. The challenging look in his eyes disappeared.

The young brown-haired girl beside him made a small sound, a laugh, almost as if she were used to such reactions when women met this man. She caught my eye and gave me a faintly mocking, though not unkind nod. Then stepping forward she extended her hand to me in what I thought was a faintly masculine gesture. "My name is Lesley Adams, Miss Ancona."

"I'm sorry. I should have introduced you," Nicholas said. But even though his apology was smoothly made, I had the feeling that Miss Adams was not an intimate member of the family. I wondered what her relationship to them was, but did not feel confident enough to inquire.

"I hope you will excuse me, Victoria," Nicholas said, bowing slightly. "I must attend to some business matters. We'll talk after you've rested and had something to eat."

"Yes," I answered, still too distracted by these unusual people to know what to say.

He turned to go into a room just off the hallway. Miss Adams followed him and closed the door.

I was alone with the petite woman who so obviously did not want me here. "Did you happen to see a small boy outside when you came in?" she asked.

"Yes, I did. He ran off into the fog," I answered.

"That was my son Tad. I sent him to show you the way into the house. I hope he was not rude to you." Her eyes denied the statement, though, and she looked to be pleased at the prospect of her son's rudeness.

The idea of a mother who would encourage such behavior angered me. I was not about to give her the satisfaction of knowing he had frightened me.

"Why, no, he wasn't," I lied.

She looked at me oddly. "I'm glad to hear it, for if he's misbehaved he shall be punished."

"Oh, no," I said. "I assure you he did not bother me in the least."

"I'll show you to your room, Miss Ancona," she said abruptly.

"You are Captain Hayne's daughter?" I asked.

"Yes. I am Frances Canfield, Nicholas's older sister. My son and I have lived here since the war ended. I lost both my husband and father in that war." Her voice was bitter.

"I'm sorry," I said.

She turned slightly toward me and her eyes flashed disdainfully. "I don't need your pity, Miss Ancona."

"But I . . ." I stopped. It seemed nothing I said pleased her and I wondered why I even bothered trying to be pleasant.

"Mother wants to see you as soon as you've rested. But I must warn you—arthritis has crippled her badly and weakened her heart, although her mind remains as alert as ever. Just don't be surprised when you see her and be careful that you do not overtire her."

"Yes, of course," I answered.

I followed her up the stairs. It was there, in the light of the upper landing, that I glimpsed the rich red flash of her silk underskirt. The woman wore the black garments of widowhood, but could not resist a splash of color where no one else could see. It surprised me, yet I understood exactly how she must have felt. I was even more surprised that we shared this quality.

The upstairs hallway was cold and drafty. As we entered the bedroom that was to be mine, I was grateful for the fire that burned in the small grate. The fall air here at the ocean seemed damp and left me feeling chilled through and through. I felt immediately better once I was inside my room, yet all the same wished I had never come. I tried to remember specific things my father had told me about the Hayne family, but his words would not come. Even though I knew very little about them, in my desperation and loneliness after father's death, I simply turned to the first offering of help . . . and here I was.

After Frances Canfield left, I looked about the room. It was nice enough, though plain and simple. There were bright rag rugs on the bare wood floors and the large bed was covered with a handmade quilt of varied colors. I splashed water on my face and hands at the washstand and looked in the mirror above it. My face seemed pale and unfamiliar in the dark bonnet and cape which rose high upon my neck. How solemn I had become. A few weeks ago I would have laughed at the rudeness of someone like Frances Canfield and her son. Indeed, their quaint behavior was laughable, now that I reconsidered it.

I smiled then, life flickering again into my gray eyes, and instantly I felt more myself. I would determine exactly what financial situation Father had left me in, make some sort of arrangements about his partnership with the Hayne family, and leave this place.

If only Lawyer Jacobsen had been in charge of Father's finances, I never would have had to come here. I still did not understand why the matter was being handled by the company's law firm.

Perhaps it could all be settled quickly and I could return to Salem and accept the position as a teacher at my college as I had planned to do before all this happened.

I removed the bonnet and fluffed my dark curls

about my face. I wanted to change into something bright and becoming before meeting Mrs. Hayne. She was the lady of the house and the one who had asked me to come. Her welcome surely would be one of understanding and kindness, and would make Frances Canfield's rudeness retreat into the background.

I remembered then something Father had said about Denise Hayne. He said she had been the belle of North Carolina, a favorite with all the young men. He had spoken of her with affection as if he knew her well. I wondered as I sat looking out toward the fog-enshrouded sea, exactly what their relationship had been.

Chapter II

I changed into a dress of emerald green crepe which was delicately tucked around the hem. After I fastened the wide black sash about my waist, I felt more ready to meet Mrs. Hayne. If it had not been for the anxious pounding of my heart I would have felt entirely normal.

I pulled a chair near the large paned windows and watched as the bleak grayness of evening faded into ebony. I hoped tomorrow would be nicer for I had greatly anticipated seeing the ocean here at Cape Fear.

Soon one of the house servants brought a supper tray to me and left without speaking. I ate and put the dishes aside with still no word from Mrs. Hayne. The hour grew very late with the quiet evening stretching slowly toward midnight.

It was obvious that Mrs. Hayne would not receive me at this hour of night. I had just decided to go to bed when there was a soft tap at the door.

"Mother will see you now," Frances announced tersely.

"Oh, I had thought she would not since it is so late."

"She rarely sleeps throughout the night, usually for only an hour or two at a time. When she awoke, she asked for you." Her eyes flicked over me coldly, taking in the green crepe dress. She made no effort to disguise her ill will and I had no patience for trying to understand her reasons.

I followed Frances into the hallway and down a long corridor lined with what appeared to be ancestral portraits, lit at intervals by sconces. The candles flickered as we passed, casting shadows upon the walls.

At the end of the corridor three steps led to a small landing where the hallway turned and continued across the great house.

Frances Canfield opened a door and stood aside for me to enter. The room was large and brightly lit. The heat from a roaring fire surrounded me like a heavy woolen blanket and I wondered how anyone could breathe in such an atmosphere. Firelight glimmered on mahogany furniture and flickered upon cut-glass mirrors and candlesticks. The sultry air contained an odd blend of spicy perfume and the hint of medicine.

The small figure lying on the large canopied bed was almost lost in the fluffy lace-covered pillows surrounding her.

"Come closer, Victoria. Let me see your face," the soft voice said.

As I grew nearer I was captivated by the woman's piercing blue eyes. Her ivory skin and pale silvery hair seemed to blend together with the pillows and her eyes peered up at me as if from a snowy cave. She looked terribly frail and weak; her skin gleamed in the lights like fine cream-colored silk. Her hair was almost completely silver with only a few dark strands to show what once had been. For all her frailty she was still a handsome woman and I thought with a twinge of sadness how beautiful she must have been once and how strange that we must all come to this.

She stretched forth a thin, delicate hand, the fingers

curved and slightly deformed by her illness. She motioned me to a plush velvet-backed chair beside her bed. I waited self-consciously as she candidly studied my face. It was then I noticed the strange gown she wore. It was actually quite beautiful—a silk kimono of peacock blue and orange. It only seemed odd on the tiny colorless woman.

"You are quite lovely," she said, "although I had hoped you would look more like Anthony. You must be like her." Her words, almost an accusation, surprised me. There was nothing fragile or delicate about the voice that spoke to me now.

"My mother, you mean?" I asked. "You knew her?"

"No, I never knew her. She was not the social type, Anthony used to say. She preferred her home and garden and tending to her little family." Her words were tinged with sarcasm. "I always thought your father was too dynamic a man to be tied to some little country mouse!"

Her rude words angered me. "If you think she was that," I said, "then you definitely did not know my mother! And as for my father, if you were friends, you must have been aware of how much he adored her." I could feel my cheeks grow warm with anger.

She laughed. "You have at least the Ancona spirit! Good! Good!"

"On the contrary," I said coolly, "Father always told me I received my temperament from my mother." I could not keep myself from sparring with her.

Her face changed then, the blue eyes growing glacially cold and aloof. I could see I had angered her, but at the moment I was annoyed and I forgot Frances's warning not to upset her.

"You, young lady, need a good dose of discipline, and if you were my daughter, I would see you got just that!"

I stood up. "Mrs. Hayne, I'm sorry if I seem rude. But you must understand I have been on my own for several years now and I am therefore accustomed to speaking my mind, perhaps more than other girls my age. As for my mother . . . I have never heard anyone speak ill of Anna Ancona. She was a wonderful mother to me and a loving wife to my father. I will not sit here and have you, or anyone, speak insultingly of her!" I turned to leave the room when I heard her gasp.

I looked back at her. Her blue eyes were the color of icicles and her pale skin was flushed with anger. Her fleshless hand clutched the front of the brilliant kimono and she seemed to be having trouble breathing.

"What is it? What shall I do?" I asked. What had I done? What if my anger and obstinate way of speaking caused the death of this tiny old woman?

"Nicholas . . ." she gasped. "His room . . . two doors from you . . . Get Nicky!"

I ran from the room, leaving the door open behind me. I could hear the sound of my own heart pounding in my ears as I ran down the hall.

I stopped, gasping for breath, hardly aware of my fist beating against the wood of the door.

"Please, God," I whispered. "Don't let her die!"

Nicholas Hayne swung the door open quickly, his eyes surprised as he frowned at me. "What's wrong? Is it Mother?"

"Yes, she's . . . There's something wrong. Please come."

But he was already past me, his long legs striding toward the landing. He took the steps in a single hurdle and burst into the perfumed room.

He went quickly to her, as if he had done this many times before. She was lying back now, still struggling for breath. Her eyes darted about desperately. Seeing her son calmed her somewhat. He pulled her gently forward until she was sitting up.

"Hand me that bottle," he demanded, pointing to a dark green medicine bottle on the night table next to me.

I handed it to him, along with a spoon. He did not take the utensil, but instead held the opened bottle beneath her nose. The scent of camphor and eucalyptus drifted toward me. There was another scent I could not identify—some unusual, exotic aroma that was strong, almost overpowering.

"It's all right now, Mother. Breathe deeply, slowly. That's it. . . . Slowly . . . slowly." He coached her as he lifted her shoulders gently and rhythmically in time with her labored breathing.

I stood on the opposite side of the bed from him, feeling helpless and unable to assist him. Finally Mrs. Hayne's breathing became slower, her eyes less frantic. She took a long shuddering breath and lay back weakly against the pillow.

My legs trembled as I sat down heavily in the chair next to the bed. "I'm so sorry. . . ."

Nicholas Hayne looked up from where he stood beside his mother. The force of his gaze stunned me. In that strange interlude I saw that his eyes were not black as I had first thought, but a deep blue, the color of cobalt.

"What did you say to her?" The voice I had thought so kind, that had warmed me upon my arrival, was now hard and accusatory.

I opened my mouth, but words would not come. I could only stare into those penetrating blue depths, my limbs still trembling from the fright of what had just happened.

"Answer me, dammit!" he said between clenched teeth.

"No, Nicholas," his mother said, placing her hand on

his arm. "It was not Victoria's fault. I became choked on some tea and lost my breath, that's all. I'm fine now."

His shoulders relaxed, but the muscles in his jaw still tensed with anger. It was obvious he did not believe her.

"You should try to rest now," he said, finally looking away from me and back to his mother.

"No, I need to speak with Victoria—only for a few moments, then I promise I'll rest."

He stood for a moment, looking as if he might deny her wish, then he bent to kiss her. As he straightened, his eyes again caught mine and I saw in their depths a silent warning. At that moment I knew, despite his earlier cordiality, that Nicholas Hayne was not a man one would want for an enemy.

After he had left us, Denise Hayne smiled at me as though nothing had happened. There was a look about her, a smugness and a determination that I had missed before. I felt she was actually gloating over her son's devotion.

"May I get you something, Mrs. Hayne . . . some tea? I'm truly sorry that I caused you to become so disturbed," I said.

"Nonsense, child. It was not your fault. Oh, the doctor insists that emotions often trigger the attacks, but I for one refuse to believe it. As you can see, I'm a woman completely in control of my feelings."

I smiled at her, wondering if she really believed what she had just said.

"You spoke your mind, just as I've always done. Never apologize for that." Then she laughed. "It's just that you aren't exactly as I had imagined," she added.

"Oh?"

"I had thought—hoped for a quiet, obedient girl. Someone more . . . pliable."

"And why does it matter to you what I am? As soon as the legal arrangements are made, we probably will never see one another again," I said.

The look she directed at me then chilled me and her words brought back the feeling I'd had earlier of being in a dream world.

"Oh, my dear Victoria, you will never leave Moonwatch. You might as well know that I invited you here for my own selfish reasons. I want you to marry my son." She paused expectantly.

"What?"

"Ancona and Hayne Shipping has been almost in ruins since the war and it cannot survive without your share of the partnership. Your marriage to Nicholas, my dear, will enable us all to continue in our present custom. Surely you can see the practicality of it?"

"Marry . . . Nicholas?" I leapt from the chair. "Are you insane? Is everyone in this house insane? I have never heard of anything so preposterous!"

"Don't be foolish girl!" she laughed. "You must realize you will have nothing if you don't do as I say. None of us shall. Together we can prosper, but alone, we will fail. What if I tell you you have no choice?" She smiled smugly at me.

"Oh, I assure you I have a choice!" I said. "Even if what you say about the business is true, why can't you simply allow me to continue on in my father's name?"

"It's not as simple as that. Do you seriously think that you, a naive schoolgirl, could partner such a business as Ancona and Hayne?" she scoffed.

"I could learn. I could—"

"No, it won't do! Besides, I want an heir! I want the blood of Anthony Ancona and John Hayne merged to continue the dynasty. It's what your father wanted for you!" Her pale eyes blazed with intensity and I began to think the woman was demented.

"*You* want an heir? I cannot believe this! Your son does not seem the kind of man to enter into such a bizarre arrangement!"

"Nicholas is a man of his own mind, that's true. But I doubt even he would deny his *dying* mother's wish." She laughed then, a mocking, derisive sound.

"Dying? You would do such a thing to your own son? What kind of person are you?" I looked at her in disbelief, then turned toward the door. I paused at the foot of her bed. "I won't do it! I will never marry a man I do not love. Money or not, I'll manage alone! I will be leaving Moonwatch first thing tomorrow morning."

"Come back here, Victoria! Your spirit is beginning to become tiresome!" Her voice was cold and commanding as if she were used to being obeyed, but I did not hesitate as I walked toward the open doorway.

Suddenly, a huge figure emerged from the shadows of the hallway, blocking my way. He stood silently before me, arms across his massive chest, his skin black as the night.

He wore the rough garb of a sailor. Fastened to a wide belt about his waist was a broad sword. I'd seen his kind many times before, on the docks where Father sometimes took me as a child.

"No, Ona," Mrs. Hayne said quietly. "Let her go."

The man stepped aside, but I could feel his black eyes upon me as I hurried down the hall. Once inside my room I fell shaking onto the bed. What in heaven's name had I gotten myself into by coming here? Was this what my father had been trying to warn me about?

I lay on the bed for a long while wondering what I should do. I had learned long ago to survive on my own, and I soon began to feel the stubborn determination return. Mrs. Hayne had underestimated me if she thought me to be a naive, helpless girl. I would not be kept here against my will. Even if I had to walk I would leave this house tomorrow morning and never come back!

Quiet, tree-lined Salem never seemed so inviting as it did to me that night.

Chapter III

I did not relish spending the night in that house, in that quiet, shadowy room. I tried to focus on the next day and my leavetaking. I counted the hours left as I lay awake listening to the strange whispering noises of the house and the rustle of wind outside my window.

It had been a long, tiring day, though, and before I knew it I slept, dreaming that angry people surrounded me, pointing, accusing me. I saw myself walking up a narrow curving stairway. As I ascended, I became enveloped in a cold, swirling cloud. Before me in the mist stood Nicholas Hayne, beckoning to me, his dark blue eyes silently urging me to come to him. I could not seem to help myself as I moved toward him. From somewhere in the wind I heard the voice of my father pleading with me not to go, telling me to beware. But I did not stop, could not make myself stop. Some strangely familiar feeling within urged me to continue. The mist grew thicker. As I reached out to the dark handsome man before me, he disappeared, his laughter ringing through my head. I looked down and saw that I was standing on the edge of a stone abutment, high above the ocean. I could hear the sound of the waves as they crashed far below me. As the ledge beneath my feet began to crumble, I could not move, could not save myself. I cried out for my father but he was no longer there.

Far away I heard the sound of a woman's crying . . . a pathetic, mewling noise. I sat up in bed trembling, my heart thudding against my breast as I gasped for air. A sickening awareness washed over me as I realized the sobs had been my own.

"It was only a dream . . . only a dream," I told myself. The coverlet had become entangled about me and I surmised that that must have been the reason for the dream and the feeling of being choked by the mists. Perhaps, I reasoned, the sight of the tall house had triggered the dream, for I had always been terrified of heights. I breathed a sigh of relief as I saw that the room was filled with the dim light of dawn. I got up and walked to the window.

I could not seem to banish the vision of Nicholas Hayne from my mind. His face in the dream had been beautiful . . . irresistible as he beckoned me to him.

I shook the image from my mind and looked out the window. The sight of the ocean stretching out before me fairly took my breath away. The mists had cleared and the tinge of pink and gold in the east was a comforting spectacle. How flat and calm was the sea now, so different from the evening before . . . and my dream. Moonwatch was much less ominous by daylight and I felt the terrors of the night begin to fade away.

A sound outside my door caused me to turn, a quiet, shuffling noise. I threw on a robe and reached for the door handle. I was determined not to allow myself to be intimidated by these people any longer. I opened the door just in time to catch a glimpse of a small figure dashing into the next room.

There before my door lay a large brown spider, its

huge hairy legs spread about as if preparing to leap off the floor. How I hated spiders! I reached back into the bedroom to a table beside the door, never taking my eyes from the horrid creature. I groped for something—anything—with which to kill it. My hand closed around a book and without conscious thought I dropped its heavy weight flatly on the spider. Shuddering, I pushed the book and the squashed insect aside and walked quickly to the room where I'd seen the boy disappear.

He wasn't hiding from me. On the contrary, he stood defiantly before me, an angry, accusing look on his small face.

"You killed my spider! You didn't have to kill it!" he shouted. He was still wearing the clothes he'd worn the night before and his hair was tousled and uncombed.

"What did you expect me to do, Tad, invite him in?" I asked.

"Why weren't you afraid? Most girls hate spiders!"

I didn't intend to let him know that I was certainly included in that majority, lest he be tempted to bring another of his "pets" to my room.

"Is that why you put it there before my door, then? To frighten me?"

"I don't want you to stay here. I don't want you to marry Uncle Nick!"

I wondered what they had been telling the boy, or, more likely, what he had overheard as he lurked silently about the house. It was apparent to me that he had little supervision and was left alone to wander as he pleased. Remembering my own lonely childhood, I felt a twinge of sympathy for him.

"But I told you before, Tad, you don't need to worry about that. I have no intention of remaining here and certainly no intention of marrying your Uncle Nicholas."

"But he likes you. Mother said so. She said he thinks you're at . . . at . . . attractive."

I stared at the boy, silently chiding myself for the pleasure that swept through me on hearing his words.

"That does not mean he would want to marry me," I said.

"I hope not! Besides, you're probably a thief, just like your father!" he blurted angrily.

"Whatever do you mean?" I asked, grabbing his arm as he tried to rush past me.

I looked up to see Frances Canfield standing in the doorway, her eyes horrified at seeing my grip on her son. "Miss Ancona! Let him go at once!" To Tad she said, "Tad, please go to the kitchen and have Cook find something for your breakfast."

Tad left obediently, but not before turning to give me a look of bitter disgust.

Frances Canfield stood before me, challenging me to argue with her, it seemed. This morning she wore a white lace collar over another dark unattractive dress. The collar was at least flattering to her complexion and her silver-streaked hair. But her displeasure at seeing me was still there and she did nothing to try and disguise it.

"If you stay at Moonwatch, I'm afraid I cannot keep Tad from frightening you," she warned.

"I was not frightened of the boy and as I told your mother last night, I will not be staying." I deliberately kept my voice cool as I spoke to her.

She regarded me imperiously, a mocking smile on her face as if she did not believe me. But there was also a sense of relief in the look she gave me.

"Your son just accused my father of being a thief. What did he mean by that?"

She did not seem surprised at my question and did not bother denying my words. "No doubt he was speaking of the Ching tê chên pagoda," she said coolly. "It was brought from China years ago on Father's first sailing trip there. The porcelain is worth a small fortune. It is one of a kind, trimmed in diamonds and emeralds. And my son was correct . . . Anthony Ancona stole it from us! Unfortunately, he died before it could be regained and it is probably lost to us forever!"

"You are mistaken, surely. My father was not a thief! You cannot really believe he would steal from his partner and oldest friend?"

"How very little you know of your father!" Her eyes blazed at me as she grasped her bustled skirt and swept from the room.

"Wait!" But it was too late; she was gone with no further explanation.

What a cold, hateful woman she was. No wonder Tad seemed so angry and defensive. He probably received very little love or gentleness from his mother. Still, I could not simply overlook their accusations. I walked to the window in the guest bedroom, which had the same spectacular view as my own, and I mused on what had just transpired.

Below me I saw a man walking on the beach. Even from this distance there was no mistaking Nicholas Hayne or the masculinity of his long-legged stride. I knew little about men, having been quite sheltered from them, except for my father before he abandoned me at school. He himself had been a gentle, loving man, eternally patient and kind.

I sensed the man on the beach was nothing like my father. Oh, he had been kind enough to me upon my arrival. Yet when he had looked at me in his mother's room last night, I sensed a shadow of something in his eyes, some dark unspoken danger. No, I doubted there was any true gentleness in him and I shuddered at the thought of a forced marriage.

I went back to my own room and began to pack when a knock sounded at the door. It was Ona, his massive size filling the entire doorway.

"Mistress Hayne asks you to come, please."

His voice was a deep rumble, compatible in every way with his enormity.

"I'm preparing to leave," I said.

"You will come, please," he said, not moving from the spot inside my doorway.

Under the circumstances, there was nothing I could do but obey.

Denise Hayne's room also seemed different this morning. It was bright with sunlight and the exotic, spicy scent still lingered pleasantly in the air. Mrs. Hayne was seated in a chair by the window. She indicated that I sit across from her in the other velvet chair.

"I was watching my son down on the beach." She looked at me slyly as she spoke. "He is a handsome man, even you will admit that?"

"Yes . . . I suppose," I said.

"One of the servants thought we had a prowler last night. Nicholas is looking for clues as to who it might have been." She looked at me pointedly, as if she expected me to ask about it. When I said nothing she motioned for Ona.

As if knowing what she wanted, he silently wheeled a teacart between us.

"I hoped you would have breakfast with me, Victoria."

"Well, I—"

"Can't leaving wait?" she asked. Her voice today was all too solicitous and pleading. "Surely you can spare a few moments so we might decide what to do about our . . . partnership?"

Was she indicating she had had a change of mind and would now allow me to take my father's place? I nodded, knowing it would be in my best interest to have it settled now. I never wanted to have to return to this house again.

Ona served us from the cart. The delicate gold-rimmed plates were exquisite; the simple meal of baked fruit and hot buttered bread was well prepared and appetizing. The large black man poured our tea in a surprisingly nimble manner. Then he walked to the door and stood, still and silent, eyes looking straight in front of him. I watched him curiously from the corner of my eye. What a strange combination these two made.

"You're wondering how it is that a well-bred lady of my years would choose such a companion . . . a black man like Ona?" she asked.

"Well, yes, I suppose I was."

"Captain Hayne brought him home from the islands . . . one called Jamaica. There had been an epidemic of smallpox among the natives and Ona's entire family died. The men on ship almost mutinied when John carried the poor sick boy aboard. He was not infected with the disease, but was almost dead of malnutrition. But he grew strong again and well, rarely leaving my husband's side from then on. His illness and the fever left him slowly. Ona is loyal and good, much gentler than he appears. But we are his family now and he sometimes tends to be overly protective and we are the same with him. I can understand, though, why you might find that strange."

I glanced at Ona and wondered if he heard or understood what she was saying. It was almost as if he were in a trance.

"Breakfast was delicious, Mrs. Hayne. Thank you," I said, rising to go.

"I thought you might be uncomfortable having breakfast with the others. I hope you will overlook my daughter's behavior. The loss of her husband has left her embittered and old before her time. She was not always that way. I had hoped she would recover, but . . ." She sighed and shrugged her thin shoulders. "Have you met Miss Adams? Now there's a pleasant, intelligent woman with whom you might be friends."

"I met her briefly when I arrived," I said.

"Nicholas, of course, runs the business, but I don't know how we ever managed without Lesley. Our accounting system was sadly lacking before she came. She seems perfectly content living out here on the coast, away from the city and people her own age. But she's quite ambitious really for a woman, and has set herself the task of learning every aspect of our business. As a matter of fact, it was your father who recommended her for the position."

"Oh?" I was surprised for I'd never heard Father mention the young woman. But then perhaps he'd only met her after I went away to school.

"Why yes, they seemed to be quite *intimate* friends," she added, looking curiously at me.

"My father did not communicate with me often the past few years, so I really wouldn't know."

Her eyes were sympathetic as she watched me. "I hoped I might persuade you this morning to stay . . . just for a few days until we've become better acquainted and can reach some sort of agreement."

"I don't think so. I really must leave today."

"Please, my dear, humor a sick old woman. What difference could a few days make to one as young and full of life as yourself?"

There was a softness about her then; I wanted to think an affection. At that moment she reminded me so much of my mother that I found myself swayed by her words, even though I suspected she had no compunction about using her illness to get what she wanted.

"Mrs. Hayne, I'll be perfectly honest with you. I have no intention of marrying Nicholas, or anyone for that matter."

"I think you made that clear enough last night," she said with a sparkle in her eye. "You will stay a few days longer?"

"Only if we drop the subject of marriage," I said.

She laughed. "Of course, not that I wouldn't be delighted to see my son captivated by you. And I believe with your spirit and intelligence you could be just the one to do it. I'm afraid Nicholas has been a pursued bachelor too long and has grown content with his ability to seduce any woman he wants. You might be just the girl to tame him."

Her words about his ability to seduce sent a small chill through me. And the thought of a *tamed* Nicholas Hayne was hard to imagine . . . but intriguing.

I shook my head as much to clear my thoughts as anything. "No," I said. "I think not."

"All right. I will not pressure you again about the marriage. But you will stay?"

"Only for a few days, until we clear up the details of the business."

"Ona, you may take the cart now." She took my hands in her long thin ones. "I'm so happy. I want to get to know Anthony's daughter better."

I did not feel any easier about staying at Moonwatch, and was not at all sure I'd made the right decision. Since I'd told her I would stay, though, it would give me the chance to explore the unusual house and find out more about my father's relationship with this family.

I left Denise Hayne's room and walked downstairs.

Frances and Lesley Adams were in the entryway, talking quietly. As I descended the stairs Frances turned and walked up past me. Her eyebrows were arched and she stared straight ahead, not bothering to acknowledge my presence.

Miss Adams stood watching, a small quirk upon her lips.

"Why does she dislike me so?" I asked. "She does not even know me."

"I imagine it is because of your father," she said unpretentiously. "She's extremely loyal to her mother and anyone opposing her is automatically disliked. She feels your father wronged this family."

Her voice was quiet and soft, as one who had been trained in the best schools. But earlier I thought I detected a slight accent of some kind. There was, however, not a trace of it now.

"Because of the pagoda?" I asked.

"Why don't we go into the study where we can talk privately, Miss Ancona," she said, pointing toward the room where she and Nicholas had gone last night.

A few weeks ago, I could have taken this woman at face value, and trusted her with no uncertainty. I judged her to be near Nicholas's age, twenty-eight perhaps, although I had thought before she was younger. She was not a beauty, with her round face and inconspicuous brown hair and eyes. But I could not help noticing that beneath her tailored, unfeminine clothing was quite a voluptuous figure, with a shapely bust and a small narrow waist. I wondered just where she fit into the picture here and what her relationship with Nicholas might be, whether it was business or otherwise.

I had not realized I was staring until she smiled knowingly at me. "I can almost read your mind, Miss Ancona. Was there something you wanted to say?"

"Oh, I . . . no." She had taken me by surprise and I hoped that she had not actually guessed what I was thinking.

But she walked into the study ahead of me, quickly dismissing my protests.

The room was small, but elegantly furnished. I guessed that much of the beautiful brass-trimmed mahogany furniture in the house had come via Ancona and Hayne Shipping, much as the objects in our own household had. I could remember Mother's excitement over the boxes which would accompany Father when he came home from one of his trips.

I was surprised at the feminine touches in Lesley Adams's office for she did not seem the type. Her desk was gracefully and ornately carved from beautiful rosewood. Upon the desk sat a Wedgwood letter holder in rose and cream. The lighted hurricane lamp gave off a pink glow through its rose glass shade.

"What a lovely room," I exclaimed. It was obvious that I found this surprising.

Sitting before the fire in the lovely, cozy room I began to relax for the first time. I felt quite at home here and felt a surge of gratitude for Lesley's kindness. Perhaps Mrs. Hayne was right; perhaps Lesley was a person with whom I could be friends.

Chapter IV

Lesley Adams sat opposite me in a small tufted rocker. Her look was inquiring, dryly questioning. I thought I had seen sympathy in her look before, but now I wasn't sure.

She smiled. "What would you like to know about our strange household? How can I help you?"

Although I was concerned and curious about many things here at Moonwatch, the thing uppermost in my mind were the accusations against my father. Without hesitancy, I told her. As she watched me, her face was expressionless.

"Mrs. Hayne told me you were recommended for this position by my father."

"Yes, that's right. Your father was most kind to me and I could be no less so with his daughter."

Still, she did not mention the Ching tê chên pagoda.

"Do you believe he was a thief?" I asked, watching her face closely.

"No, of course not. Anthony was a good and decent man. But . . . the piece *did* disappear from the locked cabinet in the parlor the night he was here."

"Was he ever confronted with this?"

"Unfortunately he died that night." She turned her

head slightly as if she did not want me to see the pain on her face. "I'm sorry I can't help you more."

"You have helped me just by listening. It's good to know that someone here in this house cared about Father."

"I have heard of Mrs. Hayne's plans for you—your marriage to her son." The grief was replaced with curiosity, her eyes now alive and sparkling.

"I cannot believe anyone would still think to arrange a marriage for their son or daughter. And as I've told almost everyone in this house, I've no intention of marrying Nicholas Hayne."

"Ah, but does he know that?" she smiled. "I'm told he's quite irresistible."

"I . . . Why no, we haven't discussed it and I doubt very much we ever will!" But I could not hide the blush that burned my cheeks, that seemed to persist every time someone mentioned the subject of my marriage to Nicholas.

"Then you are not as clever as I thought you to be, certainly not as clever as Anthony, for he never missed the opportunity to acquire a new treasure." She leaned from her chair and took a small gold case from a nearby table. I watched, fascinated, as she removed from it a long brown cigarillo which she placed between her lips. She lit the end and took a long, deep breath. If she intended to shock me, she did not, although I certainly had never before seen a woman smoke.

"Treasure?" I asked. "I believe I can manage very well without the finances of Ancona and Hayne if I have to. I shan't be wealthy, but I will manage," I answered firmly.

She laughed aloud then and blew a trail of aromatic smoke into the air.

"The treasure to which I refer, Miss Ancona, is not

money. Are you so naive that you do not know what I mean?"

I was caught off guard by her comment and her evident desire to discuss Nicholas in a more personal way.

"And what is there about him, Miss Adams, that I would find so valuable?"

She smiled with a lift of her brows, like a child who has gotten its way.

"Why everything, my dear . . . everything! Not the least of which is his handsomeness, but of course you've already taken note of that." She paused only slightly as I looked away from her. Of course she had seen me look at him so blatantly last night upon my arrival. It was something I wanted to forget.

"And then there is the power that he uses so well. There is nothing more appealing to a woman, I think, than power. Especially when it rests so easily upon one as it does Nicholas. He's brilliant, creative, ambitious, strong, persistent . . . why, I could go on all day." Her look was derisive, filled with mischief.

"Yes, I'm sure," I answered dryly, "but I was wondering—"

"What?" she interrupted.

"Other qualities—kindness, gentleness—does he possess them?" I stopped, smiling at her, challenging her.

She laughed again, the sound ringing in the small room.

"Very good, Miss Ancona." She leaned forward upon the desk, seeming to relish the good-natured sparring between us.

"But you realize, of course, that only very young and very naive girls really care about such things. A grown woman would prefer being overwhelmed by a man like Nicholas, gentle or not. She would not take a great stallion and reduce him to a mere gelding." She looked at me pointedly, still intent on shocking me, it seemed.

And I was uncomfortable, for I had not expected the bantering to go so far. Her face had changed. It was no longer teasing, but instead there was a defiance there in the lift of her brows and the flare of her nostrils.

I ignored her last reference to Nicholas Hayne and pressed further about the lost pagoda.

"Please, can you tell me nothing more about the pagoda? I don't want to leave here until I have cleared my father of this accusation."

She sighed, evidently preferring to talk more of Nicholas. "I only know that it was acquired in China on one of the *Galatea*'s first journeys."

"My father's ship?" I asked.

"Yes, it was one of his greatest designs and one of his last. Both Captain Hayne and Anthony were aboard for that trip. And both claimed to be the owner of the pagoda. It was worth a small fortune, even then, and is certainly worth much more now. But Captain Hayne kept it here at Moonwatch. No one, not even Denise, was allowed to take it from its locked case. But the night your father came here, the same night he died, it disappeared."

"They think he broke into the case . . . here in their own home?"

"It would not have been difficult to do. The doors have double layers of glass, but the lock was nothing exceptional. It had been pried open with some kind of sharp instrument. It would not have taken long and the noise would not have been noticed."

"So you think Father took it then, that night?" It sounded too incredible to be true.

"It's not what I think, but, yes, the family here seems to be in agreement that he took it then. After all, he often claimed the captain had stolen it from him. And there was a tremendous quarrel that night between him and Mrs. Hayne, after which he stormed out of the house. It was the last time I . . . we ever saw him." She sighed and looked away from me, but not before I saw the glitter of tears in her brown eyes. She certainly seemed to be a very changeable person.

"But if he took it with him, was it not recovered in the house? The fire, I understand, did not destroy everything." It was difficult still to discuss the accident that had taken place at our home.

"It could very well be there," she said. "Of course the Haynes would not go there and search for it. You, on the other hand, could." The tears were gone now and provocation filled her eyes.

"Perhaps I shall. And if I find it, won't that put Frances Canfield in a huff?" I said, almost to myself.

"I would not concern myself with Frances. She is all bark. She carries absolutely no authority here, or in the business, which is perhaps one of the reasons she is so bitter. And then she has always been of the opinion that Moonwatch and Cape Fear is the turning point of the world. She cannot tolerate outsiders, anyone who disturbs her narrow vision."

I could see that part of what she said was true. Frances did seem to resent outsiders. I believed, though, that her dislike of me was more personal.

"Yes, I can see that," I said. "Frances seems so different from Nicholas, even from her mother."

"Well, I don't mean to gossip, but Frances is treated very differently by her mother. Mrs. Hayne seems much less tolerant of her daughter than she is of Nicholas. But that, of course, is probably because Mrs. Hayne has always preferred the advice and company of men to that of women."

"Well, yes . . ."

"And you realize that Frances would be left very

little if Nicholas should marry and have an heir. As it is, Tad is now the one who would carry on the Hayne traditions and I'm sure that's as she wishes."

Lesley took another deep breath of the cigarillo and smiled that strange enigmatic little smile. "I hope we can be friends, Victoria."

"Yes, so do I," I answered. "I'd like that very much. . . . Heaven knows I could use one in this house."

At the moment I didn't mind whether her warmth was sympathy or genuine friendship. I only knew it felt good to be regarded with a little kindness.

"As I told you, your father was my friend and I could not rest if I didn't offer you a helping hand. If at any time you need me during your stay here, you've only to ask."

"Thank you, Lesley."

For the first time I caught a hint of sweetness and softness in her which made me feel infinitely better. Even though she was only an employee of the Hayne family, I was glad for an ally.

There was no one in the hall when I left Lesley's office, so I slipped quietly out the front door. I wanted to get a better look at the house and its environs.

Father once told me that Captain Hayne set the house here on the jut of land so that he would always be able to see the Atlantic Ocean. He wanted to know that anytime he chose he could sail across that wide stormy expanse to another world. He even built a tower onto the stone house and used it as a lighthouse. The captain liked watching the moon and stars from there, thus dubbing his home Moonwatch. I had always been fascinated by the name, even as I was now by actually seeing it.

I walked down the pathway between the stubby, stunted patches of grass and tall rustling spires of sea oats. I turned and looked back up at the structure. The house was large and rambling with several different levels and cupolas. The gray mansion was certainly imposing, though not classically beautiful. At the north end the tower stood, tall and round with narrow windows at different intervals, probably at each turn of the interior stairway. There were two separate levels of multi-paned glass windows which went all the way around the top of the tower. The irregular stonework and spires at the top of the roof reminded me of a medieval castle. At almost every corner of the house and on the rounded lighthouse crouched taloned gargoyles and winged animals that peered menacingly down at me. I shivered and turned away to watch the crashing waves upon the beach.

Watching the ocean fascinated me. I never grew tired of its changing colors and moods. And always, as now, when I was filled with many questions and thoughts, I could watch the sea and let everything fall away. That is what I missed most in the gentle inland hills of Salem.

When I watched the sea I often thought of Lord Byron's words:

> There is pleasure in the pathless woods,
> There is rapture in the lonely shore,
> There is society, where naught intrudes,
> By the deep sea, and music in its roar.

Cape Fear lay on a strange, uneasy part of the Atlantic, rough and storm tossed. It was the area of hundreds of shipwrecks; a graveyard of ships, some called it. I could almost feel the ferocious undertow as the waves crashed rhythmically. As a small girl I was always frightened by the power of the ocean and its great unknown depths. I think Father was a little disappointed in me for that, since I was to be his only child. I still was not enthusiastic about sailing, although I had to admit that now the sea held a certain terrifying fascination for me, with an almost hypnotic quality.

And now that fascination somehow included Nicholas Hayne and his unusual home. I had to stay here long enough to rid myself of that spell and to find out what happened to the precious pagoda. I had to stay, even as some small voice within urged me to go.

Chapter V

Turning back toward the house I caught the flicker of movement above me. I looked quickly toward the windows of the lighthouse. Someone had been there watching me, I was sure of it. I had caught the flash of white as they moved back out of sight.

I did not like the disquieting feeling it gave me knowing I was being watched. What did the watcher imagine I was going to do that would be so interesting to see? And I was certain I was the object of his scrutiny, otherwise why would he step back out of vision? If he thought to frighten me away somehow, he was in for a surprise. At that idea, stubbornness filled me with more bravery than I might normally have felt.

The wind whistled coldly about my skirts so I did not venture down to the beach. I walked back into the house just as Nicholas came down the stairs and we faced each other at the bottom. Could he have been the one in the lighthouse just now? He was wearing a white shirt which was open at the throat to expose a portion of tanned skin. But I didn't think he was the kind of person to skulk about, hiding his actions from anyone. No, I expected he would do as he pleased regardless of what I saw or thought. If he had been in the lighthouse he would have met my look boldly and defiantly; he would not have bothered stepping away from the window.

Here in the light of day he was even more handsome than he had appeared last night. He had the look of a man who knew his worth, and his attraction to women. For some reason I was irritated by his charisma. And as everyone always told me, I could never hide my feelings."

"Good day, Victoria," he said, smiling at me.

I looked up at him skeptically, wondering at his change from last night. He had been fiercely angry with me when he thought I had caused his mother's attack.

Seeing my look he said, "I wanted to talk to you . . . to apologize if I was too harsh last night."

"No, it's quite all right," I said coolly. "I should not have upset Mrs. Hayne." I was not going to lie to him and deny that I had caused her attack.

"I worry about her . . . and I was upset. But I was unduly rude and I hope you will forgive me."

"It's forgiven," I said, smiling shyly at him. How could I not forgive him when his look was so appealing and so sincere?

"What do you think of Moonwatch and our view of the mighty Atlantic?" he asked.

"Your home is quite beautiful, in its own special way," I said. "And I've long been acquainted with the Atlantic."

"Yes, of course, although I understand the ocean is not your favorite place," he added with a sardonic lift of his eyebrow.

"And how would you know that?" I did not try to hide my irritation. Surely Father had not discussed me in such detail with a man who did not even know me.

"Your father spoke of you often. He was concerned about you, that's all." He frowned and seemed puzzled by my abrupt question.

"Yes, wasn't he?" I answered slowly. Something made me want to argue with him, deny the words he spoke about my father. Didn't anyone here realize how he had abandoned me and how much it hurt?

"So concerned that he left me for five years at Salem with barely a word." I had never expressed my bitterness to anyone and I immediately regretted my words. I rarely discussed my most private feelings with anyone, not even close friends. So, why, of all people, did I say anything to this man, a virtual stranger?

"Under the circumstances, I think perhaps it was best," he replied. He watched me carefully, his dark blue eyes reflecting genuine interest.

"What circumstances do you mean? Everyone here seems to think they know more about my father than I do!"

"Victoria, your father was a good man. He treated me like a son. But he was a man with weaknesses just like anyone. He really believed you would be better off away at school. But I can see that's made you very angry and bitter." He stepped forward as if to touch me, comfort me, but I moved away, shaking with anger.

I knew only that I must get away from him, before I said more than I wanted, before his kindness persuaded me to let down the guard I had so carefully erected over the years.

He moved in front of me. I did not look up to face him. I was confused and felt out of control. What was wrong with me that I was being so foolishly emotional?

When he spoke, his voice was low, caressing and soothing me. "You have nothing to fear from me, Victoria. I only want to help you. Even if I had not promised Anthony that I'd take care of you, I would still want to do that. Can you not trust me only a little?"

"He asked you . . . to take care of me? When?"

I asked.

"Several months ago actually, but . . ."

"Why don't you hate him . . . like everyone else here seems to?" My mouth trembled slightly as I stared at him defiantly.

He took a deep breath. His eyes were kind as he looked at me. "Victoria . . . I loved your father. He was more to me than a friend and nothing he could do would make me hate him."

His words and the sweet way he said them made the tears come finally that I'd been trying to hide. I looked up into his handsome face, at the curve of his mouth. I knew it would be so easy to let him take care of me, to fall into his arms and let him comfort me. I was so tired of being alone, trying to be strong, without tenderness or understanding. And now that it was offered so sweetly, the appeal of it frightened me and the powerful feeling Nicholas stirred within troubled me.

"I wish you could help, but you can't," I mumbled, the words coming stiffly from between my teeth. "If I could make you understand . . ."

"I want to understand . . . but you have to help me, Victoria," he urged, placing his fingers under my chin, tilting my face upward toward him.

But I had already begun to rebuild the shield about me. I could not trust too soon and risk making a fool of myself with a man I hardly knew.

"All right," he said, seeing my closed look. "I won't pressure you now. But we should talk about this later . . . whenever you're ready. Can you at least agree to talk to me about your future soon?"

I could not look away from his eyes that were so expressive and warm. In my young life I'd never been exposed to a man such as he, one whose masculine appeal was so overpowering. Yes, I wanted to shout. But that voice of caution within warned me to proceed slowly and not to trust too soon. I would only be hurt again, perhaps abandoned again. And instinctively I knew I could never survive the loss of such a man as Nicholas Hayne.

"Yes," I said, keeping my voice cool and detached, betraying none of the turmoil he instilled within me. "I will agree to talk about it later."

"Good." He watched me as I walked hurriedly up the stairs. I trembled, unaware of why he affected me so.

I almost ran down the hallway to my room. The day had been filled with such emotion for me, and conversations were now crowding my mind with confusion. I only wanted to shut myself away for awhile in the quiet and privacy of my bedroom.

Once inside I quickly locked the door and splashed cool water into the wash basin. Slowly washing my face and hands I allowed the soapy lavender fragrance to soothe me.

I wanted to undress and lie in the darkened room, to think about all I'd heard today. And I needed to decide how to go about clearing Father of the ridiculous charges made against him by the people in this house.

I removed my gray wool skirt, leaving on the gray-striped petticoat and white cotton blouse. As I reached out to turn down the bed quilt, I saw a bit of color underneath the pillow. Remembering Tad's spider I jumped away from the bed instinctively. I could feel the hammering of my heart at my throat. But the object did not move and as I looked more closely I could see it was a vibrant green color. I lifted the pillow slowly away from the bed.

"What on earth . . . ?"

Underneath the pillow lay a small doll made shabbily of cloth, its arms and legs tacked on in an unskilled, haphazard way. But it was not the doll itself that sent cold prickles up the back of my neck. Its head was covered with dark wiry hair; tied about its body was a piece of emerald green material, remarkably similar to the crepe dress I had worn last night. The doll had no face. It had been charred, leaving only a round black hole in the material. The stench of smoke rose toward me and I felt suddenly ill. If this were another of Tad's deeds, he was a very disturbed little boy.

I dropped the doll on the bed and ran to the tall wardrobe where my clothes hung. The emerald dress was there, cool and undisturbed. Pulling it from the closet I threw it across the end of the bed and frantically ran my hands over the yards of material. It seemed intact.

Still holding the dress I sat down on the bed. My hands were trembling badly as I clasped them together. Again I felt the urge to run, to leave this place and never come back. But I knew I must force myself to think, not feel.

"Think, Victoria, think," I kept telling myself. "What is the message here?"

I picked up the doll again, turning it over in my hand. The material was the same I was certain of it. But had it come from my dress? Was the doll supposed to be me? And the hair—it looked so real. I went to the mirror, feverishly examining my hair. I looked down at the hairbrush—was that the source? Had someone come into my room, taking hair from the brush?

I turned back to the dress crumpled on the floor, and picked it up. It was then that I saw the rust-colored stain on the inside of the hem. As I turned it over, I knew that someone wanted to make sure I saw what had been done. A small piece of material on the inside of the hem had been torn away and around it were several small carmine-colored dots. They looked like dried blood. I threw the dress away from me and stepped back.

"Think, Victoria. Don't let your emotions rule you." I could almost hear my father's voice saying those words to me as he had when I was a girl.

I looked again at the doll. It was shoddily made, but not childishly so. I could not believe Tad had gone to such elaborate lengths to frighten me. But if not Tad, then who? And was there some special meaning to the doll's charred face?

Suddenly I remembered where I had seen dolls such as this one. Once when I was a little girl, my parents had taken me to the market stalls along Pinckney Street in Charleston. We'd shopped and laughed all day as we strolled among the colorful vendors, looking at the items for sale. I could still see the black women, their hair tied up in bright scarves, weaving their baskets of palmetto and swamp grass.

That was where I'd first seen the dolls. An old woman sat quietly outside the market, a basket at her side filled with small cloth dolls, dolls covered in bright calico, dolls with no faces. I'd been fascinated and bent automatically as a child will do to clutch one in my hand, looking up toward Father, smiling, for I knew he would buy it for me.

Instead he snapped, "No, Victoria, put that down!"

"But Father, I want a doll," I pleaded, surprised by his denial.

The old woman smiled at him. "Buy the little missy a doll, Captain Ancona?" Her mouth was toothless and slack-jawed as she looked at him.

He did not answer her, but instead took me by the hand and led me away, with Mother following behind as puzzled as I by his behavior.

After walking rapidly for at least a block, Mother gasped, "Anthony! For heaven's sake. Can we stop for a moment to catch our breath?"

We were nearing St. Phillip's Church, with its tall

white steeple rising above us. The black iron gate was open and the white marble benches scattered about underneath large magnolia trees looked cool and inviting.

Father laughed uneasily and tried to dismiss his odd behavior. "Here, why don't you two beautiful ladies rest in the shade while I bring us some refreshing ices?" With that he walked across the street to a vendor.

I looked up at Mother. She was watching him, a look of worry on her smooth, olive-skinned face.

She put an arm about my shoulder. "Never mind, dear. You may buy a doll some other time . . . a more beautiful one."

"But I've never seen dolls like those."

"Yes, I know. But Father is a superstitious man, darling, and he would never allow you to have a voodoo doll. He would be frightened for your safety."

"What is voodoo?" I asked.

"A kind of witchcraft, dear. The doll was made by the old Gullah woman. Her people live on an island off the coast and it's rumored that they practice this kind of witchcraft. They use dolls similar to those we saw to cast spells or to punish someone. It's said they can even cause a person's death." As warm as the day, I can remember that my mother shivered. "I don't really know much about it, but it sounds most repulsive," she added. As she spoke, her gray eyes searched anxiously among the passersby for Father.

Soon he came, carrying three colorful raspberry ices. We sat in the cool churchyard and ate, and he acted as if nothing had happened. The sea breeze carried with it the sweet scent of the tea olives and I soon forgot about the cloth dolls. Father was again the happy, the jolly father I knew.

The subject of the doll never arose again. Instead, I had quite forgotten it until today as I looked at the one in my hand.

"Gullah," I mused.

Was voodoo practiced in Jamaica, the island from which Ona came? The image of the huge, silent man lurking about in my room caused me to shudder.

Still, I had to consider the other possibilities. The doll might not be authentic. Anyone could make such a simple toy—certainly Frances Canfield or her son. And even though I did not want to admit it even to myself, I knew that Nicholas spent a lot of time in Charleston and would have access to the Gullah traders.

Suddenly the room where I had sought comfort seemed threatening. The crash of the waves outside and the constant winds seemed to whisper to me like human voices. The sound was ominous and frightening.

I checked the door to make sure it was locked. And even though it was mid-afternoon, I lit one of the lamps for solace. I had to think what I should do now.

My head pounded miserably and my body ached with renewed tension. I hid the doll in the bottom drawer of the dresser, underneath my chemises, then I returned the emerald dress to the wardrobe.

I lay on the bed and glanced about the unfamiliar room. I could hear the sounds of those in the house, an occasional voice or footstep in the hallway.

And I could not stop my mind from turning over the events of my stay at Moonwatch again and again.

Why was Denise Hayne so anxious for me to marry into the family? Had Nicholas intended to mention the marriage to me this afternoon? Surely that wasn't his wish any more than mine . . . to be married to a stranger.

Only the thought of Lesley Adams comforted me. For surely she was one I could trust if for no other reason than the fact that she cared for my father . . . a relationship I was not yet ready to delve into.

But I could wait. Something told me I should show the doll to no one, not even Lesley. Perhaps the only reason for its presence here was to frighten me and if I said nothing, chances were that whoever was trying to scare me would not bother me again.

With that thought in mind I soon drifted off to sleep, awakening only when one of the servants knocked on my door much later.

"Miss Ancona. Dinner in one hour."

Chapter VI

By the time I'd dressed for dinner I had convinced myself that the doll was merely a ploy to frighten me away from Moonwatch. And I was more determined than ever that I would not go until I had solved the mystery of the missing pagoda and returned it to its rightful place in the locked cabinet downstairs.

I glanced in the mirror and saw a person I almost did not recognize. There was no young, frightened girl looking back at me, but a confident, mature young woman. My dark hair was gathered back at the sides and uplifted in the back so that tumbles of curls fell from the top of my head to my shoulders. My cheeks were flushed, but not unpleasantly so. My soft blue cashmere dress, shirred at the upper arms, left my neck and shoulders bare. The color made my eyes look more blue than gray and that pleased me. The skirt that was trimmed in matching blue quilled ribbon was soft and full. I knew I looked well and I felt confident, ready to face any adversary.

I had thought much of Nicholas's words to me this afternoon. He had seemed so kind and genuinely concerned for my well being. How much easier it would be for me if I knew I could trust him, place myself in his charge. But even if I were unsure of his sincerity, I could not deny that I was looking forward to seeing him again.

Dinner turned out to be surprisingly pleasant. Frances and her son, although not exactly friendly to me, were nonetheless not openly antagonistic. I watched the boy from time to time to see if perhaps he might show any evidence of having played another trick on me, but there was nothing. He was extremely well behaved for once.

Denise Hayne was present and the towering Ona close behind her. As I looked at her from the corner of my eye, I was surprised at how well she looked.

She had been watching me all evening, a polite smile upon her lips. "You look lovely tonight, Victoria," she said loud enough for everyone to hear.

Nicholas was sitting at the head of the table and I could sense his dark azure eyes upon me as his mother complimented me. He looked very elegant and distinguished, his dark jacket enhanced by a steel gray satin waistcoat and immaculate white ruffled shirt. I had been watching him discreetly as he spoke quietly to Lesley Adams, who was seated on his left.

Lesley was dressed plainly, almost dowdily, as if she wished to disguise the curvaceousness of her figure. As I watched the two of them my breath caught in my throat. Nicholas, with his high cheekbones and straight, aristocratic nose, the curved sensual lips, was not a man any woman could ignore. But even as my thoughts strayed in that direction I caught the look in Lesley's eyes as she laughed with him, and I was stunned. In that look was avid hunger . . . greedy and searching. It was so private a look that I quickly turned my eyes away and down to the food before me.

I could not hide my discomfort from Mrs. Hayne. "Aren't you hungry, dear?" she asked. I could feel her gaze upon me, studying me closely.

"I . . . no, I suppose I'm not."

"My son is very handsome tonight, don't you agree?" she whispered.

"Yes," I muttered, not looking back at him. "He is."

"Miss Adams's attraction to him is inconsequential, I can assure you," she smiled, keeping her voice low so that no one else could hear.

"I . . . I had not noticed," I lied. "And, of course, it's none of my business."

She laughed gaily like a young girl. "You're lying, of course, but in this case, I'm quite delighted. You can be honest with me, my girl. I can see how much it bothers you, seeing them together. When you're alone tonight, why not ask yourself why that is." Her voice was bantering, but in a quiet, more friendly way.

I was more than ready to change the subject. I did not want to think about why her son disturbed me so.

"Mrs. Hayne . . . I would like to go to Wilmington tomorrow. Would it be possible for me to borrow a carriage and a driver?"

"Of course you may. Everything here is at your disposal. You need not even ask, although I would like to know where you go, for your own safety."

I hesitated a moment, sensing her concern. "I . . . I would like to see the house."

"I see . . ." she said, seeming to study my words. "I was afraid of that. Do you think that is wise?" she asked. "Going there alone could be a very frightening and painful experience."

"I prefer to go alone. And you might as well know I intend to find out what I can about the pagoda and my father's role, if any, in its disappearance. I will never believe he was the one who took it, but I must know."

She sighed. "You are stubbornly loyal . . . like your mother I'm sure. So tiresome. But I suppose you must find out for yourself. So I will not oppose you on this; however, I do wish you would allow someone to accompany you. I could send Ona with you."

"No," I insisted. "It's something I must do. Besides, I'm sure I will be able to find some of the house servants to help me. I understand only a small portion of the house was burned."

"Yes," she said. "I believe that is true." She looked now toward Nicholas and I realized he had been listening to us all along. He had made no attempt, though, to interfere or to enter the conversation. "Very well then. You must tell me what you find . . . if anything. Ona, I would like to return to my room now."

The black man stepped forward to wheel her chair away. I looked straight up into his face. His black eyes were cold and unemotional, but there was a flicker of something else there . . . distrust perhaps, or a warning? I could not be sure what he intended to convey, if anything, but I watched him thoughtfully as they left the room.

Without my being aware of it, Nicholas had come to stand beside me. His hand touched my elbow, sending my head reeling.

"It's early. Would you like to walk outside for some fresh air? The winds usually die down in the evening," he said.

Unconsciously, I looked across the table. Lesley still stood there, and a smile flickered across her face as she observed us. She arched her eyebrow at me, in a mocking, but not unfriendly way. Our earlier conversation flashed into my mind, making me feel more self-conscious than ever. I smiled at her, and acknowledged that I knew what she was thinking.

Nicholas followed my look and as he gazed at Lesley, a small frown furrowed his brow. As if she'd been dismissed, she smiled and turned to go without a word to either of us.

In the entryway Nicholas reached to the hall tree and lifted a cape from one of the ivory hooks, and placed it about my shoulders. "October nights can be quite cold here at Moonwatch," he said.

My skin tingled where his hand touched me and I did not look up into his blue eyes.

Once outside we soon walked from the shadows of the great house toward the beach. It was dusk and the sun's last rays shimmered upon the top story of the house, turning the gray stones into muted gold. The fierce wind had died somewhat, but the breeze was still brisk against my skin. I felt invigorated by the wind and by being outside, delightfully aware of all my senses and, I had to admit, of the man beside me.

"Did you find the prowler?" I asked.

He looked at me thoughtfully. "How did you know there was a prowler?"

"I saw you on the beach. When I had breakfast with your mother she mentioned there had been someone about last night."

"There was no one. Probably just a drunken sailor wandering down the beach. You need not concern yourself about it." But I had the feeling he was not telling me the whole truth of the matter. Perhaps he was afraid it might frighten me.

We stood on the beach, silently looking out to sea. The view was an unforgettable sight, one to memorize and keep forever. The ocean murmured gently, its waves moving rhythmically in and out, bringing a calm, a peace to everything.

We both stood as if hypnotized, drinking in the beauty before us. Nicholas's face was serene and I could see how very much he loved the ocean. It was easy imagining him at the helm of a tall ship, riding the powerful waves with mastery and defiance.

I continued to watch him as I spoke, "Perhaps the prowler was for my benefit," I said. "I believe someone here is trying to frighten me away. Do you know anyone who would want to do that?"

He turned to me, the calm gone from his face. "What do you mean?" He had not attempted to deny what I'd said and I felt a certain gratitude for that. And the concern in his eyes was genuine, I was sure of that.

"I found a doll under my pillow this afternoon. A Gullah doll, I believe." I described the doll to him and explained how my emerald dress had been torn and splattered with the rust-colored dots.

"And you don't think it was Tad?" he asked.

"No, I really don't believe it was."

He walked away from me and looked out toward the sea, then back toward the house.

"Victoria, listen to me. I don't like the sound of this. And to be perfectly honest, I'm as puzzled as you. But I think we should take it seriously. If someone is trying to frighten you away, as you say, then perhaps it might be best if you did return to Salem."

"No!" I said, looking at him in surprise. "I'm staying here until I find the pagoda or at least what happened to it. If my leaving is exactly what this person wants then I shall not give them the satisfaction of thinking they've succeeded."

"Don't be so stubbornly foolish, lass," he warned, his dark eyes glittering at me in the growing darkness.

We stood facing each other warily, two enemies almost. His eyes wandered over my face to my hair blowing wildly about my cheeks, then down to my lips. His eyes darkened as he gazed down at me. I almost gasped at the powerful emotion surging between us so suddenly and so unexpectedly.

"You are the strangest sort of girl, Victoria," he said

quietly. Slowly his head came down toward me until his mouth was upon mine, warm . . . softly shocking me with its touch, its intimate searching.

I was lost as his lips explored and gently moved against my own. I had never felt this before, this exquisite fire singing through my veins, sparking such odd excitement deep within me. I never dreamed I could feel this way about any man and certainly not Nicholas Hayne.

When he pulled away from me I felt drugged. My lips felt warm from his kiss, my eyes languid and heavy. He held me tenderly against the length of his body.

"Why, little Victoria, such a prim and proper schoolgirl," he teased. "Be careful you do not bewitch me." He held me away from him, smiling down into my eyes as he spoke.

As I looked at him, I knew I did not want to talk, or to banter about what I was feeling. "Nicholas," I whispered, reaching for his lips once more. I felt strangely like someone else, as if this were not really happening to me. And if my actions were perceived as bold or wanton, I did not care. All I wanted was to be close to him.

He pulled away, only momentarily, looking with surprise at me, but his mouth met mine again, hungrily, smothering my moans as his kisses became deeper and more desperate. I was frightened, trembling at what would happen next, but I would not try to stop it. Whatever this mystery was between a man and woman I was suddenly more than willing to learn.

"No, Victoria," he said finally, gently holding me away from him.

I felt as if all the light had left the earth as he continued to keep me at arm's length. Only then did I begin to feel the embarrassment of my actions. He was a stranger to me and yet I had thrown myself at him, practically begging for his love. Had this place and this man bewitched me as well?

My face felt warm as I pulled away from him, away from his touch so that I might think more reasonably. But even then I could not truly distance myself from him, could not loosen myself from his spell.

"I . . . I'm sorry," I managed to stammer. "I've never done this . . . never felt this way before . . ."

"Shhh," he whispered, his fingers warm against my lips. "I know . . . do you think I don't know that?"

He pulled me gently back into his arms and I clung to him, never wanting him to let me go. I was strangely aware that the ocean, the wind, and the sky had all fallen away from us and we were alone, only the two of us, it seemed, in the huge beautiful universe. And even though I lacked experience in such things, I knew instinctively that this was how it should be between a man and a woman, a husband and wife. It was the first time I'd let myself admit it . . . I wanted to be his wife, probably had since the first time I saw him. Had it not been for Mrs. Hayne's suggestion and everyone's remarks, I would have recognized it then instead of trying so hard to deny it.

I felt no apprehension that I had known him only a few hours, or that I was rushing into something that Denise Hayne wanted so desperately. For then I did not relate her desperation to her son's actions. Nor did it ever occur to me that my father's neglect and now his death had left me alone and starved for affection.

I was young. And I only knew that I was hopelessly, desperately drunk with love for Nicholas Hayne.

Chapter VII

But Nicholas did not mention marriage, nor did he speak about the business partnership as I had expected him to. Instead he turned and directed me back toward the house.

The night about us was black, the only light being those from Moonwatch and the distant glitter of stars above us. I noticed the bright beam of light from the lighthouse as it shone brightly out into the night, toward the ocean's horizon.

"You still keep the lighthouse?" I asked awkwardly, not knowing what to say in the silence between us, wondering why he had grown so quiet.

"Yes, Ona tends the light now. I think somehow in the simplicity of his thinking he hopes my father will return and he wants to be sure the light is always there."

"How very sad."

We were at the house before Nicholas spoke again. His silence disturbed me. Had my passionate reaction to his kiss bothered him . . . displeased him in some way? I wanted desperately to know, to speak to him about it, but I could not bring myself to say the words.

Just before we went in Nicholas looked up once more to the lighthouse. "I'll take you up there one day and show you how the light works. The refracting prisms and glass rings are quite beautiful."

"Yes, I'd like that," I murmured.

"You might even spot a ship far out in the ocean," he added. His voice was warm when he spoke as if nothing was wrong, but still I sensed he was troubled by something.

The house was quiet when we entered, with only a light shining beneath the door of Lesley's office. I saw Nicholas's quick glance in that direction. Then he put his hand upon my waist and guided me up the stairs.

We stopped at my door and I turned to face him. A spark of pleasure ran through me as he pulled me against him, close and warm again within his embrace. It was where I belonged . . . I knew it. But was it really possible to fall in love in such a short time?

I wanted his kiss, wanted to rekindle the exquisite fire I'd felt before, still felt deep within, that waited only for his touch to ignite.

But he kissed me softly on the forehead as if I were a sister. When I made a small sound of protest, he smiled. "Victoria . . . I shouldn't have let this happen," he said.

"But why?"

He sighed, leaning his head back to look upward. "You're so young . . . you're father has just died. I don't want to take advantage of your position . . . your vulnerability."

"No," I protested. "You're not. You—"

"No, listen to me!" he said almost angrily now. "I'm responsible for you now, and I want you to be happy and secure. This was not what I had intended." He looked away from me, pulling back out of my reach.

"Nicholas . . ."

"Goodnight, angel," he whispered. "Sleep well."

I could hardly keep myself from following him, pleading, crying, begging . . . anything to be in his arms again. What had I done wrong? And how could he lead me into such delightful, intoxicating emotions and then tell me it was not right?

My bed had been turned down and a lamp glowed cheerily on a nearby table. The curtains had been drawn, giving the room a cozy, sheltered ambiance. I locked the door and quickly searched for any sign of disturbance. But my mind was elsewhere and the doll seemed far away and insignificant now.

Denise Hayne's earlier words came to mind. She had said it bothered me, seeing Lesley and Nicholas together and asked me to question myself as to why that might be. I had not been willing to admit it to her then . . . nor even to myself. But here, in the solitude of my room, with only the vision of blue eyes before me, I knew I could no longer deny it, could no longer push away the disturbing attraction I felt for Nicholas.

I should have slept well for it had been an exhausting day, filled with wringing emotions. But I was consumed by a restlessness that I did not understand and did not know how to banish.

I woke the next morning feeling little rested. But somehow, as the dawning of a new day has the power to refresh and revitalize, I was filled with optimism and eagerness to be up and about.

I dressed with care, not because I was going to Wilmington, but because of Nicholas, for I had to admit I wanted to look my best for him. I planned to leave immediately after breakfast so I carried my dark green wool cape with me and my new black jockey hat with its jaunty plume of emerald feathers.

I could not help but smile as I entered the dining room, expecting to see Nicholas and to be in his magnetic presence.

"My, but aren't we happy this morning?" Frances Canfield's voice taunted emptily in the room. She looked at me languidly as she bit into a piece of toast, and smirked at my glance about the room.

"Nicholas has already eaten," she said.

"Yes, I see." It was too late to hide my disappointment from her prying eyes.

But she only smiled smugly. I had not fooled her for an instant. I wondered how she knew of my newfound feelings for her brother. Had she seen . . . had he told her? The thought of their discussing me, perhaps mocking me, assailed my thoughts and without another word I whirled to leave the room.

"In case you're wondering, he's gone to Charleston . . . with Lesley. Business, I believe," she simpered.

I stopped, stung by her words and her insinuation. She laughed, pleased I was sure, to have inflicted doubt and pain within me. I lifted my chin and marched steadily out of her sight and outside to the carriage that waited at the front steps.

It was late afternoon when we arrived on the outskirts of Wilmington. I had thought of little else than Nicholas on the trip. He had not even mentioned to me last night that he was leaving this morning. Had not even bothered telling me good-bye.

"This be it, miss." The driver's voice abruptly brought me back to reality. I had not even realized we sat before Ashford Place. My childhood home had been lost to me these past five years and I'd often longed to see it. But now there was no feeling of homecoming, only sadness for this was where I had so painfully said good-bye to my dying mother and now where my father had died. I shivered, feeling uneasy and apprehensive about what I would have to face inside.

Father had built the place for his bride, his lovely Lady Ashford, and had named it after her ancestral home in Sussex, England.

As I stood for a moment watching the delicate afternoon sunlight play across the front of the house I thought of how very much I had missed it. I had forgotten how beautiful it was. And there was no visible evidence of the fire on the outside at least.

Ashford Place was a three-story house built in the Adams style with Carolina gray brick laid in Flemish bond. The tiled roof sloped down to a long porch across the front which was supported by large fluted columns. At each end of the house were bowed piazzas with large glass windows. The formal English gardens surrounding the house were still kept beautifully and were filled now with mounds of colorful chrysanthemums and marigolds. Set among the flowers were oleander, azaleas, and jessamine. The scent of camellias and tea olives filled the air, almost overpowering in their honeyed aroma, and bringing a pang of bittersweet memories to me.

I walked up the long brick walkway and no sooner had my foot stepped upon the porch, than the large door swung open.

I stepped forward expectantly, thinking to see Samuel, the black man who had been with our family as long as I could remember. Instead, the man who greeted me was a stranger. His dark eyes were almost level with mine and his stocky, muscular frame seemed to fill the doorway. I could only guess at his age, probably forty, certainly much younger than our Sam. His swarthy complexion contrasted oddly with his pale sun-streaked hair. He had the look of a corsair, and surely did not seem to fit the part of a majordomo.

"Welcome home, Miss Ancona," he said. He did not smile, but his voice was friendly and pleasant enough.

"Thank you. You are?"

"Roberts, miss . . . Eric Roberts." He stood aside and swept a brawny arm toward the entry hall.

"Where's Samuel?" I stopped in the entryway as I spoke.

"I'm sure I do not know, miss," he answered coolly.

"But . . . how long have you been here?"

"I came shortly after your father's death. I should like to offer my condolences, miss."

"Since his death? But . . . how? Who hired you?"

"I was already employed at the shipyard of Ancona and Hayne. I transferred here at Mr. Hayne's request."

"Nicholas Hayne?" Why, I wondered, would Nicholas take it upon himself to hire someone in my home?

Then the man stepped into the lights from the doorway and I could see that he was not as old as I had first thought. His dark face was heavily lined, as if from years in the sun, but he could not be more than thirty-five.

"Yes, miss. Would you like something to drink, a rest perhaps before your inspection?"

Eric Roberts watched me, probably noting the tug of memories which my face reflected. He seemed cool, but not entirely unsympathetic.

"No . . . I . . . nothing right now. How did you know I was coming?"

"A telegram from the law firm, miss," he replied.

"Mr. Jacobsen?"

"No, miss. Ashley Brooks is the lawyer."

"But . . . I'm not familiar with the name. Has Mr. Jacobsen taken a partner?"

"Mr. Brooks works for the shipping company."

"The shipping . . . ? Ancona and Hayne, you mean?"

He lowered his eyes as I stared at him.

"That's correct."

"I see. That will be all for now, Roberts."

He seemed surprised at my dismissal and not at all anxious to go. Perhaps he intended to dog my steps all day. To report my findings to his employer? He walked down the long hallway toward the back of the house.

"Roberts?"

"Yes?" he said, turning toward me.

"Where are the other servants?"

"They've been dismissed, miss, except for Cook and a cleaning maid. The gardener comes once a week."

"Dismissed by Ashley Brooks?" I sighed, knowing the answer before I asked.

"Yes, miss, there was no need for such a large staff after your father—"

"Yes, I see. Thank you then."

I was completely baffled as to Nicholas's motives and the company's involvement. Surely they did not have the legal right to do this. As Father's only child I was the rightful heir and this house had nothing to do with the shipping company. I could not believe no one had mentioned this to me before I left Moonwatch. Mrs. Hayne, although discouraging, had certainly not warned me of this. And even Lesley had challenged me to come here and search for the pagoda. Had she known about this? I had to believe she did.

I was so distracted that I had not noticed the faint acrid scent of smoke which still lingered in the cool, silent house. I stood now in the hallway and let the familiarity of the house jog my long hidden memories to life. Nothing had been changed and there was much to remind me of the happy years we'd once had here, when there was just the three of us.

Mother's prized Elfe gate-legged table still stood in the same place in the hallway. There were always fresh flowers on it, just as there was now. Although the house had obviously been kept up I could see by the lack of changes that Father's heart had left the house with my mother.

I removed my cape and hat and took a long deep breath. Seeing the room where Father died would be hard, but I had no choice but to do it. I did not expect what I found when I opened the door.

The room was filled with new, unfamiliar furniture and new paneling. There was no visible damage. The study had already been completely redone. The only clue as to what happened in the room was the odor of newly painted wood mingled slightly with smoke.

"What on earth . . ." I turned, stalking back to the hallway.

"Roberts!"

The dark muscular man appeared almost instantaneously as if he'd been lurking nearby all along.

"Miss?"

"I suppose Ancona and Hayne's lawyer was also responsible for the renovation of the study?" My voice trembled with anger and frustration.

"Yes, miss."

"On whose authority was this done?"

For the first time the look of arrogance left his face and he did not meet my eyes.

"I can't really say, miss."

"You can't? You mean you won't!"

"Can't. It was done before I came."

"Then I take it this was done immediately after the fire?"

"Yes, I think so."

"I understand that some items were salvaged from that room. Where would they be?" I was becoming more and more impatient with him, having to drag every response from his lips.

"I'm not at liberty to say."

"Not at—!" I was shaking now with anger. I wanted to strangle the man with my bare hands. I could feel the blood rush hotly to my face as I stood before the haughty stranger who dared to challenge me in my own home.

All the frustration I'd been feeling for the past few days seemed to gather within my breast and I wanted to scream at the man. But I said quietly between clenched teeth, "Let's understand something between us, Roberts. This is my home and any possession of my father now belongs to me! I will not have an employee stand before me blantantly telling me it's none of my business!"

"That was not my intention, Miss An—"

"Do not interrupt until I am finished! Whatever is going on in this house I shall find out for myself and neither you nor the Haynes nor anyone else will prevent that! Do you understand me?"

By now the cook and cleaning maid stood gaping through the kitchen door, wondering no doubt what the shouting was about.

"Yes, Miss Ancona, of course," he said. His voice was quiet enough, but the muscle in his jaw twitched with anger and his already dark skin was crimson.

"Good! Your services are no longer required." I turned to go up the curving stairway.

"What?" Suddenly he came to life, his eyes blazing as he looked up the stairs toward me.

"You heard me," I snapped. "You are no longer an employee of this household. I suggest you have Mr. Hayne return your old job to you. Good day."

"You can't do this!" he insisted.

"Oh, but I already have, Roberts."

I saw the scurry of skirts as the two watchers fled back to the kitchen. I would attend to them later. For now I watched Eric Roberts as he stalked away, his steps ringing across the cypress floors of the hallway.

Undoubtedly the house already had been searched and even if the pagoda had been brought here, I knew it probably was not here now. My mind kept thinking of reasons why Nicholas would do this, or even excuses why he could not possibly be involved. But I felt betrayed.

There was one thing no one else knew, not even Nicholas and his mother. I ran quickly up the curving white stairs. Father had always kept a journal, a throwback to his sailing days. I was sure I could find it; I could only hope he had written of Moonwatch and the treasured pagoda.

I went directly to his bedroom. In the northeast corner I turned back the thick Oriental carpet. The small door fit so snugly into the pine flooring that it was hardly noticeable except for the tiny hinges. Inside, just as I remembered, were two journals. Joyfully I clasped them to me. I could hardly wait to read them, savoring every word he wrote. Perhaps he had even written of me; spoke of his love for me. Tears filled my eyes as I once again felt the pain his neglect had caused me.

I flipped quickly through one of the books, but nothing of significance caught my eye. I would wait until I returned to Moonwatch before reading the journals. At the moment all I could think of was seeing Nicholas, and have him explain why he had taken such outrageous liberties with my home.

I spent the remainder of the evening in the attic. Going through Father's room proved fruitless. There was no sign of the pagoda, or indeed of anything unusual.

I walked through the still house to the kitchen where Mrs. Fitzgerald, our cook, stood polishing various pieces of silver. Her tall body was as thin and gaunt as I remembered. There was still no gray in the curling reddish brown hair which sprang from beneath a white day cap. Although I knew she was near my father's age, she hardly seemed older than when I was a child. She had always treated me with a kind tenderness as she now did, coming forward to take my hands in hers.

"Ah, Miss Victoria. 'Tis so sad we all are for the loss of your dear Father," she said.

"Thank you, Mrs. Fitzgerald. It's so good to see you're still here. Whatever has happened to everyone else?" I asked.

"I'm sure I don't know. It all happened so fast."

"Were you here then? When . . . when my father died?" I asked.

"No, dearie. None of us were here except of course for Mr. Roberts who discovered the fire and tried to rescue Mr. Ancona, God rest his soul." Tears filled her hazel eyes as she spoke of my father.

"Eric Roberts? The man I spoke with today?"

"Yes, and it was good for my poor heart to see how you set that brash one straight! He be needin' it, he did. A high and mighty man he is, as cocky as God ever put on this green earth." I had never heard Mrs. Fitzgerald speak so of anyone.

"But he told me he came *after* the fire." I wondered if perhaps I had misunderstood him in my anger.

"Oh, he came to work afterwards, 'tis true, taking Sam's place. But he worked at the shipyard and was here off and on the past year doing odd jobs. He just happened to be here the night of the fire."

"This is all so strange," I murmured. "Why was there no one else about?"

"Why, your father rarely stayed at Ashford Place after you left. There was no need for servants except for special occasions. Jane and me came by once a week to clean or cook if Mr. Ancona needed us, but other than that, we were free to seek other employment."

"But why did old Sam leave?" I asked.

"Well, Sam was gettin' on in age, you know, and sometimes he did speak out of turn. He and Mr. Roberts didn't get on too well either." Her eyes were bright, resentment glittering there as she spoke of Sam.

"*Mr.* Roberts?" I said slowly. My voice must have reflected my astonishment.

"That be about it!" she replied.

"Mrs. Fitzgerald, after I've gone I want you to find Sam and bring him back here. Tell him he has a home here at Ashford Place as long as I have anything to say about it. You do know where he is?"

She smiled broadly. "Yes'm, he's living with his sister down on Marco Street. I knew you'd set things aright, Miss Victoria. 'Tis the answer to my prayers that you came back!"

"And, of course, I hope you and Jane will stay on here too. This is your home, and even if I decide to sell it I will make arrangements for you both."

"Sure and I'll be glad to, Miss Victoria. And you be a living angel, just like your dear mother!"

She hugged me to her as if I were still a little girl. She still smelled of fresh bread and clean starched cotton.

"Oh, yes," I said. "One more thing. While cleaning did you ever see any Chinese pieces—a porcelain pagoda, for instance?"

She thought for a moment. "Why, there's several fine pieces of Chinese porcelain in the house, but, no, I don't recall such a one as you speak of."

I was not surprised at her answer, for if the pagoda had ever been here I was certain it was not now.

"I'll be leaving early tomorrow morning, so don't bother about breakfast for me," I told her. "And I shall be in touch with you about Ashford Place. In the meantime, just consider this your home. I shall make arrangements with Lawyer Jacobsen about money."

"Bless you, Miss Victoria. And you take care of yourself now."

Chapter VIII

The drive from Wilmington seemed interminable, so anxious was I to be back at Moonwatch. The journals, hidden safely away inside my cloak, seemed to burn where they lay against my body. But I did not want to read them until I could be safely and privately back in my room.

We followed the same road as I had come on my first day here. So very much had happened in those few days that my mind was fairly cluttered with thoughts and questions.

I was still perplexed by the strangeness of the household, the rudeness of Frances and her son, and Denise Hayne's obsession with my marrying her son. Yet none of these things seemed important now. Not even the mystery of the pagoda could intrude for long upon my unquenchable curiosity about Nicholas.

In the light of day my passionate response to him two nights ago seemed bizarre and unreal. And yet, picturing his face before me I felt the same tingling sensation shake my body as then. Even the mere thought of his lips upon mine sent a warmth surging through my veins.

I tried to concentrate on the splendid scenery before

me. The ocean was now in view, and as we drove through dark, dense stands of pine, the water sparkled brightly through the trees, catching me as always in its magic spell. I reveled in the atmosphere as the scent of evergreen mingled with the salt breeze. The cry of seabirds was loud above us, and could even be heard above the swish of sand beneath our wheels.

But nothing could keep Nicholas from my mind for long. I was puzzled by his actions at Ashford Place, but the anger I'd felt then had dissipated somewhat and I told myself there must be a good explanation for what he had done.

My trip to Wilmington had taken two days and I knew Nicholas's business in Charleston could not have been concluded in such a short time. I was disappointed that he would not be at the house upon my return, but it would give me time to read the journals and to think.

It was late when the driver helped me from the carriage. The evening was clear and cold with millions of twinkling stars appearing above me in the autumn sky. One of the servants let me in and hurried away to the kitchen to find supper for me. No one else appeared in the dimly lit hallway, and I quickly went upstairs to my room. By the time the maid arrived I had changed into my dressing gown and sat warming my feet before the crackling fire.

She placed the tray before me and smiled. This girl with her dark curling hair and bright blue eyes had been here before and I had noted then her cheerful smile and kind eyes.

"Will that be all you'll be needin', Miss Ancona?" she asked softly.

"Yes, Millie, thank you. It's really more than I expected this late in the evening."

"Mrs. Hayne has given us all orders that you're to

be treated as a daughter of the house, miss," she said.

"Oh?" Her words surprised me.

Millie left quietly without another word. Perhaps she thought better of having told me as much as she did.

The hot soup and thick crusty bread tasted more delicious to me than anything I'd eaten in days. I realized I had not felt so relaxed since leaving school at Salem. Millie's attitude toward me and her words about my new status in the house pleased and soothed me and I knew that was the reason for my calm.

The bitter words of the past few days and my anger with Mrs. Hayne seemed far away. I was actually beginning to feel comfortable at this strange place by the sea. Even Tad's childish pranks were forgotten as I settled myself into bed with Father's journals.

The first few pages contained notes made while at sea. Most of the writings were technical with notations about the trade winds and currents. I was disappointed that there were no personal memoranda, no mention of home or of me. I should not have been surprised. Father was ever the efficient captain of his vessel and while at sea, no doubt, felt himself in another world entirely.

I blew out the lamp beside the bed. The cozy room and tasty meal had warmed me and the flickering patterns of light from the fireplace played upon the wall, lulling me into a sweet and dreamless sleep.

The next morning before breakfast, I tucked the journals safely away in the bottom of my trunk and covered them with other books which I had brought with me.

I stepped out into the hallway and walked quietly toward Denise Hayne's room.

When I knocked at her door it swung open immediately and Ona stood looking down at me.

Without hesitating he said in his deep voice, "Please to come in, miss." Standing aside, he motioned me toward his mistress's pillow-laden bed.

Mrs. Hayne sat propped up in the bed reading. She wore another magnificent silk gown, this one in magenta and emerald green. The large sleeves swung back and forth gracefully as she waved her hand to motion me forward.

"Victoria, my dear child. I'm so delighted you've come to me on your own. I had so hoped you would." She smiled at me almost tenderly. "Sit here and chat with me awhile. Would you like tea?"

"Let me do it," I said, reaching for the delicate blue willow teapot. I poured the steaming amber liquid into two cups.

"You seem unusually subdued this morning, my girl. I take it you did not find what you were looking for in Wilmington?"

"No, unfortunately I found nothing." I looked directly into her faded blue eyes. I had no intention of telling her, or anyone, of the journals, nor did I feel I should mention Eric Roberts. That was something I would take up with Nicholas. But something in her eyes, the way she smiled, told me she already knew what I had found.

"Ah, well, I was afraid you would be disappointed. Forget the pagoda, Victoria. It's of no importance. If it had any significance at all it was to my husband and your father. I would not like to see it come between anyone else that I love."

"But I thought it was worth a great deal of money." I looked at her questioningly.

"Oh, yes, to be sure. But the money is nothing if there is no one with which to share it." Her voice was quiet and it seemed her mood had become somewhat melancholy.

I was afraid she might lapse once again into the illness as she had before. She was a strange woman, seeming so strong and determined one moment, and the next a frail, empty shell with too many sadnesses in her life. And when she spoke of love, did she refer to her husband, or my father?

"Are you all right, Mrs. Hayne?" I asked, taking her teacup from her trembling fingers.

"Will you excuse me now, dear? I'd like to rest for awhile." Her eyes had grown distant and her voice was soft, almost imperceptible.

Before I could answer, Ona stepped behind my chair as if to escort me from the room if I hesitated—away from his mistress.

I had learned nothing from Mrs. Hayne that would help me unravel the mystery of the pagoda. Perhaps I should forget it as she suggested. Yet some intuition nagged at me, filled me with doubts and questions about the strange love/hate relationship between the Hayne family and my father. I knew I could not simply forget it.

I decided after leaving her to find my way up to the lighthouse. I was curious about Captain Hayne and, like him, I was fascinated by the violently beautiful Atlantic.

I went to the front of the house to the landing at the top of the stairs. The corridor there led across to the lighthouse addition. Just as I reached the turning point, the front door opened below and Nicholas and Lesley entered. They did not immediately see me so I stood there waiting for my chance to speak to Nicholas. Suddenly, though, I was aware of a certain intimacy between the two of them, something felt rather than actually observed. I should have turned and walked away from what I saw, but something held me there spellbound. I stepped back into the shadows of the hallway.

He took her cloak from her shoulders and she turned to look up at him. She was standing very near, almost touching him, and I could see on her face that same hungry look as before.

"So Nicky, you didn't answer my question before. Are you going to ask the sweet young Victoria to wed as your mother wishes?" Her voice teased and mocked him gently.

I stiffened when I heard my name. I knew I should go. Eavesdropping was not a habit I was fond of, but I could not move. I was compelled to hear his reply.

"That, my dear Lesley, is none of your business." His voice was soft and teasing as hers had been. The intimacy in his tone tore at my heart as I watched uneasily from my unseen place.

One of my mother's sayings returned to me and I knew exactly what it meant now—"Eavesdroppers rarely hear good about themselves." I did not want to hear if he mocked me, and I could not have withstood seeing him kiss her. I felt as if someone had twisted my heart within my chest. Turning quietly, I fled along the corridor to the steps leading upward to the lighthouse.

I hurried up the curving stairway, not even pausing for a view at each landing. Tears threatened to blind me and my throat burned painfully as I rushed on, anxious to find a hiding place. I was such a fool to ever think a man like Nicholas could care for me.

Finally I reached a doorway at the top of the stairs. Quietly I pushed the door open. After the dimly lit stairwell, the sunlight in the room was blinding. I closed the door and leaned against it gasping for breath and letting the tears finally come to wash away the ache in my heart. Knowing I was safely hidden away I could let my guard down more freely than I had been able to do since Father's death.

"What are you crying about?" a small voice asked.

I looked up, my heart lurching in fright at the unexpected sound. I brushed my fingers across my wet cheeks and stared at the boy sitting in the chair before the great windows.

"Tad," I said dumbly.

He did not speak, but sat turning the wooden chair back and forth on its swivel base. In his lap was a large book, but he was not looking at it. Instead, he watched me as he swung back and forth. The look he directed at me held none of the earlier anger and hostility.

I walked to him and sat on a stool beside him. "I thought this was the light room," I said.

"No, this was Grandpa Hayne's room. The light room is up above here." He pointed up at the ceiling.

"Oh." I found it hard to make conversation with him. He seemed like another child today.

"Do you miss your daddy? Was that why you were crying?" he asked. "Sometimes I come up here where no one can find me. . . . Sometimes I cry when I miss my daddy."

I had thought that was a very unusual question for him to ask. But now I knew he was relating his pain with mine. "Yes, I do miss him, Tad, very much. I suppose today is just a bad day for me, that's all."

"This is my place now," he said possessively, "but you can come here too if ever you miss him real bad."

His sweetness made the tears come again and I smiled at him. "Thank you," I muttered.

"I don't cry much anymore," he said, "since Uncle Nicholas came back here to live. And even though I missed him today, I have this book he gave me to remind me of him . . . Daddy and Grandpa too." He held the book out proudly for me to see.

It was a history of sailing ships, splendidly illustrated with colorful sketches of the proud tall ships as they had been in their halcyon days before the war. I was filled with pride at the number of graceful ships pictured there that were built by Ancona and Hayne.

"It's beautiful, Tad," I said, feeling a great peace in the little room that sat high above the world. And the companionship of the boy was certainly part of that feeling.

I looked out at the sea, my breath catching at the beauty before me. The pale autumn sky was clear, a cerulean blue, with only the faintest wisps of clouds here and there. The ocean gleamed and sparkled, looking from this distance to be alive with its millions of whitecaps as far as I could see.

"This is magnificent," I whispered.

"If Uncle Nicholas was home he could tell you things, and show where fishes swim beneath the surface." His voice was wistful as he looked out to sea.

"You love your uncle very much, don't you?" I asked.

"Yes," he answered quietly.

"Then you'll be very happy to know that he just arrived home only a few moments ago."

"He did?" His eyes became large and very bright. Then he bounded down from the chair.

He then hesitated and turned back to me, his face very expressive and eager. "You may look at the book while I'm gone if you'd like."

In his innocent face I saw sympathy and kindness and I felt the urge to reach out and hug him. But I dared not risk jeopardizing the fragile bond of understanding that had formed between us.

"Thank you," I said, taking the book as he bounced out the door.

As I looked out at the sea, I thought of Nicholas and the conflicting emotions he had stirred within me since our first meeting. Here alone in the quiet I had to be honest with myself. I could not keep from wondering about his friendship with Lesley Adams. He was an overwhelmingly attractive man and she seemed to have no qualms about showing her desire for him. How many men, living within the same household, would feel the need to resist such a woman? It was foolish of me to think that his words to me and his stirring kisses were anything more than simply a man's curiosity for a new woman. And I had certainly been more than willing to accommodate his curiosity.

I glanced about the masculine room, obviously the captain's private hideaway. The woodwork was a rich, dark mahogany with gleaming brass lanterns hung between the windows. A large telescope stood pointed out to sea, before the captain's chair. Below the windows, bookshelves filled to capacity lined the entire room. Here and there on the shelves were various mementos of his travels or brass fittings from a ship.

In the floor where the structure curved away from the oceanside stood a gracefully carved figurehead, beautiful in its unpainted state. The barely draped figure of a woman stood proudly forward, arms raised slightly to reveal full, rounded breasts, her hair blown sensually back by the wind as she looked watchfully toward the heavens. She was a mythological sea nymph and I was captured by her beauty once again. I had seen her before, years ago, on the great clipper named for her, the *Galatea*, the ship my father designed and captained.

As I stood admiring the figurehead I heard a scraping sound outside the door.

"Tad?" I called. There was no answer.

I opened the door and looked about, but I saw no one, or anything which might have caused the noise. As I looked into the gloom of the granite stairwell, I felt a chill course through me and suddenly I wanted to be away from the tower and back to the warmth of the main house below.

Quickly I closed the door and started down the narrow stone stairway. I had been so distraught on my way up that I had paid little attention to the heavy maroon-colored velvet curtains that hung over the windows in the winding tower. For a moment I thought I saw a movement there, but I told myself it must be a draft stirring the curtains. I hurried past the windows and began the descent to the next level. With a start I saw that the gas lamps here had been extinguished and my pathway would be in total darkness until I could go around the curve to the next set of windows.

Something told me to turn and go back up the stairs to the security of the study. But then what? I asked myself. I could not stay there indefinitely. There was nothing to do but proceed carefully, feeling my way along the cold stone walls as I went.

I took a deep breath that echoed eerily in the murky enclosure, then I started down the steps. I felt rather than heard the presence of someone behind me. As I turned, fear gripped my heart and I caught only a glimpse of a figure dressed in a dark robe. That was all I saw before the blow fell on the back of my head and neck and I plunged forward into the darkness.

Chapter IX

I had the feeling of being in my room, but I was confused and disoriented. I could not remember where I was or how I had gotten there. A small cry escaped from me as I tried to raise myself from the bed. The shattering pain in my temples was unbearable and for an instant I felt the light in the room grow dim. My body felt light and free; the pain began to ebb from me.

"It's all right, angel," I heard a deep masculine voice say. "Don't try to move now. The doctor says you must lie perfectly still."

The pillow was cold beneath my head. As my vision gradually returned I was able to see the person beside my bed.

"Nicholas?" I whispered.

"I'm here," he answered.

I felt his large hand envelop mine. I had not realized how cold I was until I felt the warmth of him. He held on to me tightly, anchoring me down as my lifeless body threatened to drift once more into darkness.

"Cold . . . I'm so cold." I closed my eyes, giving in to the weakness that shook me.

"Millie," Nicholas said. "Get more blankets, and bring a warming pan. She's freezing." His voice was hoarse as he spoke.

"Yes, sir," Millie answered from somewhere in the dimness of the room.

Then another voice came to me through the haze. This one not as friendly or caring. "She's only chilled, Nicholas. She's going to be perfectly fine, for goodness sake. You shouldn't fret so over her." I knew it was Frances Canfield even though I could not see her.

"That's enough, Frances!" Nicholas's voice cut through her words. He left my bedside, probably so I would not hear. But the rumble of his voice in the quiet room came to me clearly.

"If Tad had not gone looking for her she could have died there in the cold. It's time you contain your resentment for the girl. It's hardly her fault that her father was Anthony Ancona . . . or that Mother is obsessed with having the blood of Ancona and Hayne united in an heir!" His last words were spoken more quietly, but his anger was still evident.

I tried to speak to them, to protest, but my mouth felt dry and my lips only moved silently.

"Well, I never thought to see you act so foolishly over any woman!" she said.

"If you can't help, then get out. You're upsetting her," he rasped angrily.

"Oh, all right. I'll go help Millie."

"Tell Mother that Victoria is going to be all right. I don't want her frightened into another spell by all this," he added.

I wanted more than anything to speak to him, thank him for defending me. And I wanted to ask him why they hated my father so. While he had spoken so coolly of the two of us producing an heir, the very idea of it set my heart pounding, but I could not speak for my chattering teeth and the throbbing pain that beat inside my head with an intensity that threatened to blind me.

I could see Nicholas moving about the room, then coming to my bedside to lean close to me.

"Victoria, can you hear me?" he asked softly.

I opened my eyes wider, trying to focus on his darkly handsome features.

"I want you to take this medicine. It's laudanum that the doctor left for you."

He lifted my head upward, his hand gentle and easy. I swallowed the bitter-tasting liquid, quickly chasing it with the water he held.

"Please," I said. My words were barely audible as I grasped at his sleeve. "Don't leave me alone." I was more frightened by the memory of that dark stairwell and the hooded figure who had suddenly appeared than I could express to Nicholas. I did not want to be alone, but I was too weak and ill to make him understand.

He looked at me, a questioning frown furrowing his brow.

"What is it? Can you tell me what's wrong?" His look was anxious.

But I could not. I shook my head slightly from side to side. The pain was beginning to dull and I could feel consciousness slipping away from me.

"Promise . . . me . . . you . . . won't," I managed to whisper. Each word seemed to take all my strength.

"I promise," he said quickly as he looked intently into my face. "Don't worry, I won't leave you alone."

I smiled, content now to let the waiting mists envelop me and carry me quickly away, rocking me gently, so gently.

For the next few days I drifted in and out of reality, my body wracked with fever and chills, the dull ache always within my skull.

I was sometimes aware of movements in the room, of people coming in and out, but I was no longer frightened, for each time I woke to sip the hot broth and tea, Nicholas was always there. And he made sure I knew he was.

His dark blue eyes watched me, almost tenderly I imagined, and his firm hand strengthened me during the hallucinations brought on by the fever.

I'm sure he could not have been there night and day, but I thought he was and that was what mattered most. I had not felt such personal concern from anyone since Mother died. It was that concern which sustained me and gave me the will to get well.

Once I was awakened by the touch of a cool hand upon mine. I opened my eyes and saw pale hair that gleamed in the lamplight. It was like spun sugar, giving the woman's face a muted, angelic glow.

"Mother?" My voice was a whisper of disbelief.

"No, my dear. It's Denise." A look of pain crossed her face and she clutched my hand tightly.

I blinked my eyes and looked again. Nicholas was there beside her and I knew the look of worry on his face must surely be for his mother. I could not hope it would be for me.

"Oh, Mrs. Hayne . . . of course. I must have been dreaming." My words did not come with much force, although I was feeling much better.

"You're going to be fine, child," she said. "It will take time, but you will be all right. I don't want you to worry about anything. Nothing matters now except having you well again." The words were hers, yet the voice was different, the tone more kind somehow.

I could only nod my agreement.

"The next time I come to see you I hope you will be sitting up. Then you can tell me what caused the unfortunate accident."

As was her way she had spoken her mind and was now ready to go. But as Ona took her away I frowned. Accident? But didn't they understand what had happened? I lifted my hand to motion her back, but my voice was only a whispered croak.

"No. . . ."

Nicholas sat on the bed and captured my hand in his. He held it firmly against his chest to quiet its movements. The wool of his jacket felt coarse and cool, and I could feel the slow steady beating of his heart in the pulse of his hand.

"What is it?" He watched me quietly.

"Nicholas . . ." My voice was weak as I tried to make him understand. I felt panic arise within me at my inability to express myself.

I shook my hand for emphasis, its movement barely making a difference in his hard, firm grasp.

"Easy," he said. "It's all right, I'm here. Whatever you need to say will wait."

"No!" I said. "Please!"

He frowned and looked closer into my face. "What is it, Victoria? Take your time. I won't leave until you've told me everything you need to say."

A great swell of relief surged through me and for the first time I felt the mists of the past few days lift from my mind. It was as if I were emerging from a long, dark tunnel where no one had been able to see or hear me.

I took a great gulp of air and closed my eyes in gratitude. Nicholas brought a glass of water and put it to my lips so I could feel the cool rim of the crystal goblet.

I spoke quickly then, my voice hoarse at first, but growing stronger.

"Your mother said accident. It was no accident, Nicholas. Someone pushed me. The lights were off on the landing and someone was there waiting for me!"

Panic beat within my breast at the memory.

Nicholas sat on the bed. He looked puzzled, as if he could not comprehend what I was trying to say.

"Nicholas." I clutched his coat in my hands as I tried to make him understand. More than anything I had to make him know the terror and the fear that I felt that day and even now on recalling it.

"I'm sorry. This is just so unbelievable." He took my hand again and looked into my eyes. "It's all right. Just slow down. Tell me everything you remember."

He moved closer to me and gathered me into his arms. Holding me against his chest, he leaned back against the headboard and stretched his legs out on the quilt-covered bed. His hands moved gently over my hair, quieting me as one would calm a wild colt. I relaxed against him and felt the tightness in my chest vanish as I took another long, shuddering breath.

"Now," he said, his voice a deep rumble beneath my ear. "Tell me what happened."

I felt the movement of his lips against my hair as he spoke, and a warmth of belonging spread through my entire being. I felt safe and not even the thought of someone coming through my door to see the compromising picture we made could disturb me.

I chose my words carefully and tried to speak calmly. I did not want him to think these were the ramblings of a girl half-crazed with fever or a flighty female prone to imagination and vapors.

"Someone was waiting for me in the shadows and pushed me down those steps. It was not an accident and I did not imagine it." My voice sounded a bit more firm and convincing now that I knew he believed me.

I could feel his body tense and he was silent for a moment. I turned my head to look up at him and his face was serious, thoughtful as he looked at me.

"But who?" he asked. His jaw clenched tightly and

his eyes narrowed as he waited for my reply. "Did you see who?"

"I . . . I don't know. I only caught a glimpse of him. One of the lights was out on the landing and I was frightened, but I could see the glow from the next level, so I started down. There was a movement behind me—someone in a cloak. I felt the hands shove me and . . ."

His face was angry as he pulled me close again, his arms tightly encircling me as if to protect me from whatever fear I was reliving.

I could almost feel him thinking, his breathing still and waiting. Finally he spoke. "I don't know what to say, how to explain something like this happening here, when you should be protected." He turned me to face him. "I'm so sorry, Victoria. I'm so sorry it was you."

"Then you do believe me?" I felt such relief now that I had finally put my fears into words.

"Of course I believe you. Did you think I would not?" Even though his jaw was still clenched and his gaze fierce and angry, I knew it was not directed at me.

As he looked at me, the anger was suddenly gone, replaced by the kindness I had seen there when I first met him. His face was very close to me. Against my will I looked down to the curve of his lips that hovered only a breath away from mine. I was trembling at the nearness of him, of being in his arms and feeling the strength he offered . . . demanded that I take. I knew he felt it, the heat that passed between us was like quicksilver spreading instantly through my body.

His eyes closed for a moment, long lashes lying against his dark skin. When they opened languidly there was a quiet warning within them that drew him away from me.

I must have murmured a protest for he smiled and touched my cheek as he stood up and bent toward me.

"You need to rest now," he said. "But I promise you

have nothing to worry about. No one will harm you."

My eyes followed him as he walked across the room, turning back to me as he reached the door. "And now that you're better, perhaps I should keep my vigil *outside* your door."

I smiled at him helplessly. I was very tired and lay back wearily against the pillow, staring at the soft firelight that splashed upon the walls, filling the room with his warming glow.

There was no caution left within me, no thought of Denise Hayne's warning that I would never leave this house. Even the changes Nicholas had made at Ashford Place seemed insignificant as were his unemotional words to Frances about an Ancona and Hayne heir. I cared about nothing except being here with him. Everything within me yearned to belong here, to Nicholas Hayne. I only knew I could never bear to lose the feelings that he stirred within me, that I felt whenever he was near. And I knew instinctively I would never feel that with anyone else.

As weary as I was, sleep would not come, for everywhere I looked I saw Nicholas's face and the blue fire that flickered deep within those cobalt eyes.

"Nicholas," I whispered into the silence of the darkening room.

Chapter X

The night that I told Nicholas about the intruder seemed the turning point in my recovery. Within two days of his visit I was allowed to be up and about in my room as long as I stayed warm and did not become overtired.

Millie placed a chair near the window for me so that I might look out upon the ocean. I had not seen Nicholas alone since that night and I began to wonder if I might only have imagined the strong emotional response that passed between us. Perhaps, I told myself, it was a result of my illness and fever and nothing else, only my imagination.

I had almost convinced myself of that, and under the circumstances became grateful that at least I had not expressed my feelings aloud and made a fool of myself.

My thoughts were interrupted by a noise outside my door. I stiffened, watching warily. My heart lurched and a tingle of fear raced to the tips of my fingers. The darkness of the lighthouse stairs came rushing back. But as the scratching noise continued, I realized it was only someone attempting to open the door. I could even hear the mutter of words.

When the door sprang open, Tad was fairly propelled into the room by the action. He looked up at me sheepishly as children sometimes do in their clumsiness. In his hands he carried a telescope, a much smaller version of the one in Captain Hayne's study.

"Tad, I'm so glad to see you!" I had not seen him since that day in the lighthouse.

Almost shyly he walked toward me and there was no sign of the bitter look he'd had when I first arrived. "I thought you might like to look for dolphins. It's terribly boring being sick."

"Yes, it is," I agreed. "And I would very much like to look through the telescope. It was very thoughtful of you to think of it."

He grinned at me as if my words had pleased him. But he was such a strange little boy that I could not be sure what he really was thinking.

He brought the instrument to the window and pulled a table closer to place it on. He worked silently, his mouth set seriously as he arranged the three-legged stand upon the table. Then he adjusted the lens and stood back proudly.

"There," he said.

I hesitated a moment before bringing my eye to the telescope. "Hmmm," I murmured, hoping he would recognize the teasing in my voice. "There is no shoeblack on the end is there? I should not like to have a black eye."

Tad's blue eyes grew large and I could see that my words had taken him completely by surprise. Then he laughed, an easy, carefree sound, the first time I'd heard him do so. It altered his face from the rude, sullen little boy I'd first encountered and I could not resist laughing with him.

"No, here," he said. "I'll show you." Then he bent down and placed his eye at the eyepiece. "See," he said, rubbing his eye as he straightened again. "No black eye."

He stood close beside me as I viewed the blue-green expanse beyond the house. The wind was very brisk, causing whitecaps to dot the ocean as far as I could see.

"See anything?" he asked eagerly.

"No, I don't think so. You look." His interest in the ocean was obvious as was his impatience for his turn at the glass.

I was amazed at the transformation which had taken place in Tad in the days since my arrival. Perhaps it was because he sensed an interest within me or perhaps it was simply that he had never been exposed to other people outside the family—someone he could talk to on his own level. Whatever it was it was certainly a striking change and one I hoped would continue.

Tad turned back to me, a look of disappointment on his young face. "Nope. The sea must be too rough today."

"Tad, you must not bother Miss Ancona with your silly daydreams." Frances Canfield had entered the room.

Instantly Tad's face changed once again and I could see the repressed anger within him.

"He's not bothering me at all, Mrs. Canfield. In fact my afternoon was quite dull until Tad came."

She made a small, sniffing sound as if my words were too ridiculous to answer. "How are you feeling?" she asked.

I'm sure I must have looked at her oddly, for it was the only time she had spoken civilly to me. But I remembered one of the nights I had been so ill when I heard Nicholas's harsh words to his sister. Perhaps that was what had made the difference.

"I'm feeling much better, thank you," I said. "In fact, I thought I might come downstairs to dinner tonight."

Her dark eyes flashed and her prim lips tightened

slightly. "Well, that's splendid. We shall all look forward to it, I'm sure."

I almost laughed at the absurdity of our conversation. I was positive even if her words were politely given that she did not welcome my presence at dinner any more than she ever had.

She focused her attention again on her son. "My goodness, Tad, wherever did you find those clothes? I'm sure Millie could find something more suitable."

At the look on Tad's face, it was obvious he was used to her constant criticism, if indeed one ever grew used to it. I felt sympathy for him and wanted with all my heart to comfort him, but the distant, skeptical look had returned and I feared he would only reject me.

"Is it all right if your son stays with me awhile?" I asked as she turned to go.

"If you're sure he won't disturb you." Her voice was cold and sharp and I had the feeling she did not really care if he disturbed me, but rather felt she should give such a reply.

"On the contrary, I should enjoy his company very much." I looked at Tad and smiled encouragingly, but he was looking distractedly out to sea.

"Just remember, Tad, any more tricks and you'll have your Uncle Nicholas to answer to."

The boy did not speak, but stood stiffly, his back still turned to me as he looked out the window. It was as if his mother's indifference had embarrassed as well as angered him.

"I'm glad you came today, Tad," I told him. "I've wanted to thank you for rescuing me."

My words caught his attention and he turned to me with a look of shy surprise on his face.

"Rescue?"

"Your Uncle Nicholas said I might have died if you had not come looking for me that night in the lighthouse."

"He did? Uncle Nicholas said that?" He seemed so childishly pleased at his uncle's approval that the sweetness of it tugged at my heart. I found myself more and more able to relate with Tad and the hurts and anger of my own childhood.

"Yes, he did. Your uncle is very proud of you, you know."

Tad sat back against the wide window ledge, looking at the toes of his shoes.

"Mama says that if you marry Uncle Nick, I shall be turned out without a penny. She says he will have boys of his own and will have no use for me any more."

When he looked up at me his blue eyes were filled with pain and confusion. I could almost see his young mind working, his instinct for natural friendliness conflicting with what his mother had told him about me. I was furious that she could treat him this way.

"That's not true, Tad! Your uncle cares for you deeply, and I think you know he would never do anything to hurt you."

"But if he had a wife . . . if you were his wife and you told him to . . ." He looked at me with distrust, waiting for an answer.

"Your uncle is not the kind of man to allow his wife to run his affairs. And I would never do such a thing, Tad, I promise." Then I realized the folly of my words and added, "Of course, I'm not marrying your uncle, so there's really no need for you to fear anything, is there?"

"Then why did you come here?"

I had to wonder exactly what he had been told and I was glad for the chance to tell him the truth. "I've been away at school since my mother died. I had no other family except my father. So when he died, I had no idea what I would do. Your grandmother graciously invited me here—only temporarily, mind you—until I can decide what I will do about the business." I paused, watching him carefully, but he had no comment to make.

"There are . . . complications about my father's interest in Ancona and Hayne shipping. But believe me, Tad, I did not come here to marry Nicholas. I'd never even met him until a few days ago. It's just a misunderstanding."

He was thoughtful for a moment, then he turned to gaze out the window again. When he spoke his voice was muffled. "But what will you do if you leave here?"

"Oh, I'll probably be a teacher. It was what I'd planned all along, but it can wait until my father's business is taken care of. And of course I do have a home, a lovely one, in Wilmington. But it's quite large and after the accident I . . . Well, I thought coming here might be better."

"You loved your father?" he asked. There was an odd look on his face as if he found it hard to believe I could.

"Of course I loved him. He was my father. And no matter what he might have done to anger your family he was not a bad person. And I cannot believe he was a thief." I tried to keep the resentment from showing. After all, he was only a child, unduly influenced by his mother. I could not put him in the position of taking sides against her.

"Well, I suppose I'd be angry if someone accused my father of doing something like that, especially if he was . . . dead . . . and couldn't fight back." He looked at me apologetically when he used the word *dead* as if he were afraid it might somehow offend me.

"I do hope you understand, Tad. I did not come here with the intention of hurting anyone, or causing any problems in your family."

"I wish I could go to school." Childlike, he abruptly

dismissed our conversation and went on to one which interested him more.

"You've never been to school?"

"No, but I've had a few tutors. They didn't last long. No one wanted to live out here in the middle of nowhere and the ones who did . . . didn't stay." He looked sheepishly at me.

"Oh, I see," I said. "Did someone frighten them away, perhaps . . . with spiders or toads?"

"Maybe," he said. I could see he still did not trust me enough to divulge his most guarded secrets.

"If you'd like, you and I could have lessons while I'm here," I offered.

At my words his eyes lit with a bright curiosity and I felt I'd gained a small foothold with him.

"When can we? Today?" Then he hesitated. "Oh, I don't suppose you feel up to it yet. Boys are a trial, I guess."

"I've always found boys to be delightful." I smiled. I wondered if he had heard his mother express such sentiments. "I'm sure I'll be able to do it within the next couple of days, at least for a little while each day. It will give me time to prepare a lesson. Does that sound all right with you?"

"Yes, ma'am!" he answered.

"But first I must make sure it will be all right with your mother and your Uncle Nicholas," I warned.

"What was that about Uncle Nicholas?" I recognized the deep masculine voice that asked the question and turned to see Nicholas standing at the door watching us.

"I'm going to fetch some of my books, Miss Ancona." Tad looked at me urgently as if reminding me to ask his uncle. I only smiled and nodded as he ran away, throwing a hopeful look at both of us as he went.

Nicholas walked across to where I sat and pulled a

chair near to me. He carried a small square package wrapped in tissue paper which he placed on the table where Tad had left the telescope. Suddenly I was conscious of every aspect of my appearance and wished I had brushed my hair, or put on a more flattering robe. I felt as if I were meeting him anew, for I found our relationship had changed significantly and I had hardly been aware of it.

But, I reminded myself, there were so many things I needed to discuss with him, not the least of which was Ashford Place. I wanted to know exactly how much he had to do with the changes in my home, including the presence of Eric Roberts.

He sat in the small stuffed fireside chair, his long legs extended out before him. His muscular frame seemed incongruous in the chair and even in the confines of the room. He seemed a man who would be more easily matched with the elements and the great expanse of the heavens and ocean. Yet I had noticed before how effortlessly he made the transition to the indoors and the social amenities. His dress and manners were always impeccable and I wondered at his versatility.

"You're looking much better today," he said. He had leaned back into the chair with his head cocked to one side, his chin resting on the fist of his right hand. His cobalt blue eyes surveyed me unflinchingly, and I found myself becoming self-conscious and awkward in his presence.

I could have laughed, for at school I had been the outgoing one, the girl who always dared to step forward and speak her mind. This gauche behavior was something new for me and I was always surprised at his ability to affect me so.

"Yes, I'm feeling much better. In fact, I told your sister I would probably be down for dinner tonight."

"Excellent," he said quietly. He reached out for the

package he had placed on the table.

"I brought you something from Charleston." He handed the package to me.

I must have looked surprised for he laughed softly. "Unwrap it."

I tore the flimsy paper away to reveal a picture, framed in soft burnished walnut. It was a watercolor of a ship, the most magnificent I thought I had ever seen. The colors were soft and muted, making the ship at full sail seem to be floating in the mist like a great ghost ship. I had studied all of the great clipper ships, but this was one I did not immediately recognize.

I frowned and looked at Nicholas. He was looking at me oddly with a quiet, secretive look. "Look at the engraving," he said.

At the bottom of the frame was a small brass plate engraved with the words, "The *Victoria*."

"The *Victoria . . . ?*" I whispered. "But I don't understand."

"This is a painting of the last ship that Anthony Ancona designed. He named it for you." He spoke quietly, allowing his words to sink in. "I took it with me to Charleston and had it framed properly . . . as a gift to you."

Tears filled my eyes before I could will them away and I found myself speechless. I could not believe my father had done this, or that Nicholas had been so thoughtful.

"But, he never told me. . . . He was always so distant and . . ." I could not finish, for tears spilled down my cheeks as a childish ache of love and longing filled me. The same longing I'd always felt when I thought of my father.

Nicholas moved forward and took the picture from my hands, placing it on the table. Then he clasped my elbows, pulling me from the chair and into his arms.

"I'm sorry. I didn't mean to hurt you. I thought it would make you happy."

I allowed him to hold me as I cried for all the lonely nights I'd spent without a family, for all the times I hated my father for withholding his love from me. Nicholas said nothing, letting me vent all my pent-up resentment as he soothed and murmured quiet words to me.

I pulled away from his disturbing embrace and turned to look out at the blustery sea. "It does make me happy. I just never dreamed he had done anything like this."

I turned back to him and smiled. "It was very kind of you to bring it to me. Please don't think I'm ungrateful. It's just—"

"What is it, Victoria?" he asked. "Can you still not trust me?" From the tone of his voice I knew he was hurt by my continued withdrawal.

I shook my head, not sure that I could make him understand the anguish of a young girl who had lost her mother and quickly found herself banished from the security of her home, abandoned by a father who did not seem to care.

I took a deep breath and wiped my face with my hand. When I sat back down, Nicholas did also. "When my mother died and we buried her, I clung to my father. We'd always been so close, the three of us. All I wanted was for him to take me home and tell me everything would be all right. Instead he sent me away." I looked at him and he solemnly nodded for me to continue. "I was confused at first . . . and hurt, but I began to tell myself that he would soon come for me . . . and tell me he loved me. He would take me back to Ashford Place. It was a year before I could admit to myself that he was never coming. I hated him then, Nicholas, hated him! And he died without my ever forgiving him!" Perhaps the last part was the hardest for me to admit.

I jumped up and whirled about to pace the room, the anger toward my father which I'd always suppressed threatening to spout forth like an erupting volcano. "He left me there with no word until the next Christmas when he came, smiling and posturing for everyone to see what a wonderfully generous man he was with his trunkful of gifts!" I fairly spat the words out with disgust, almost unaware now of Nicholas's presence.

"Did you tell him then how hurt you were?" Nicholas asked, in a voice that was gentle and patient.

"No! Why should I have to tell him? Why couldn't he see what he had done?" I could feel myself growing more and more out of control, an unpleasant feeling. I took a deep breath and continued more slowly. "No, I never told him. I've never told anyone except . . . except you. I compensated by being the best student at school, by achieving every goal and winning every award I could."

"But it didn't help." He seemed to know exactly what I meant.

"No," I said through trembling lips. "It didn't."

Nicholas frowned and shook his head slightly. "So in all those years, when you and your father were together, neither of you ever spoke of the bitterness you felt—you hid it from him?"

"Is that so hard to believe?"

He smiled then, and there was something in his look that told me he did know exactly what I meant. It was almost a sharing of the anger and frustration I felt.

There was a sorrow deep within his eyes and I realized it was not only for me. He had been hurt too. That look caused my heart to quiver strangely and I longed to reach out to him and tell him he was not alone.

"But . . . you and your father were close, weren't you?"

"Oh, yes, I suppose. Close enough. As long as I fulfilled all his expectations of me, as long as I loved the sea as much as he did and devoted every waking hour to studying it. My father could be a stern man, intolerant of those who did not share his zeal. And I was young."

"But . . . but you do love the sea, the ships. I can see it when you talk. That's not something that can be forced upon someone."

"You're right. It can't. Problem was I didn't realize how much that love and interest was a natural thing to me until after Father died. When he was alive I resented him much the same way you did your father."

"I'm sorry," I said simply.

He looked up then and smiled, the sorrow immediately gone from the blue depths. "Don't be. I'm happier now than I've ever been. I have everything I could possibly hope for." His smile changed to one of playfulness. "Well, almost everything."

I smiled back at him, aware of the incredible lightness I felt, the burden that had been lifted just by sharing it with him.

"You know, Victoria, Anthony never seemed the kind of man that you've just described. He talked of you constantly. It was obvious to everyone how much he doted on you." He picked up the picture of the ship. "He wanted this last great design to carry your name. The spirit of his beautiful Victoria, he used to say."

I closed my eyes at the pain his words struck within me, and the guilt. My chin trembled again with the crushing emotions I felt.

"Would it be best if I took the picture away?" he asked.

"No . . . really. I'd like to keep it. Perhaps someday I will understand why he left me the way he did. Talking to you, to someone who knew him so well, helps."

"I'm glad if I've helped."

I took the picture from his hand and studied it. "The ship was never built then?"

"No, unfortunately he only finished the design a few weeks before his death. It was still on his drawing table at work."

I walked to the window and stood looking out at the great ocean my father loved so well. Perhaps it had been his one all-consuming love and there was just not enough room for me.

I was surprised to see great billowing clouds rolling across the water. The blustery weather we'd been experiencing all day had finally pushed a storm our way.

"Victoria," Nicholas said.

I looked around at him, allowing the dark blue eyes to rivet me where I stood. There was no pretense between us then, no girlish imagination of love and romance. The look I saw and recognized there was one between a man and a woman and I felt weak at the intensity between us.

"I want to help you, angel." His fingers touched my cheek, traveling down to caress my chin with his thumb. "Come to me if you need to talk—if you need anything. Will you do that?"

I could not take my eyes from his wonderful face. He was so handsome that just looking at him almost took my breath away. I was mesmerized by his look and his deep, husky voice.

"Yes," I whispered, knowing I was saying yes to so much more than his offer of help.

His eyes narrowed slightly as he smiled. He seemed to be making a conscious effort to keep a certain distance between us and I had not forgotten our conversation the night he kissed me. He seemed to have fought his feelings then just as he was doing now, and that gave me more hope than doubts.

"I'll see you at dinner then." He reached out to brush a wisp of hair from my eyes and I was again amazed at his ability to tame me, to make me like clay, waiting only to be molded into whatever form he chose. A few months ago I would never have thought any man could do that to me.

Only after he had gone did I remember what I wanted to ask him about . . . all the questions I had about Ashford Place and Eric Roberts. But he seemed to have that power . . . the power to make me forget everything except him.

Chapter XI

The approaching storm grew nearer and more intense as the hours passed so that by late afternoon the house was dark and shadowy. The winds whistled loudly against the windows and even the distant crashing of waves could be heard plainly within my room. The sea seemed to be nearer . . . seemed to be all around us.

I dressed carefully in a crimson velvet evening gown, one of my favorites. At least Father always made sure I had every material possession a girl could wish for. The dress had a wide tucked band at the top, falling just slightly off the shoulders. The fitted waist was a bit loose since my illness, but it would have to do. The wide skirt, made simply in a full flaring style rustled faintly against the silk underskirt as I walked to the dressing table to arrange my hair. Looking at my reflection, I thought I'd made the right choice by wearing no jewelry. The dress was elegant enough by itself.

My face was pale and very thin, causing the mass of dark curls to seem even wilder and more unruly looking than before. I pinned my hair up as tightly as I could, leaving it full in the back. But soon curly tendrils fell about my face, refusing to be contained.

By the time I left my room and entered the hallway, great streaks of lightning slashed the sky across the ocean. The flickering light moved eerily along the hallway, playing tricks with my vision as I walked, making me feel dizzy and unsteady.

Downstairs the lights were a little better and I lost the unsteady feeling. The dining room was well lit, but the room was large and the wallpaper was of a flowered burgundy pattern, so that the corners of the room appeared somber and shadowy.

I was the last to arrive and I was pleasantly surprised that everyone seemed so concerned with my well being. Nicholas rose and pulled a chair out for me, then took his place at the head of the table.

"You hardly look as if you've been ill," Lesley commented. She was seated tonight at my right and I was on the corner near Nicholas. "I wanted to visit you, but you were so sick that I thought it best to wait."

"It's all right," I told her. "I appreciate your concern . . . everyone's." I looked across at Frances and Mrs. Hayne. Ona was not with his mistress for once.

"We were terribly worried about you, my dear," Mrs. Hayne said. "That was a nasty accident, but we're happy that you've recovered so nicely."

"Accident?" I looked at Nicholas and from the warning look on his face it was obvious he had not told his mother the truth about the attack.

"Thank you," I murmured, going along with Nicholas's wishes. I was happy when he tried to steer the conversation to something other than my health.

As the various courses were brought to the table, we could hear the sound of the storm outside, even through the thick stone walls of the house. The floor vibrated with the thunder and the windows rattled in their frames. But I had never minded storms so I concentrated on the creamy tomato bisque and the delicately flavored baked fish. As wonderful as the food tasted, I was able to eat only a small portion, not being used to such a large meal. I declined the rich dessert of rum cake and drank a demitasse of steaming coffee while everyone talked about the storm outside.

"Has there been any talk of a hurricane, Nicholas?" Frances asked. She seemed frightened, looking about as she spoke.

"No," Nicholas assured her. "It's only an autumn storm." As he spoke he leaned toward her and took her hand in his. Immediately her face was flooded with relief and she pressed his hand tightly in gratitude. I was surprised at the look on her face. She seemed almost normal for a change and I thought how much more attractive she looked, even pretty.

"Oh, Frances, for goodness sake, try not to let every little storm frighten you out of your wits!" Mrs. Hayne always seemed critical of Frances, a great contrast with the admiration she heaped upon her son.

Nicholas looked coolly at his mother, his gaze stopping her from whatever else she might be tempted to say.

"Franny is fine, Mother," he said. "She's not exactly hysterical with fear. There's nothing wrong with a little healthy caution." He spoke pleasantly enough, but there was a wryness to the tone, enough to make his point.

Frances's look at her younger brother held something close to adoration and for a moment I felt a bond with her, a wish that we could be friends.

For me the storm was exhilarating, although I had to admit it was almost too violent for my taste. I had never been exposed to such raw weather, having been raised further inland. But I had often heard Father speak of the furious storms out on the ocean. Here at Cape Fear

I was able to experience that ferocity for the first time and I relished it.

As we talked quietly, Vickers, one of the servants, came into the room and spoke quietly to Nicholas.

"Excuse me," Nicholas said, rising to follow Vickers out into the hallway.

Through the open doorway I could see a man who had just come into the house. He wore a yellow rain cape glistening with water. His form and stance seemed familiar, but I could not see his face. He seemed to be staring straight at me through the door until Nicholas walked to him and took his arm, pulling him out of sight to the end of the hallway. We could hear the low murmur of their voices from the dining room.

Mrs. Hayne glanced back over her shoulder, but the man was no longer in sight. Everyone at the table seemed to be waiting for something; I could not understand exactly what it might be. Only Lesley seemed calm and uninterested in the conversation going on in the hallway.

When Nicholas returned, his eyes appeared almost black and he seemed angry. His bearing was stiff as if he held himself in check. His mouth was tightly set and straight. He looked toward me only briefly, and I thought I saw a touch of regret there that we had not had time to talk as perhaps he hoped.

"I'm afraid you will have to excuse me. Business. Lesley, I'll need you." That short statement was all the explanation he offered even to his mother before he turned and walked quickly from the room with Lesley following behind him.

I was too tired to be very curious and my evening downstairs had drained me more than I thought. I also excused myself. I was anxious to go upstairs and change, looking forward to lying in the big soft bed while the storm raged on about us.

As I stepped on the stairs, the door at the end of the hallway which lead to the kitchen opened and the man I had seen earlier came through it. He was surprised to find anyone in the hall and stopped suddenly, looking directly up at me, his face illuminated by the gaslights.

"You!" I gasped. It was the man I had fired at Ashford Place, the man hired by the Hayne family lawyers. Nicholas had left the dining room so hurriedly to see Eric Roberts!

He looked away from me as if he had not even seen me and went into the small room that was Lesley's office.

I stood for a moment looking at the closed door and a small alarm jangled somewhere deep in my mind.

Thunder cracked throughout the house as if the lightning had struck something nearby. Hurriedly I ran up the stairs and along the hallway with its ghostly wavering lights and into my room. It too seemed gray and shadowy. I went about hastily turning up the wicks in the lamps and placing more coal into the grate. Finally the room was bathed in a warm golden glow, outshining even the flash of the storm outside. Only then could I relax and banish the cold fear that crept along my spine.

Nicholas had seemed so different . . . angry and impatient. I knew he had a quick temper, I had seen it the first night I came. But this was different. This seemed somehow to have something to do with me.

As tired as I was at dinner, I now found myself tossing restlessly, unable to sleep. I listened for Nicholas's footsteps and even considered going to look for him, but what would I say?

The lights and the fire had warmed the room cozily. Finally I blew out the lamps and crawled back into bed. I must have fallen asleep as soon as I did so.

I don't know what time it was when I first heard the

voice. I was dreaming, or so I thought, of someone in my room, someone close beside my bed. I tried to open my eyes, but I was so sleepy that my eyelids felt heavy and unnatural. I tried so hard, feeling a panic rising within me as the voice continued to whisper so close. I knew I was in danger and needed to wake myself, but was unable to do so.

"Victoria," the voice whispered almost in my ear. Then I realized it was no dream and I was filled with horror, a feeling of evil and death.

Suddenly I was awake, sitting up in bed. The fire had gone out and the room was in total darkness except for the sporadic light from the storm which seemed to be raging even more violently than before.

"Victoria." The voice sounded again in the stillness of the room and I felt my skin prickle with terror. This was no dream.

"Who's there?" I asked, my voice sounding more resolute than I felt.

There was laughter then, a harsh, guttural sound somewhere near the doorway. I saw a sliver of light as the door opened and closed. Whoever had been in my room was gone.

Quickly I jumped from the bed, not even bothering to grab a robe or slippers. I ran to the door and opened it, but I could see nothing in the dim hallway. There was only one light visible down near the landing just above the stairway.

I don't know what prompted me to go into the hallway in search of the intruder. Perhaps my anger and curiosity overrode my fear and I had to make sure I was not dreaming.

I tiptoed past Nicholas's room, two doors from mine, but still I saw no one. Just ahead in one of the alcoves I thought I heard a noise. My blood froze as the whispered voice called my name once more.

"Victoria . . ."

I wished more than anything for a light, knowing it would somehow give me more courage. But I was determined and walked quietly to the curtained alcove right next to Nicholas's room. My hand closed upon the heavy brocade curtains and I threw them aside. There was a heavy door of grilled ironwork across the small nook. Outside, beyond the door, I could see in the flicker of lightning a rounded balcony. But the entire area was visible and there was no one there. Curiously I turned the handle and the heavy door swung back in my hand. I stepped out just under the eaves of the house. Instantly the sound of the boiling ocean crashing onto the shore rose up loudly toward me.

It happened so suddenly—the shadow of movement behind me, the hands at my back pushing me brutally out onto the small balcony. With disbelief I grabbed the wide stone bannister which stood slightly above waist level. When I turned to look back at the door, it slammed shut.

"No!" I stepped to the door. It was locked! I pressed my face against the glass panes, but the heavy curtains inside made it impossible to see the interior of the house.

The rain slashed across the house and balcony in heavy sheets. Within seconds I was soaked to the skin. The heavy drops were ice cold, propelled by the violent wind. It stung my face until I could hardly see and peppered against my bare arms. It was only then that the reality of what had happened struck me. It was well after midnight and I was hopelessly locked outside in the raging storm with only the sheer walls of the house above and below me. I felt the glass panes in the door, but they were completely covered with heavy grillwork, making it impossible to break, even if I'd been afforded some instrument with which to work.

Still, I could not accept it. I would not sit down quietly and cry, waiting and hoping someone would look for me come morning.

I went back to the banister and leaned over, looking around the side of the house. I had to shield my eyes against the icy pinpricks of rain. The windows to the next room were less than six feet from me but it was impossible to make my way across the slippery stone walls of the house.

My foot touched something on the floor of the balcony. I picked up the small clay pot which probably had been placed there for summer flowers. Without hesitation I dropped it, breaking it into several large shards.

I leaned over the balcony and threw a piece of the pottery at the window to Nicholas's room. It clanged loudly against the glass. I could detect no movement from within and by now I was shivering almost uncontrollably in the cold rain. My hair hung heavily over my face and shoulders. I threw another piece and then another, but still there was no response. The thought entered my mind that this window could be a sitting room or that possibly Nicholas was not even in his rooms. I tried not to allow myself to think so negatively and continued throwing the pieces of clay at the window until I was tired and shaky from the effort.

It was no use. With the storm raging so heavily outside, no one would be able to hear the small noise against the window. Even if it was heard it probably would be attributed to the wind and rain.

In despair my shoulders began to tremble and I sank heavily to the floor, crying helplessly, for I knew it was no use. I scooted back as far against the door as I could, but the rain and wind still beat down upon me unmercifully.

Then I heard the smallest sound, as if a window were being opened. I ran to the edge of the balcony once more. There was a dim light showing through the window.

"Nicholas!" I screamed. "Help me!"

I saw his head emerge from inside, his profile looking so strong and comforting that I felt weak with relief. But now I could do nothing but cry, managing only to breathe a weak sigh when I tried to speak his name.

"Victoria? For the love of God!—" His voice faded away and the window closed. Within seconds I heard the rasp of the key in the door behind me and Nicholas was there, pulling me inside.

He didn't waste time by demanding an explanation. He seemed intent only in gathering me inside out of the rain. Swiftly he picked me up into his arms and in a few long strides had carried me to my room and placed me on the bed.

I was shaking uncontrollably and my teeth chattered so badly I could not have spoken even if he had demanded it. He efficiently went about lighting the lamps and stoking a fire back to life. Then he took one of the large towels from the washstand and walked to where I sat.

Gently he dried my face and shoulders and rubbed my dripping hair. I could not stop shaking and at this point I could not be sure if it were from the cold or the sheer terror I had felt.

His face was deadly serious and his beautiful eyes were dark, shining in the light from the fireplace.

"You'd better change," he said, handing me the towel. "Where are your nightclothes?"

I pointed to the armoire and he went to it, quickly bringing me a soft clean gown which he placed on the bed beside me. Then he turned and walked to the fireplace, keeping his back toward me as I pulled the soaking gown over my head. I quickly dried myself and slipped on the clean gown. It felt warm and comfortable, helping to ease the shivering that wracked my body.

He came back to me and without words indicated I should get into bed. I did so, but continued to sit up. I took in every movement Nicholas made, more precious to me now than before . . . every minute facial expression I wanted to etch into my mind, for now I was suddenly very unsure about my safety.

Nicholas took the towel and sat beside me on the bed. He began to slowly dry my hair. Somehow this most basic of tasks touched me more than anything he could have said or done and I felt a quick wave of warmth move over me. It disturbed and excited me both and I reacted by touching his hand.

All the questions and doubts I had earlier about him simply dropped away. I was captured by this man . . . engulfed in feelings so powerful that I wondered if anyone had ever experienced this beautiful anguish before.

"Victoria," he murmured as he moved toward me. "What am I to do with you?" The shadow of his face blocked out the light as his mouth moved swiftly to capture mine, warming my cold lips with his touch.

There was an urgency in him now and I felt myself responding to it as his kisses grew deeper and more passionate. Desperately I wound my arms about his neck moving closer until I felt a tingle of electricity where my breasts met the smooth contours of his muscled chest beneath his robe. I gasped against his mouth at the shocking pleasure it sent through me.

I felt, rather than heard, his small groan as he pulled away from me. He took a long, deep breath and smiled oddly at me. He seemed bewildered and amused, perhaps by his own response.

"As hard as I try, I can't seem to stay away from you . . . or stop touching you," he said softly. "You're like an enchanting siren from the sea." His eyes continued to hold mine with a look of intimacy and passion, making me want to reach for him once again. But I could feel him drawing away from me again.

"Would you like to tell me exactly what you were doing on the balcony in the midst of a storm?"

He rose from the bed to stand beside it and I could see the effort he had to make at composure. I think that, more than anything, caused a feeling of hope to leap up within me.

"You'll think I've lost my mind . . . perhaps I have." Saying it out loud somehow made the whole episode seem ludicrous. The thought was already nagging at me that I had dreamed the voice. And couldn't the draft have caused the door to close, trapping me outside? But I shivered as I remembered the feel of those hands pushing me out onto the balcony. No, I could not possibly have imagined that.

"Tell me," he said, his voice firm and unrelenting.

I told him about the voice that woke me and my belief that someone had been in my room. When I related how I had followed the intruder down the hallway, Nicholas threw me a look of disbelief and turned to pace the floor angrily.

"Dammit, Victoria, what were you thinking?" his voice rasped with exasperation. "You could have knocked at my door! How can I protect you if you insist on going about chasing ghosts in the middle of the night?"

"It was no ghost!" I snapped, hurt by his disapproval. Even though I knew he was right and I had acted foolishly, his scolding made me feel like a child. "Besides, I'm used to taking care of myself!"

"It always comes back to that with you, doesn't it?"

Then he sighed, the sound a mixture of disgust and frustration. But he did try to maintain a more patient demeanor. "Did you ever actually see anyone?"

"No, not really. Only a shadow as he pushed me onto the balcony. Why does someone want to play these ridiculous games with me?"

"Games? Surely you don't believe this was a game! You could have died from the cold and rain, especially after having been so ill. And you . . . you played right into his hands when you followed him into the hallway alone." I could almost see his mind working as he concentrated on what I had just told him.

"Well, I suppose I'm not the most popular person at Moonwatch at the moment."

Nicholas only looked at me, a small frown worrying his brow as he waited for me to explain my statement.

"I mean it's fairly obvious that Frances resents me. She's tried her best to turn Tad against me, poor lad. And everywhere I turn Ona seems to be watching me with those odd, accusing eyes."

"No, no, Victoria. Ona may look frightening, but believe me, he's as gentle as a lamb. He would never harm anyone. And Frances . . . ? That's too ridiculous to even deny."

I was angered by his attitude, and hurt. Even though I knew he would defend his sister, I felt a sense of betrayal that I had no right to feel.

"Then who? Perhaps it was your friend Eric Roberts." I deliberately kept my voice calm as I spoke the name.

Nicholas's blue eyes were cool as they regarded me with an unreadable expression. "I wondered when you would get to that," he said quietly.

"Tell me, Nicholas, was he also here at Moonwatch when I had the other *accident* in the lighthouse tower?" My tone was dispassionate, as if I did not really care, but inside my heart skittered crazily as I waited for his denial.

"No, he was not."

"I thought it was your mother who hired him at Ashford Place—hoped it was. But it was you, wasn't it?" I did not want to believe it, even now, but his face reflected the truth he had wanted to keep from me.

"Why, Nicholas? Please tell me why."

I could see his slow, reluctant acquiescence as he walked toward the bed. He pulled a chair close and sat down, making no effort to touch me now.

"Are you warm?" he asked.

"I'm fine," I answered, sitting patiently in bed, the quilts pulled up to my waist. I felt no self-consciousness in his presence, no sense of false modesty.

"I'm sure you have many questions," he said slowly.

He would not make it easy for me, would not volunteer any answers. Instead he was going to leave it to me to find out what I could.

"On whose authority was my father's study renovated after the fire?"

"Mine," he answered tersely, his eyes meeting mine boldly.

"Nicholas, why don't we dispense with this cat and mouse game and you simply tell me what made you do such a thing."

He leaned forward, seeming to relax a bit as his elbows rested on his thighs. His fingertips were pressed lightly together as he stared thoughtfully at his hands.

"I can imagine how angry you were, Victoria. I should have told you all this before you went back to your home. But whether you believe it or not, whatever I did was for you . . . and for your peace of mind as much as anything. I didn't want you to see the place as it was . . . the way it looked after the fire. And I didn't want to have to explain why I had the authority to do what I did."

"Authority? I don't understand."

"Ashford Place is mine, Victoria. Your father deeded it to me months ago. I have the papers if—"

"No!" I interrupted. "What are you saying? Why would he do such a thing? You mean Ashford Place is no longer mine and you let me go on thinking—"

"Victoria, listen to me. I know your father's death was a tremendous shock for you. And coming here has been hard too. I didn't want you to know all this until you had time to accept everything that has happened."

I was unable to speak for the choking tears in my throat. I knew without a doubt that the look in his eyes was sincere and I dreaded what he was about to say.

"Your father was very unhappy after your mother's death, more I think than you ever knew. He gambled a great deal. Ashford Place was frequently filled with guests whom I'm sure he would not have wanted his young daughter to associate with. There were years of it—too much drinking, too many gambling debts. And women—more women than he could even remember. He wanted to stop later, to bring you home, but it was too late for him. I think he grew to hate himself for his weaknesses, but he could not seem to help himself."

Tears fell slowly down my cheeks as I shook my head, but I was hardly aware of their presence. I simply could not imagine my father behaving in the way Nicholas had just described, but I knew in my heart it was true. It explained so many things.

"Go on," I said hoarsely.

"Your father borrowed money from the company secretly. More and more of it as time went on . . ."

"Borrowed? You mean he stole it!" I said bitterly.

"It was his money too. He told me he intended to pay it back, always after the next card game, or the next horse race. And I believe he meant to, but . . ."

Nicholas spread his hands helplessly and gazed at me apologetically.

"Did he actually come to you and tell you he'd taken the money?" I hoped my father had at least been honorable enough to do that, but the look on Nicholas's face told me differently.

"No," he said quietly.

"You're trying to make it seem as if he did nothing wrong. Why? To protect me?"

Nicholas did not answer my question, but the look of pity in his eyes told me it was true.

"By the time we discovered the losses, the company was almost in ruins. He insisted on telling Mother himself and naturally she was shocked. When they quarreled, as they often did, she became very ill. She's been bedridden ever since. That's why Frances is so bitter toward Anthony, even though Mother eventually forgave him. She could forgive him anything you know, except for loving your mother, instead of her." Nicholas looked at me pointedly as if he wanted to make sure I knew what he was telling me.

"I knew there was something there, but I could not be sure exactly what." I wanted to know more about Mrs. Hayne and my father, but I knew this was not the time.

"Your father placed the deed for Ashford Place in my name as partial payment for the losses. I had hoped we would not have to sell it and I kept it the way it was . . . for you." He paused, waiting I knew for my response.

I was exhausted, as if I'd been running for hours. I lay back against the pillows, trying to think clearly enough to comprehend what all of this meant.

"And what about Eric Roberts?" I asked, staring blankly at the ceiling.

"We had to let all the household help go, except only

the most necessary ones. Eric worked for us on the docks. Lesley mentioned to me that he was exceptionally bright and thought he would be able to look after the place well enough."

"I fired him." I sat up straight and challenged him to defend the man. "He was rude and secretive and I fired him."

Nicholas smiled crookedly, his eyes twinkling with real amusement as he surveyed my indignant face. "Yes, I know." His voice drawled sarcastically. "I suppose the social graces are not exactly Eric's forte. But we'll work on that. In the meantime he will be here at Moonwatch helping Lesley.

"There's one other thing I'd like to know Nicholas. And I'd like you to be honest with me."

His eyebrow quirked and he nodded. "Of course. What is it?"

"The Ching tê chên pagoda. Do you think my father stole it the night he died?"

He leaned back against the chair and expelled his breath softly. Then he looked up at me, his cobalt eyes meeting mine with a look so direct and yet so gentle that my heart seemed to stop for a second.

"Yes, angel, I think he did." His voice was kind as if he hoped to take some of the sting from his words.

"No!" I blurted. "I'll never believe that! If he did, then where is it now? I searched at home—" Then I realized that the house I'd considered home was no longer mine. "—Ashford Place, and I found nothing. Surely if he had taken it, it would still have been in the house."

Nicholas hit the palms of his hands against his thighs in a gesture of frustration and stood up. "I don't know," he sighed. "I admit I haven't the faintest idea, just as I have no idea who would want to hurt you. But I can promise you one thing, I intend to find the answers."

"Good," I said. That, at least made me feel better. Even the terror of the night did not seem so frightening when I was with him.

He looked at the clock on the mantel. "We've talked the night away." The gray light of morning was now visible outside the window.

He walked back to the bed and sat beside me. "How are you feeling, Victoria? No chills?"

"Nicholas, I'm fine," I replied firmly.

"That's a relief, but under the circumstances I think it might be wise if you stayed in bed today."

"Absolutely not! I'm not about to let this person frighten me into an illness, and I won't stay in bed to give him the satisfaction of thinking he frightens me!"

Nicholas looked surprised, but he grinned. He had a beautiful smile and I found myself longing to reach forward to touch his lips and feel the rough shadow of his chin where he needed a shave.

"You are a stubborn lass," he murmured. His eyes flicked downward to my mouth and I could see the color of his eyes darken. "But I find I like you more every day." His voice was a mere whisper.

Just when I was in danger of throwing myself at him, even if I had to beg him to kiss me, he abruptly stood up.

"I'll go downstairs and see if breakfast is almost ready. Could you at least let me have it sent up here?"

"No," I insisted. "I'll dress and come down as usual."

"I thought as much," he replied, smiling. The room seemed empty and cold when he had gone, leaving me anxious to be up and about so that I could see him again at breakfast.

Chapter XII

I looked out the window as I dressed, surprised to find it still raining. The gray haze of fog floating at ground level and the fine spray of rain seemed to engulf the entire world. I could see the ocean only as far as the shore where great billowing yellow-green waves continued to crash loudly.

I put on a cream-colored cashmere wool dress with long full sleeves and a soft full skirt. It was trimmed at the neck and down the bodice with a pale blue braid, set off by small gold buttons. I needed the warmth of such a dress, for although I would not admit it to Nicholas, I was still cold. I had tried to dry my hair before the blazing fire, but it remained slightly damp. There was nothing to do except pin it into a loop at the back of my head.

I passed the darkened alcove where I had been stranded and could not repress a shiver that ran through me.

When I entered the dining room, Denise Hayne sat near the large fireplace in one of the wing chairs. Nicholas stood nearby and I sensed from their expressions that he was telling her what had happened to me during the night.

Frances, who sat near her mother's chair, looked up as I came in, but there was no sympathy in her eyes. Even Tad seemed aloof toward me this morning. But I did note his clean clothes and neatly combed hair.

We all sat down at the table to a huge breakfast of sliced bacon and scrambled eggs, freshly baked bread, baked apples, pancakes, and a pitcher of hot buttered syrup. I poured myself hot tea and began to eat, feeling quite hungry after the ordeal in the rain.

Nicholas was watching me. He smiled and seemed pleased at my healthy appetite. I concluded the hearty breakfast must have come on his orders.

Moments later Lesley came in, dressed in a more flattering gown than usual, of black and gold striped silk. And her face, as she smiled, seemed to have a special glow about it. I wondered if the man following her had anything to do with her cheerful disposition, for they seemed to be spending a great deal of time together.

Eric Roberts, dressed in a well-cut black jacket and beige waistcoat, looked quite different from when I last spoke to him. Across the vest dangled a gold watch chain. Today he looked for all the world like a lawyer or a successful businessman. I wondered exactly what his position would now be at Ancona and Hayne.

I'm sure my glances at him made him feel self-conscious and he seemed to avoid my eyes as he seated himself beside Lesley to my right. When Nicholas related the story to them of my adventurous night I would like to have seen Eric's eyes, for I still did not quite trust him.

But Lesley turned to me, her dark eyes full of concern. She watched me as she took her bread and tea.

"It's lucky you weren't hurt badly, or taken ill from the cold."

"Well, I for one think this is just ludicrous. How

could anyone have gotten into the house? And where did they come from? I mean we *are* isolated here at Cape Fear." Frances's words seemed to be aimed at placing doubt upon my story.

But I was not about to let myself get into a debate with her about the validity of what had happened. So I only shrugged and went on with my meal.

"Maybe it was Grandpa Hayne's ghost," Tad said almost shyly.

I looked at him, the amusement quickly fading from my lips as I saw his face. He stared at me angrily, resentfully, and I could not imagine what had caused this change in him.

"Tad! We'll hear no more of that," his mother snapped.

"Vickers saw him and so did Millie," the boy insisted defiantly.

"Tad, you heard your mother," Nicholas said quietly. His voice was stern, but he was plainly not disturbed by the boy's words.

"Victoria," Denise Hayne said. "I'm terribly sorry about all this. I hope you won't be frightened into leaving us."

I realized then with a bit of surprise that I no longer wanted to leave Moonwatch. I looked at Nicholas. There was more determination to stay now than before and I realized it had not so much to do with clearing my father as it did with being near the master of Moonwatch.

"Grandpa Hayne doesn't want her here. Can't you see that?" Tad was as belligerent as I'd seen him and I could only stare at him in disbelief. What had I done to provoke such anger? "He didn't want your father here and he doesn't want you either!"

"Tad," I began. "What—"

But before I could speak, Frances swiftly took the

boy's arm and pulled him from his chair, practically dragging him from the room. "That will be quite enough from you, young man."

I had never felt so sorry for anyone as I did for Tad at that moment. It must have been extremely embarrassing for him.

He threw a look toward me filled with both disillusionment and pain. I stood to protest for I could not bear seeing his mother treat him so coldly. But she had already whisked him from the room.

"Let him go, dear," Denise Hayne said. "The boy's head has always been filled with whimsical notions." There was annoyance in her gestures, but it was obvious to me that she was visibly disturbed by Tad's words about the ghost of her husband.

"I'm going to find him," I said, walking swiftly from the room and up the stairs toward Tad's room.

As I neared the corridor leading to Frances and Tad's quarters I heard someone behind me. I whirled about, my heart beating hard at my throat.

"Ona!" I exclaimed.

He did not answer me. He stood instead in the shadows and watched me for a moment before turning and walking away. He made no attempt to try and conceal the fact that he had been following me.

Frances was just outside the door and her dark eyes appraised me coolly.

"Let me talk to him," I said, moving past her.

"He's not there. He got away from me. I don't know where he went." Her words were clipped and impersonal as if she were speaking of a stray animal rather than her son.

"Why was Tad so angry with me?" I asked. "What have you told him to make him hate me so?" My voice became louder with agitation and I wanted to shake her, make her see that she was using her son for her own petty grievances.

"I'm sure I don't know what you mean," she said disdainfully, but her cheeks were flushed with color, betraying the anger she felt every time she was near me.

Quickly she brushed past me and walked down the hall.

"Oh!" I said in frustration. My fists were clenched by my side and I thrust them downward in an angry gesture, then turned and walked straight into Nicholas's arms.

"Where is Tad?" he asked.

"I don't know. Frances only said he ran away from her. I know she's your sister, Nicholas, but honestly, the way she treats him sometimes, I just want to strangle her!"

He laughed softly. "Remind me never to make you angry." Then he took my arm. "Come along, I think I know where we can find him."

I followed him down the hall to where the landing above the stairs lead to the lighthouse. Of course. I should have guessed where he would go. I hesitated only a second before going back to that section of the house, but it was long enough for Nicholas to take note of it.

He turned and looked down into my face, then slowly reached to take both my cold hands in his. "It's all right, angel," he soothed. "Don't you know I would never let anything hurt you?"

His dark blue eyes were hypnotic, urging me to him, pulling me gently along with him. Deep inside a memory rang silently in my mind and I knew his look and the power it seemed to have over me were exactly as they were in my dream. But in that dream he had lead me to the edge of danger and then stepped away, laughing as I fell. Quickly I brushed aside my ridiculous thoughts and followed more closely behind

Nicholas as we came to the curving stairwell.

It was the first time I had been back, but with Nicholas I found I was not afraid and we hastened up the steps to the study.

The door was locked. Nicholas tapped softly upon the massive wood. "Tad," he said quietly. "Let me in, son."

Slowly the door opened and Tad stood facing us defiantly. When he saw me he turned and went back to the captain's chair before the wide expanse of windows. He looked through the telescope as if we were not even there.

I didn't feel as if I should interfere so I sat down, allowing Nicholas to handle his nephew.

"What is it, Tad?" he asked. He stood beside the boy and placed his hand on his shoulder. "Why were you so rude to Victoria?"

"I wasn't," he insisted sullenly.

Nicholas, seeing Tad's reluctance, did not try to force him as I felt most men would do. Instead he leaned closer to him and looked out to sea along the line where Tad looked.

"What do you see today?" he asked patiently.

Tad shrugged his shoulders indifferently and continued to look out to sea.

The fog finally had lifted and the rain had also stopped. The wind continued to howl fiercely about the tower, although the sky seemed to be clearing. I could make out small spots of blue far out over the ocean.

Suddenly Tad leaned forward eagerly and raised his eyes from the eyepiece to squint out into the ocean. "Look there, Uncle Nick!" he exclaimed. "It's a schooner. Can you see it?"

Nicholas leaned down and looked into the telescope. "So it is, lad," he said. "How many masts does she have?"

"Four!" Tad exclaimed. "She's got four! Gosh, ain't she a beauty?"

I had never seen Tad so excited and I smiled as I watched the two of them there together, talking with such enthusiasm about the ship on the horizon.

Tad turned to me somewhat self-consciously. "Would you like to see it?" he asked.

I rose and walked to him. He slipped from the seat to allow me in. Nicholas leaned close to me and pointed out the direction where the ship lay. I gazed through the telescope until my eyes found the ship.

"Oh," I whispered, drawing in my breath with wonder. I never tired of seeing the beautiful ships upon the water. This one was large, riding at full sail and it was miles out to sea. But even at that distance her grace and superior structure were evident. "It's magnificent."

We watched the ship sail across the horizon until it finally disappeared into the blurred distance. Then we all fell silent, sad that it was gone, even as we remembered the rare beauty of such a sight. It was like watching a rainbow disappear.

"I didn't mean what I said about Grandpa's ghost not wanting you. I was just mad." Tad did not look at me as he spoke.

"But why were you angry, Tad? I had hoped we were becoming friends," I said.

"We were—we are." He looked at me then, the pain and confusion evident in his eyes. "But you promised you'd teach me and you forgot. My mother said you never asked her. She said you didn't want to waste your time on a boy like me."

"Oh, Tad," I whispered, looking toward Nicholas for support. "That's not true." I felt such sorrow for the boy and I wasn't sure I had the right words to comfort him. "Of course I want to teach you. I just didn't have a chance to ask, but I was sure it would be all right. I'm sorry if you thought I'd forgotten."

Some of the anger and hurt seemed to leave his face, but I knew that winning his confidence would not be so easy a task. His mother already had ten years of such negativity to her advantage. It angered me more than I could say that she could treat her own son in such a manner.

"You do?" he asked. "You still want to teach me?"

"Of course I do . . . very much. If it's all right with your uncle . . . and your mother." I looked at Nicholas who was regarding me with a quizzical look and a tenderness that surprised me.

"It's a very good idea, Tad. Don't worry about your mother. I'll see to it," he told the child.

"Oh, boy! Can I go tell Grandmother and tell her about the schooner?"

"Run along," Nicholas said with a laugh. "I'll show your new teacher the schoolroom. I'm sure it needs some work before she can begin."

We stood for a moment after Tad left. I walked about the room touching the many beautiful things Captain Hayne had brought to this room. I paused before the carved figurehead.

"I remember her from the *Galatea*." I reached forward to touch the cool surface of the wood.

"One of the best designs your father ever made," Nicholas said.

"Yes, she took us to Charleston one balmy summer day. It seems so long ago."

Nicholas did not try to explain why the sea nymph from my father's ship was here at Moonwatch and I didn't want to know. I could only assume that everything now belonged to the Hayne family, everything that once had been ours.

I turned quickly and walked back to the window. I did not want to become caught up in the crush of memories, of times that could never be again. And I did not want to have to think about Ashford Place, or the fact that now I was left with nothing except memories.

"You're very quiet," Nicholas said. He came to stand beside me and looked out toward the ocean. "Those gray eyes of yours are like the ocean out there . . . so stormy and mysterious. I can see so much in them."

"Can you?" I asked coolly, turning to look up at him.

"It must be painful seeing your father's personal belongings here and knowing what he lost. I'm sorry. I wish—"

"You've no need to be sorry. I will manage very well on my own," I said. "As I told Tad I have a teaching position at Salem College whenever I want it."

"Is that what you really want?" His eyes were very bright and clear there in the gray light that flooded the room. I found myself disconcerted by his direct look. It was hard to remain angry when he looked at me that way.

"Of course it's what I want," I insisted. "I've always wanted to teach."

His mouth quirked oddly at the corner as if he did not believe me. I pulled my eyes away from his for I did not want him to see how very much he affected me.

"You don't fool me, you know. I've seen the way your vision is always pulled toward the sea, and how your cat eyes brighten at the sight of a ship. Somehow I can't imagine that spirit and curiosity tucked away somewhere in the staid confines of a schoolroom."

I frowned at him, for no one had ever seemed to know me quite so well.

"Your hair should never be bound up in a prim knot at the back." He reached to touch my hair, slowly removing the pins from the back and letting it fall about my shoulders. "It should be wild and free, blowing in the wind under the sails of a ship, wet with the rain . . . like it was last night. You were so beautiful."

I had almost stopped breathing. His words filled me with a longing so intense that I wanted to cry. His blue eyes reflected the colors of the sea and sky, sometimes changing to a dark gray, like the mist and rain. But his words had struck home and left me wondering if we were more alike than I wanted to admit.

We stood only inches apart, so close I could feel the rhythm of his breathing. He made no effort to touch me, but as he continued to study my face and eyes, I felt as if he had.

I looked away then, from those eyes that seemed to see into my very soul. "I've always been frightened of the sea, you know that. How could you imagine me on a great ship when the very thought of it fills me with overwhelming terror?"

"Perhaps because I imagine myself there with you," he whispered, "showing you every aspect of the sea and the great ships that attempt to conquer it. It's where you belong, Victoria! I know that. It's in your blood as surely as it is in mine and you can't deny it."

I knew he was right. It was something I had never admitted to anyone, the way my heart soared at the mere vision of a ship at sail, or the feel of the spray on my face as the prow cut through blue-green water. Just the sound of the wind whipping and cracking in the sails filled me with excitement, but my fear had kept me from ever talking about it or even allowing myself to dream that it could someday be a reality.

"Perhaps you don't know me as well as you think." I was still afraid to let him in, to let anyone really know my innermost feelings.

"Oh, I know you, Victoria," he said, his voice husky as he stood closer. "I know you as I've always known the sea, like something that's been with me forever.

And you feel it too, don't you?" he whispered.

I turned away from him then, his words threatening to break through all my barriers. I was not sure what he wanted from me and I was afraid.

"I could teach you what you've always longed to know—about the sea, about life. You won't be afraid, I promise. I won't let you be." He regarded me intently, his eyes burning into mine. "We belong together. You know it as surely as I do."

"What . . . what are you saying?" I asked, my voice suddenly shaky, as I turned to stare at him.

"Marry me, Victoria. I'm saying I want you to be my wife." He pulled me toward him.

"Marry you?" I almost gasped aloud. But even as surprise washed over me it did not enter my mind then that this was what his mother had wanted all along. I could think of nothing except the meaning of his softly spoken words . . . and his eyes.

"Is the idea so offensive to you?" he asked. His lips quirked in amusement at the stunned look on my face.

"No," I whispered. "Never that. I'm just—it's so soon. I hardly know you."

"Know me? You can't deny what's between us . . . has been since your first night here. Have you forgotten last night? The way you felt . . . the way we both feel when we're together." His words coaxed me enticingly as his lips whispered only inches away from mine.

How could I deny it . . . deny him? It was what I had hoped for, dreamed of in my innermost self.

He made it sound so idyllic—almost too good to be true. Still something deep inside nagged at me, made me doubt his words. Was he only doing his mother's bidding, fulfilling her perverted wish to have a grandchild by the daughter of a man she once loved so fiercely and could never have? Had she asked it of him as her dying wish just as she threatened to do?

"Is this because of your mother?" I had to ask, had to see his face when I spoke the words.

"Angel, how can you ask that after last night? After what we both feel right now . . . after this."

He pulled me tightly against him, his hands almost spanning my waist, and he kissed me. His lips were warm and sweet, commanding that I feel what he meant. And I did. I could hardly breathe from the joy that swept through me. I knew he could see it in my eyes when he finally pulled away.

"Marry me, Victoria," he insisted, his voice low and demanding. "Let me take care of you . . . love you."

I closed my eyes and gave in to his demands and those of my heart. There was no time to listen to anything else, not my intuition or my head. I simply *felt* and every emotion and instinct within me was saying yes to his masculinity and his sensual persuasion.

"Yes, Nicholas," I whispered. "Just love me. I want you to love me." My hands slid around to the back of his neck and I caught his thick black hair in my fingers. I didn't take time to examine the look I saw in his eyes as my mouth reached for his. There was no denying the pleasure I saw there, but only later would I remember what else I saw—a look that could only be described as triumph.

Later after we had gone downstairs he kept his hand possessively at my waist. We walked together arm in arm to the wing of the house where Frances and Tad lived. That was also where the old schoolroom had been.

I could not recall ever being so happy and it was all because of the man beside me. I could not believe my good fortune. One moment I was alone and penniless with no family or home; the next I was looking forward to marriage with the most handsome, exciting man I'd ever met. One whose eyes could set my heart pounding and whose touch was nothing less than consuming.

As he took me into the schoolroom, I had to try and concentrate on his words rather than his face. He was as distracted as I, pausing between phrases to kiss me or touch me lightly. I thought nothing or no one could ever make me as happy as I was then, and I vowed that nothing would ever take him from me.

As I walked around the room I saw a wooden table in one corner with four straight-backed chairs. I ran my hands absentmindedly over the dusty surface, feeling an unevenness as I did so. When I looked closer, I could see a name that had been carved into the wood.

"I see you've found my handiwork," Nicholas said, smiling now at me.

"Captain Nicholas Hayne," I read. The letters were scrawled in a childish scribble. "Oh, Nicholas, how old were you?"

"I don't know. About eight, I think." He smiled indulgently at me.

"And you wanted to be a sea captain even then?"

"Oh, yes, always. Even when my father and I did not agree on anything, I always wanted to go to sea. In fact, nothing could have kept me from it." His voice was warm with memories, both of the schoolroom and of the sea, I thought. But there was also a firmness and a determination in his words. This was a man who was used to having what he wanted.

"So did I," I whispered. I kept my voice low and conspiratorial, teasing him about guessing my long, secret desire.

"I know. I told you you have an expressive face." He reached to cup my face in his hands and moved closer, just as the door to the schoolroom opened.

"Oh!" It was Frances and her look was one of absolute shock at seeing us so close together with

Nicholas touching me in such an intimate fashion.

"I thought I heard voices." She was obviously not pleased at the affection she saw between us, but she did not make any further comments about it.

Nicholas put his arm around my waist, not bothering to deny there was anything between us. And that gesture earned my undying gratitude. "Victoria is going to teach Tad a few subjects. If it's all right with you, of course."

"Why I . . . Well, of course. Heaven knows he needs some disciplined study. But Tad *is* quite a handful and—"

"I don't think you need worry, Frances," Nicholas interrupted. "The boy is quite enthusiastic about it, and I think he likes Victoria."

Frances raised her eyebrows and seemed struck dumb by the looks Nicholas and I exchanged.

"Well. I'll just go get two of the girls to come up and clean in here. I presume you intend to start right away?" She was trying hard to appear unconcerned.

"Yes," I answered. "Tomorrow, if that's all right with you."

"Oh, yes . . . yes, indeed. That will be perfectly fine." She frowned at Nicholas as she left the room, her face clearly puzzled.

After she had closed the door Nicholas chuckled softly. "We've certainly managed to stir Frances's curiosity, haven't we?"

"I'm afraid so," I said, frowning slightly at him. "Nicholas, I don't want to cause any more resentment than I already have." Though I didn't say it, I certainly did not want to cause a rift between Nicholas and his family or put him in a position of having to defend me.

"Don't worry, darling," he said. "Frances will come around. She's not as cold as she seems."

"But what about Tad?" I asked. "I think this was one

of the reasons he disliked me so much. The first thing he said to me was that I mustn't marry his Uncle Nick."

"I know, and I'm sorry that happened, Victoria. I suppose I should have set Frances straight long ago and insisted she stop telling Tad such hurtful, foolish things. I'll talk to Tad."

"Would you mind if I tell him? He was so upset with me when I first came. He thought I came purposefully to steal you away from them. And now what will he think?"

"I think he'll come around with time. You certainly don't want a ten-year-old child to dictate our future, do you?" His words were straightforward, but there was a gentleness to his tone which radiated sympathy.

"No, of course not," I said.

"I'll go with you when you tell him," he offered.

But neither of us had the chance to go to Tad, for he chose that moment to walk into the schoolroom.

"Did you tell my mother?" he asked. His eyes were large and bright, full of childish hope.

"Yes, we did, Tad, and she has agreed." I smiled at his happy grin and pointed toward the table where I'd discovered Nicholas's name. "Your Uncle Nick sat here when he was almost your age. See? He carved his name."

Tad looked up at Nicholas who stood quietly watching the boy. He nodded and smiled at Tad, who seemed to be finding it hard to believe his uncle had ever been his age.

Almost reverently, Tad sat in one of the chairs at the table and ran his fingers lightly across the whittled letters.

"Tad, your uncle and I have something to tell you." I sat at the table across from Tad.

"I hope you will understand." Tad looked at me as I spoke, his eyes wide with curiosity. As I continued, I glanced at Nicholas for support.

"Nicholas and I—we're going to be married. I know I told you before that this would not happen, but, well, that was before I came to know him as I do now."

Tad looked from one of us to the other. "Does that mean you'll be living here with us forever?" His question took me by surprise.

"Well, I'm not sure about forever, but, yes, I'll be able to stay here now."

He smiled then, a quiet shy smile and if his response was not wildly enthusiastic, it did allow me to breathe a sigh of relief. I could see he no longer bore me the bitter resentment of before.

"I'm glad," was all he said.

"Tad." Nick's deep voice sounded loudly in the nearly empty room. "Nothing will ever change how I feel about you, or the position you will one day have with the company. The only thing this will change is the size of our family. I think you already know that Victoria is a very nice person and that she cares about you."

I was surprised and grateful for his words and his ability to put things into perspective. When he caught my look he only grinned that crooked smile I had come to love so much.

"You're the first person we've told, Tad," I added.

"I am?" He seemed pleased when I told him that.

"We wanted to tell you before anyone," Nicholas said. "Do you think you can keep it a secret for a little while, until we announce it to the family tonight?"

"Sure," he grinned. "You can trust me." His last words were spoken with a certain boyish pride.

"I know we can." Nicholas ran his fingers across Tad's dark curly hair.

"We'll begin your first class at nine tomorrow morning, Tad," I said as he was leaving. He turned once and smiled back at us. He seemed completely different from the boy who had met me that first evening and pulled rudely at my cape.

I was so relieved by Tad's reaction that my feet were scarcely touching the floor as Nicholas walked me to my door. I was going to have a family at last, albeit an unusual one. And more exciting and unbelievable than that, I would be marrying a man who stirred within me such emotions that I could not believe they existed. My head felt light and giddy at the thought.

After Nicholas had left, I danced gaily about the room, holding out the skirt of my soft cashmere dress as I whirled and glided across the floor. I finally came to rest at the window and stood with my hands clasped tightly to my chest.

"Moonwatch," I whispered to the sea. "I shall be mistress of Moonwatch."

Chapter XIII

I wanted to look my best for dinner and decided to wear my favorite dress, the emerald green crepe. I had almost forgotten about the Gullah doll until I pulled the dress from the wardrobe and spread its wide skirt on the bed.

I felt a tingle of apprehension sweep over me. I saw the inside hem of the dress where the small jagged edge bore witness to the missing piece of cloth. The tiny rust spots were still there and I scrubbed them with a damp cloth until they were barely visible. It did not matter that they were on the underside of the skirt and would not be seen. I did not like to think of those stains there against me.

As I arranged my hair, Nicholas's romantic words of the afternoon came to mind. I left my hair down to fall about my face and shoulders, then I stepped into the green dress. I was almost ready, just finishing the buttons at the back of the dress, when Nicholas knocked at my door.

His smile was warm and possessive, filled with a look I felt was for me alone. Silently he turned me about so he could assist with the buttons. As I pulled my hair aside out of his way he moaned slightly, a sound filled with fun and teasing.

"Your hair smells like roses," he whispered. Before I could reply, his lips were on my neck where my hand held back the hair. I leaned my head back against his shoulder and closed my eyes, giving in to the pleasure that swept through me.

He laughed softly and fastened the few remaining buttons. My attraction to him and my obvious desire seemed to please him very much. "We'd better go down while I still know what I'm doing," he said.

Every time he said such words to me, words to let me believe he was somehow under my power, I felt alive and tingling with pleasure. But I knew that it was I who was under *his* control.

When we entered the dining room together, I felt as if our feelings must be obvious to everyone, even though Tad was the only one there who knew our secret. Nicholas had asked that Tad be allowed to stay up for dinner tonight.

I looked at Tad and caught a glint of excitement in his eyes. His sweet smile made me feel not quite so alone.

I hardly was aware of what was served that night, waiting only for the moment when Nicholas would tell everyone of our plans.

"Mother, Victoria and I have an announcement," he began.

Mrs. Hayne looked up in surprise, her opaque blue eyes blinking slightly as she looked first at me and then back to Nicholas.

"I've asked Victoria to marry me . . . and she has said yes." Nicholas smiled and raised his wine glass toward me.

I heard a gasp of surprise, but I could not be sure whether it came from Mrs. Hayne or the other two women seated at the table.

Nicholas's mother clasped her hands together in front of her and her eyes grew bright with happiness. She looked steadily at me then, nodding slightly as if to thank me, or to show her approval. I could not be sure which. Her look was cool and clever, as if she were entirely responsible for the whole thing.

It seemed a blur when we all arose from the table, Nicholas and I receiving congratulations. Frances came slowly and reluctantly forward, a look of scorn on her face. But as she stood before us she did manage a smile and even clasped me to her in a cool, polite embrace.

"I hope neither of you will regret this," she said solemnly, in a voice low enough only for the two of us.

"Why, thank you, dear sister, for your enthusiastic reception." Nicholas's dry words were given with humor and a crooked smile. But I knew it irritated him. Frances only shrugged her shoulders in resignation before taking Tad by the arm and turning to leave the dining room.

"I'll see you tomorrow morning at nine o'clock, Tad," I reminded him. At my words he turned and smiled at me shyly, giving us a small wave of his hand.

Lesley, who now seemed to spend most of her time with the mysterious Eric Roberts, was smiling as she approached me.

Her embrace was warm and friendly, and she seemed genuinely happy for us. But her whispered words were only for me. "I owe you an apology, it seems. You are far more astute than I gave you credit for."

"No," I said, "it's not like that at all." Did she really think I was marrying Nicholas for anything other than love?

She held up her hand to silence my words. "Never explain your choices, Victoria." Then she moved on to speak with Nicholas.

Eric Roberts stood before me. It was the first time we had spoken since our angry confrontation at Ashford Place.

"Congratulations, Miss Ancona," he said, taking my hand in his. I was aware of the hard, rough texture of his hand.

"Thank you," I said stiffly, for I still felt uncomfortable in his presence.

"I hope that I am forgiven for upsetting you before . . . at your home." He seemed genuinely apologetic and his manner was certainly more genial than before.

"There's nothing to forgive," I said. "It was a difficult day for me . . . coming home. I'm afraid I was more distraught than I realized." But although I made my own attempt at an apology, I was not yet ready to have him back as majordomo.

"I understand completely." His voice was smooth and he bowed slightly, his action incongruous with his stocky, muscular build and swarthy complexion. He had certainly learned well in his transition from dock worker to a valued Hayne employee.

As Eric walked away, I saw Nicholas talking with Lesley. They seemed so deep in conversation that I hesitated to approach them. I surmised it must be business from her serious looks. But as she saw my brief glance, she smiled and moved quickly toward Eric, following him from the room.

There was only Mrs. Hayne and Ona left in the room with us. To accommodate her, Nicholas and I both pulled our chairs near her to talk.

"Nicholas," she said, leaning over to embrace her tall, handsome son. "This is the happiest day of my life. You could not have chosen a girl that would please me more." Then she reached out to include me, clasping my hand in a tight grip. "Victoria, thank you," she said.

I frowned, looking at Nicholas who only smiled at me quietly. "'Thank you' seems an odd thing to say, Mrs. Hayne. I'm in love with your son." I wanted her to have no doubt as to my reason for agreeing to marry him.

"Yes, of course you are!" she exclaimed. "And that makes it even more delightful. Whatever the reason, you must understand how very much you are welcomed here and are wanted as part of this family."

"Thank you," I said, watching her. She was such an odd woman. And the tears that swam in her pale blue eyes seemed imcompatible with the manipulation of which I knew her capable.

"I only hope I may live long enough to see the wedding," she said, smiling tremulously at Nicholas. "But if I do not, you must always remember how happy you've both made me today."

"Nonsense, Mother," Nicholas said gently. "Of course you shall see our wedding and many of our anniversaries as well."

"Then I hope you won't wait too long." Her words were not entirely joking, but I recognized this as another means of trying to persuade us into doing as she wished.

There was a glint in Nicholas's beautiful eyes as he looked at me. He knew exactly what his mother was up to. "We haven't had time to discuss that yet. What do you think, Victoria? Can you plan such an event within a few weeks?"

"Of course she can," Mrs. Hayne interjected. "I'll help her. We shall have it done in no time. And the place—I presume you will want to be married here at Moonwatch?"

"Why, yes, I suppose." I hardly had had time to think about all the details, caught up as I was in the magic of romance instead.

"Good. I'll see to the guest list tomorrow. Of course you must give me the names of anyone you wish to invite. We'll have Mrs. Dalton come out and design your gown. Oh! And I'd like to have a dinner party to celebrate the announcement. This is simply going to be marvelous!"

"I don't want you to overtire yourself because of this, Mother," Nicholas cautioned. "I'm sure Frances and Lesley will help."

"The date, children. What about the first of November?"

I'm sure I must have looked surprised. That was less than two weeks away. I looked at Nicholas; he was grinning widely, obviously amused by his mother's enthusiasm and my confusion.

"Is that too soon, darling?" Nicholas asked me. His look was innocent enough, but I did not miss his meaning: it was not too soon for him.

At the look in his eyes and the promise I saw within their blue depths, I could not have refused him anything and I think he knew it. I could not resist smiling with him, shaking my head in a helpless gesture. "No, it's not at all too soon," I answered.

"Wonderful!" his mother exclaimed, clasping her hands together like a child.

"I have much to think about before I sleep," she said. "Ona, I'm ready to go up to my room now. Good night, children." She leaned forward to kiss Nicholas and then me, bringing the exotic spicy scent that lingered about her like a pleasant mist.

After the night of our announcement, the house began to fairly bustle with activity. Along with the wedding plans were my classes with Tad so my days were completely filled. Nicholas usually spent most of his day at the office, which was on the other side of the Cape, about a thirty-minute ride from the house.

I had not been to the office or the docks since my arrival. My memories there were ones which always included my father. I used to be so proud when he took me around to meet the captains and the dock hands. His presence always commanded respect and we were treated regally.

Now, I once again looked forward to a visit there. I longed to see for myself the tall ships in the harbor, their reflection wavering in the clear blue-green water, and catch the scent of sun-baked wood and tar.

Being with Nicholas would make all the difference and I knew I no longer dreaded stirring up old ghostly memories of the past. We would begin our own memories and I knew they would be even sweeter ones.

I had decided part of Tad's lessons each day would consist of an outdoor study when the weather permitted. Luckily, our first day dawned beneath clear and sunny skies. The wind, it seemed, would always be with us at Moonwatch, and it was cool. But I had always enjoyed the wind, loved being out in it. I was delighted to discover that Tad felt the same.

We took a book from the schoolroom that identified various birds along the coastline. Tad ran about happily pointing out various gulls and great white pelicans that wheeled and soared above us and out beyond the water. Each one we identified was written in a small notebook which we would keep as a journal.

When we both grew tired, Tad came to walk beside me as we ventured farther along the beach, away from the house.

Most of the shoreline here was flat and smooth, devoid of rocks or plants. But as we went farther we could see a small rise of land before us which was scattered with large porous-looking gray stones. At this point the sea made a small inland jag so that the waves ran very close to the area.

"This is where the pirate treasure is," Tad exclaimed, running slightly ahead of me.

I could see a small opening in the hillock leading back into a sort of cave.

"Don't go in, Tad," I cautioned, running to catch up with him.

He waited for me at the entrance. His eyes were large with excitement and I noticed the impatience of his movements.

"I don't suppose there really is a treasure here?" I asked.

"Nah, there's nothing much inside. Sometimes people come here to look around or a sailor might wander by and rest awhile if the tide's low."

I smiled and bent down to look inside, but it was almost totally dark except for a thin stream of light farther back in the cave.

"I see a light back there," I said.

"It comes from a hole at the top," he said, pointing to the crest of the hill. "Sometimes when the sea is high and the tide's coming in, the water runs into the cave and splashes up through the hole—like a whale spout." Tad's eyes were alive with excitement.

"Oh," I mused. "I should love to see that."

"I gave it a name—the Whale Cave," he said proudly.

"That's very clever, Tad. I like it."

"Next time it storms, we'll both sneak down here to see it," he said slyly.

"Sneak? Because your mother won't approve, you mean?"

"Yes, but now we can tell Uncle Nicholas and then it will be right with her."

I was discovering that in Tad's eyes his uncle could

fix anything, knew everything. And it made me happy to hear it, almost comforted me, since Nicholas was still a stranger to me. Tad's words about him told me very much indeed about the type of man I was marrying.

"It's getting late, Tad. We'd better get back to the house."

Walking back, we were on the side of the house where the lighthouse stood. I remembered that first day I'd walked on the beach and had seen someone watching from the light room. Instinctively I looked up at it now.

Tad's eyes followed my gaze, but he made no comment. Could he have been the one I saw that day?

"Tad, did you watch me from the lighthouse when I first came here?"

"No, why?" His eyes were innocent and held a startled look which made me believe he was telling the truth.

"Oh, nothing really. There was someone up there one day when I looked up. But he stepped back out of the way as if he didn't want me to see who it was."

"Grandpa," he muttered underneath his breath.

"What?"

"It was Grandpa Hayne. It's where his ghost stays, but I don't think he would push you down the stairs." Tad's small freckled face was troubled as he spoke.

"Tad, surely you know there are no such things as ghosts?" But even as I said the words I felt a shiver of apprehension run through me.

"It's only his spirit, but when he finds the pagoda he can go away and rest." His words sounded childish, like a fairytale, but I wasn't entirely certain they came only from Tad's imagination.

I stopped for a moment and turned him to face me. "Tad, where did you hear such an idea?"

"Millie's seen him and Vickers—some of the other servants too," he insisted.

"They told you that when he finds the pagoda he'll go away?"

"No, Mother said that." He looked at me almost defiantly and I felt sorry for him. His mother had placed a heavy burden on him, by making him choose between her opinion and mine.

"I see, and what does your uncle say?"

"He said it was foolish fe—feminine nonsense." Then he smiled crookedly, reminding me at once of Nicholas.

"Oh, he did, did he?" I asked, smiling back at him.

Tad laughed aloud at my teasing. "What *is* feminine?" he asked.

"It means female . . . womanly. And I presume your uncle thinks most women have only foolish ideas." I was smiling as I spoke, for I knew better, but I wanted to lighten Tad's mood a bit.

"I guess you'll have to talk to him about it," Tad suggested, joining in the fun with me.

I laughed and put my arm about his shoulders, directing him toward the house. "I suppose I shall," I declared.

We walked silently until we reached the steps of the house and Tad looked at me, his face serious again. "Do you think it *is* Grandpa's ghost, Victoria?"

"No, Tad, I don't."

"Then who pushed you down the steps, and locked you out on the balcony in the storm?"

"I don't know that, but I do intend to find out. Besides, you don't really believe your grandpa would do such a thing do you? Would he have done such a thing while he was alive?"

"No, course not," he answered.

"Then his ghost, if there is such a thing, would not do

it either."

He looked at me in surprise, then slowly nodded as if a burden had been lifted.

Once inside the house, Tad ran upstairs to tell his grandmother about our day and the birds we had identified. As I hung my cloak on the hall tree, Lesley Adams's door opened and she walked over to me.

"I thought I heard voices," she said. "How did it go . . . your first lesson?"

"Very well. I think Tad enjoyed it."

She stood with her hands on her hips, a slightly masculine stance, her look speculative. "I think you're going to be good for the boy. I was just about to have tea. Won't you join me?"

"Thank you," I answered. "That sounds very nice."

I followed her into her office, feeling immediately comfortable and at ease in the small, cozy room. She poured our tea in cups decorated with pale pink blossoms. They were so delicate and fragile that I could see the light through them. Everything Lesley possessed was perfect—very feminine and expensive. I wondered again at the odd contrast with her outward appearance.

"You seem to have won the boy over," she said, raising the cup to her lips. "I'm sure that has been to your advantage with Nicholas."

I was puzzled by her choice of words and by her manner. Although she was always friendly and supportive toward me, I sensed a subtle change in her, some reluctance to welcome me fully into her confidence as she might have done before. I felt as if she studied and evaluated everything I said, every action I took. I remembered suddenly the conversation I'd overheard between her and Nicholas the day I was pushed down the stairs. It caused me to look at her from an entirely different perspective.

Had my coming here changed the status between her and Nicholas? That was not something I had considered until now. I had just assumed that whatever was between them, if anything, was over a long time ago. Now I couldn't be sure.

"Advantage seems an odd word to use," I said slowly.

"Well, obviously Nicholas dotes on his nephew, so if you are on good terms with him, it would certainly be pleasing to your husband-to-be."

"That is not the reason I'm kind to Tad." I looked at her forthrightly, a little irritated by her cleverness.

"Oh, no, I'm sure it is not. I didn't at all intend to imply that. It's just that Nicholas is quite a man. One would need to use every ruse available to keep his interest. I'd think it would take a very worldly woman to hold him. And quite frankly, Victoria, you are anything but worldly. And I don't intend that in a critical way." She reached into the gold box and lit one of her long, brown cigarillos.

"And so I would need to use other methods . . . such as Tad. Nicholas's mother too, perhaps?" I knew exactly what she was implying, but did she really believe what she was saying?

"Exactly. I'm only telling you this for your own good and because I want to see you happy. I really do admire you, you know. It would be a shame if something happened between you and Nicholas."

Her words were spoken with great kindness and sincerity, and I had no reason to doubt her. Yet there was a strange feeling I had about her; a sixth sense told me there was something just beneath the surface in this woman that she did not want the world to see.

"Well, thank you, Lesley. I appreciate your concern. It's good to have someone to talk to." I wanted her to feel assured that her words were well taken, but inwardly I smiled. She misjudged me if she thought I was so easily manipulated. I was marrying Nicholas because I was totally, madly in love with him. I could not believe for a moment she did not know that.

I did not bother to tell her that I believed very strongly in the power of love. I knew she would only laugh cynically and call me gullible and innocent. I would not let Lesley or anyone else spoil my wedding to Nicholas. I was determined that the next two weeks would be the kind of days of which brides dream.

"What about you, Lesley?" I asked. "You seem to be spending a great deal of time with Eric Roberts. Perhaps there will be another wedding soon?"

"Oh, no," she said quickly. She laughed, holding her cigarillo away from her. "Eric is the kind of man a woman might take for a lover, use for her pleasure . . . but marry? Never!"

My surprise must have shown blatantly on my face, even though I thought I cleverly concealed it by reaching for a small cake from the silver tea tray.

"Oh, now I've shocked you! I'm dreadfully sorry, Victoria. I keep forgetting you will enter into your marriage a complete innocent." Her brown eyes twinkled mischievously as she mocked me. She crushed the small cigar into a crystal ashtray.

"Lesley, I've just spent four years in a girl's school where the majority of nightly conversations centered upon men and the mysteries of which you speak." But I could not deny I was a little uncomfortable with the turn of the discussion. She had not shocked me, though, as perhaps she had intended. If I had been shocked by anything, it had been my first wild feelings for Nicholas. But only to myself could I admit that.

"Ah, yes. Nonetheless it is still a mystery, no? Now if there is anything you need to ask about, dear, please feel free to come to me. And later . . . if there are any problems that I might help you with . . ."

"Thank you, Lesley," I said slowly. "That's very kind of you."

Her face and words were all innocence but I was puzzled by them and by her near insistence on becoming involved in Nicholas's and my personal life. "If you'll excuse me, I believe Mrs. Dalton will be here soon and I don't want to keep her waiting. Thank you for the tea."

I left her there in the coziness of her intimate little room and I was more perplexed than ever by our conversation and by the strange woman I'd hoped to make my friend.

I didn't know if it were our talk that caused me to feel a bit anxious, but as I walked to my room I found myself overcome again by the same uneasy fears I'd had before. I realized that very little had changed except my relationship with Nicholas. What was even more perplexing was that I still knew so little about this man I would soon marry. So little that I could not comfortably go to him and tell him of the odd conversation I'd just had with Lesley. Or ask if he'd ever been in love with her.

And deep inside I knew I was afraid to discover the truth about Lesley and Nicholas, what their relationship had been before I came.

Was I being foolish to put all my trust in Nicholas, a man I barely knew, and to think that he could keep me safe in this house that was filled with such dark, shadowy secrets?

Chapter XIV

My conversation with Lesley also brought back memories of those first days at Moonwatch when she had said she and Father were friends. Now I wondered again about their relationship, for I was beginning to see she was not the type of woman who would be only friends with a man.

Perhaps I could find the answers to some of the questions that had been nagging at me. The best place to look was my father's journals. I had been attacked on my first day back from Ashford Place, followed by days of illness. Now my engagement to Nicholas had taken all my time. As a result, I had still not taken the journals from the trunk where I'd hidden them.

While I waited for the dressmaker, I pulled the trunk before the fireplace and brushed aside the clothes and books to uncover the two volumes. I sat on the floor and removed the journals.

The first one which I'd briefly scanned before proved to be completely filled with technical data from Father's various cruises. The second, however, was altogether different and I knew from the first page that this one contained his most personal thoughts.

The first entry was dated December 18, 1869, almost a year ago. It read: *Tonight the winds of the Atlantic howl fiercely outside my cabin. We lie at anchor within the Charleston harbor, having arrived late this afternoon. Tomorrow I shall face the task of Christmas shopping for Victoria.* My heart leapt at the mention of my name. *I can hardly believe the child is almost nineteen years old and as beautiful as ever her mother was. We have drifted apart over the years and I grieve to think that it is by my hand that this has happened. As I confided in Nicholas, it is my one wish to reverse the mistakes of the past so that I may once again be reunited with Victoria. But it must only be in a fashion which would make her happy.*

Perhaps by the new year I shall be able to accomplish this. But it will not be an easy task. I have made so many mistakes in my life. I don't know how I shall repay the company's treasury, but I know I must. Colonel Thompson's ships will be in by Christmas and perhaps, with luck, I shall be able to recoup my losses when I meet again with him and his cronies.

The writing sounded so much like my father, so staid and formal, and yet his words about me surprised me and filled me with sadness. Perhaps he had lost all ability to show affection after Mother's death and only here in the privacy of his journal could he say such things about me.

I turned the page to read his next entry. Christmas was past; he had already visited me at school. He wrote very little about the visit, but went on instead to what seemed to be most troublesome in his mind.

When Anna was alive, Christmas at Ashford Place was a joyous celebration. Now the house is cold and empty. How I wish, at least, that Victoria could have been here with me. She has stopped asking when she may come home and I fear she resents me very much. As well she should! What kind of father have I been to her? I must speak to Nicholas soon; perhaps he will not hate me too much. But with my heavy losses before

Christmas, there is nothing else to do except face my punishment, whatever he chooses it to be.

My eyes and throat burned with unshed tears so that I could no longer make out the words written in his bold hand. I closed the book and held it to my breast for a moment, hoping somehow to ease the ache in my heart, to capture some of the familiarity, the feeling of the man he once had been. For this poor, pathetic man was not the father I remembered, the father I longed for and adored. It troubled me that I could not even recall how he looked.

When Millie knocked at my door to announce Mrs. Dalton's arrival, I quickly placed the journals back in the trunk and pushed it again into the corner of the room.

Since Mrs. Hayne wanted to be involved in the selection of the gown, I walked up the hallway to the steps leading to her room. She wanted to see every detail of Mrs. Dalton's design, probably wanting to make sure that I chose an appropriate gown suitable for marriage into the prestigious Hayne family.

Today Ona was in the entryway outside the door. He always made me feel as if I were facing some pagan god, for he was so silent and still, never speaking except when necessary. And yet those eyes, his dark, grave eyes followed me everywhere.

At least today the room was not quite so suffocatingly hot, although the sweet spicy scent still permeated every corner.

Mrs. Dalton was a tiny woman, no more than five feet tall. Her fine reddish blonde hair was arranged in curls atop her head as if that would somehow make her appear taller. Her dress was in a plain navy faille, trimmed in tiny jet buttons. It was certainly nothing spectacular, not what one would expect from a woman whose fashions were the current vogue.

She seemed to be constantly in motion, her hands

moving as she talked and her eyes darting back and forth quickly.

"Ah, so this is Victoria Ancona. I have so longed to meet you . . . the woman who has captured Nicholas Hayne." The last statement contained a note of awe. She moved back to assess me from head to toe. I could not help smiling at her manner even as I wondered if she was disappointed in what she saw.

"Delightful!" she declared. "Tall and willowy, but not too thin. Good coloring. Some girls simply do not look good in white—'tis a pity. But you, my child, will be stunning!"

I looked at Mrs. Hayne who once again was sitting up in the large bed amidst lace and satin-covered pillows. She watched us carefully, listening to every word Mrs. Dalton spoke.

I remained silent, putting myself entirely in the capable hands of the tiny dressmaker. I had seen some of her creations and knew she designed very beautiful and intricately made gowns. I did not doubt I would be pleased with whatever she chose for me.

"I took the liberty of bringing a basic gown to which we may add or subtract as we wish. If you will slip this on, Victoria, we shall begin to create the most beautiful wedding dress the coastal plains have ever seen."

The dress which she had called her basic gown was of heavy satin in an ivory color. The square neckline was low, showing the curve of breasts and shoulders. At the arms were short cap sleeves. I breathed in the scent of the rich new fabric as Mrs. Dalton fastened the long row of satin-covered buttons in the back.

"Now," she said, moving around me slowly, looking at every detail. "Yes . . . hmmm, the waist needs taking in at least three inches, but the length is good. Hold still only a few more moments, dear, while I pin. What do you think, Mrs. Hayne?"

"I think it should be much more elaborate than

that," she replied with a worried look upon her face.

"Oh, it shall be, to be sure. It will be elegant enough even for a princess!"

The small woman fluttered about like a pretty bird, pinning the waist and pulling out the full skirt until it belled around me.

"There, we have the correct fit. Ah, my dear, your figure is divine!"

I had certainly never had anyone tell me that. But I smiled at her enthusiasm as she became caught up in her work. I had been standing patiently for at least thirty minutes while she pinned and prodded, and I began to grow a bit weary. She turned me about as if I were a lifeless dress form.

"Now for the design. Yours shall be the only one of its kind, my dear, made just for you!" She turned me toward the bed to face Mrs. Hayne who was sitting patiently watching the whole proceeding.

"She has beautiful arms and shoulders, so I'm going to leave them bare, even though it is November. A row of scalloped beading will be added to the sleeves with a longer strand of beadwork which will hang from the outside down the arm." She picked up a bolt of the satin material and unrolled a length which she held up to my waist.

"There shall be an overskirt, scalloped and embroidered with pearls around the bottom and separated in the middle to show the gown beneath. The overskirt will be embroidered with elegant jeweled designs from the floor to almost hip level, trailing into a train behind. Attached to the shoulders at the back will be a length of this—just imported from France." With great élan she rolled a bolt of the gossamer material across the bed, catching it up in her arms.

I caught my breath at the beauty of the material as it lay sparkling. The material was of the sheerest weight, its color the same as the gown. But it was shot with sparkling gold and scattered with tiny star points of light. It reminded me of butterfly wings and fairy gowns. It was unlike anything I'd ever seen.

"This shall flow like glittering wings behind her, lightly covering the train behind. Most unusual for a wedding gown, but stunning, don't you agree?" She did not really expect a reply. She almost seemed to be talking to herself.

"And to accentuate her lovely bare neck and shoulders, something new, my own creation: a scalloped collar about her neck made of satin and beaded decorations to match the skirt. Dropping from the front shall be a large teardrop pearl."

The woman stood back and sighed as if she had just finished a delectable and thoroughly satisfying meal. "What do you think, Mrs. Hayne?"

There was a sparkle in Mrs. Hayne's eyes as she approved. "Perfect," she said. "It is absolutely perfect. I want there to be no other bride like the one Nicholas Hayne shall marry."

Her words and the look in her eyes made me feel that I no longer existed, except as a mannequin. The girl standing before her could have been anyone. My value was such because Nicholas had chosen me. A cold chill ran through me as I watched her eyes. It was as if she were in a world of her own.

"And you, my dear?" The woman waited for my answer, but I knew it did not truly matter. Nothing mattered except that I be elegantly gowned and presented as a beautiful object in Denise Hayne's audience—a reflection of Nicholas's good taste.

"It's lovely," I said. But the enthusiasm had gone out of me.

"Any changes or additions you might like?" she asked, looking at me quizzically.

"No," I answered. "It's fine just the way it is."

"Ah, Mrs. Hayne, you have a treasure here! A

daughter-in-law so sweet and agreeable . . . it's a rarity, I tell you." Her hands fluttered in the air as she went about gathering up her materials.

"Yes." Mrs. Hayne smiled mysteriously. "I could not be more pleased with Nicholas's choice if I had made it myself." As I glanced at her I could see the smug challenge in her look.

I couldn't wait to get the gown off and leave the stifling confines of that room. The pale eyes followed every move I made and I could see the glory of her triumph reflected in their depths.

Each time I was with her I doubted my decision to marry Nicholas. I longed now to see him and feel the warmth of his arms about me. I needed to hear his deep rumble of laughter and see the love within his dark blue eyes. I wanted reassurance that this marriage was his wish and not his mother's. For I could see more every day that her feelings toward my father, whatever they might be, had twisted her, leaving her with a bitterness that was almost insanity.

I practically ran down the hallway to my room, quickly closing the door behind me, shutting out Ona's silent eyes and the eyes of the house that seemed to be everywhere I went.

Once again the view of the Atlantic drew me to it, bringing the intermingled longing and fear I'd always felt toward the vast mysterious depths of the ocean.

I wondered if Nicholas were home yet. I had not heard him arrive, but then I probably would not have noticed from Mrs. Hayne's room.

I looked out the window at the sky which was already growing dark and gray. The wind whipped the waves, tossing specks of sea foam into the air. It looked as if it might rain again and I shuddered as I remembered the last violent storm.

I was just turning from the window when a movement down on the beach caught my eye. In the dusk of eventide I could not make out the identity of the two people below me. I could only see that one was a woman, her full skirt billowing in the gusty winds; the other, a man.

I stepped closer to the window and squinted into the evening light. I was sure it must be Lesley and my first thought was that the man was Eric Roberts. But this man was much taller than Eric. Nicholas? Whoever it was, they seemed to be engaged in an argument. They stood close together and the movements of their arms and bodies seemed agitated. Once the woman turned to walk away and the man reached for her arm, pulling her back to face him.

Finally it grew too dark and I could no longer see, but I continued gazing at the spot. I was filled with an odd, uneasy feeling, as if intuition told me something was dreadfully wrong.

It was that same feeling I had when I first came here and I dreaded spending even one night in this room. But then I had fallen in love with Nicholas . . . perhaps from that first time I saw him. And he was master of this house, so I had not wanted to leave. My feelings for him had blinded me to everything else . . . all the initial fears. And now they were back, leaving me uncertain and afraid, longing to see him and yet unsure. Should I tell him how I felt? What kept me from trusting him completely? I didn't know. But I did know that once again I felt like the stranger, the little orphaned girl taken in by the wealthy and powerful Hayne family. I did not know what my destiny would be . . . or if I would be the one to choose it.

Chapter XV

By the time I bathed and dressed for dinner I had managed to convince myself that I was only overtired and anxious, easily stimulated by the disturbing atmosphere of the seaside manor.

When Nicholas stepped from his room into the hallway, practically into my path, I felt almost giddy with relief at seeing him.

He looked so calm and normal, easing somewhat my eerie, unforgettable feelings. It could not have been him on the beach with Lesley. I wanted to throw myself into his arms and let his strength be my own. But somehow I managed to restrain myself, only putting my arm through his and smiling happily up into his face as we went down to dinner.

Surprisingly, the evening turned out to be one of the most pleasant since my arrival. What was even more odd was the fact that Lesley and Eric, certainly Nicholas, were all in high, good spirits. I became convinced that the couple I'd seen arguing must have been two of the house servants. It was a logical explanation, since the house was the only one on this end of Cape Fear. And it was the only explanation I was prepared to believe.

Denise Hayne was still excited about the wedding

and talked of little else. Even the dour Frances made an effort to join the conversation, smiling quietly at me from time to time.

"I'd like to have a dinner party here next week, Nicholas. A kind of prewedding gathering," Mrs. Hayne said. "What do you think of the idea?"

"Whatever Victoria wants." Nicholas looked at me and smiled.

"Victoria?" Mrs. Hayne said.

"I think I would like that very much. It will give me a chance to become acquainted with Nicholas's friends."

"Then it's settled. We shall plan that for next Friday evening, two days before the wedding."

As pleasant as the evening had been, I was happy when everyone dispersed, leaving Nicholas and myself to walk upstairs alone. I felt I had not been alone with him nearly enough since we'd announced our engagement.

He paused at my door to say good-night, making no move to go inside. His circumspection amused me, for I had not thought him to be the kind of man to be overly concerned with outward appearances. It was not as if we had never been alone before.

"I don't trust myself alone with you." He smiled wryly, answering my question before I asked it.

"Nor I you," I replied, moving closer to him.

He kissed me then, gently, and pulled away sooner than I would have liked. His eyes seemed to warn me that he intended to remain unmoved by my nearness. He continued to hold me lightly, though, against him, taking some of the sting from his cool treatment.

"I have something to ask you," he said.

"I'm listening."

"I've ordered the *Galatea* home. She should be sailing into the inlet by the middle of next week."

"Yes?" I was very curious as to what he had to say about my father's ship.

"I would like us to spend our wedding night aboard her. The next day we could sail down to Charleston, visit the city, dine in the finest restaurants. You might like to visit some of the shops while we're there. What do you think? His eyes were cautious when he spoke, as if he were unsure of what my reaction would be.

"Oh, Nicholas," I whispered. "I would love it."

"You would?" He gave an obvious sigh of relief as he spoke. "And what has become of the girl who was so afraid of the sea?"

"I would go anywhere with you Nicholas . . . anywhere. Don't you know that? I've never felt as secure and protected with anyone as I do with you."

There was a look of surprise and great pleasure in his eyes as he took in my words. I felt his arm tighten around me as his eyes darkened and I was again caught up in his power to make me forget everything except his nearness . . . his touch. This time when his lips reached for mine there was no pretense at coolness and I knew I had only to move toward my door and all the barriers would fall. I felt giddy with the power I possessed.

I cautioned myself, though. This was not what I really wanted and neither did Nicholas, if we allowed ourselves only a few moments to think. Especially now that he had told me of his special plans. No, I wanted the night on the *Galatea* to be extraordinary, a once-in-a-lifetime night with the man I adored.

This time I was the one to pull away and if I was moved by the blatant desire I saw in his eyes, I said nothing, trying to resist my own desire as well.

"Angel," he whispered. "You are only saved by the fact that our wedding is within days."

I knew he was teasing me, but if I wanted our wedding night to be special, I dared not tell him I had no wish to be saved now.

"You are a very special lady, Victoria, and I'm so thankful you came to Moonwatch and into my life."

"So am I," I answered, still dizzy with what his looks could do to my heart.

"Good night," he whispered, still reluctant to release me even as his lips clung to mine.

I was still trembling minutes later when I climbed into bed alone. And, I told myself, even if he had never actually told me he loved me, at least I knew his desire for me was real. How I loved him, this tall, muscular man whose very touch made me weak with wanting and whose eyes could make me tremble. Would it always be this way? I almost laughed aloud, thinking of Lesley's worry about the mystery I was soon to discover and her offer of advice. What would she think if she knew how I felt, how I longed to learn anything Nicholas Hayne wished to teach me.

It bothered me that he never said he loved me, not in so many words. But there was no doubt about his attraction to me and I was willing to settle for that only because instinctively I knew I could make him love me. It had become my goal.

It had been a long, tiring day and I fell asleep quickly with a smile on my lips as I thought of Nicholas and our wedding.

The next few days seemed to rush by. I'd never been as busy, not even at school. But Tad's lessons and our explorations on the beach took most of the day. Then there were the daily dress fittings, for Mrs. Hayne insisted that I had a trousseau far beyond anything I truly needed. Nicholas was unusually busy at Ancona and Hayne, sometimes coming home late in the night. When he did he never failed to knock at my door so that we could say good-night.

Lesley and Eric sometimes went with Nicholas and worked at the office and sometimes they remained at Moonwatch, but I rarely spoke with the enigmatic

Mr. Roberts; he seemed as quiet and shadowy as the sinister Ona.

I could not believe the end of October was so near, but suddenly it was Friday and time for our formal dinner. I had looked forward to it with great excitement and I could sense that even Nicholas, who was usually so cool and detached about such things, was also quite anxious.

We hardly saw each other that day, both of us being busy, but Nicholas did not leave for his office on the inlet. He, as did I, spent most of the day packing and preparing for our wedding which was to take place on Sunday.

I packed Father's personal journal away for the trip, hoping I'd be able to read more of it in the atmosphere he so loved, the tall ship he built.

When it was time to dress for the celebration, I took my time, leisurely arranging my hair up and then taking it down again. Finally I decided to leave it down. I silently chided myself as I did for I knew I was allowing Nicholas's opinion about my hairstyle to influence me. I found myself lately trying senselessly to please him in everything I did.

On the bed lay the dress I was to wear. I had intended to wear the crimson velvet gown again, but Mrs. Hayne would not hear of it. She insisted instead that Mrs. Dalton design something especially for the party. I felt sorry for the petite woman, knowing the aggravation it must have caused to make this dress, the wedding gown, and the trousseau, but I had to admit I had never seen a dress like this one. It seemed to be made of spun sugar, with a filmy, billowing skirt of white silk sarcenet sprinkled with pale blue star-shaped sequins. I felt like a princess and Moonwatch my fairy castle as I walked downstairs that evening.

The large dining room had been cleared earlier in the day and the rugs rolled back to reveal the rich soft gleam of cypress wood floors. Long tables were set along two walls; one would hold the sumptuous buffet meal and the other was for seating. I could hear the music drifting up to me as I came down the stairs.

Below me several gentlemen stood talking in the entry hall. The house was filled with extra lights and candles that now illuminated the usually dark and shadowed corners. I spotted Nicholas at once, his tall dark-haired figure standing out above the others, but he had not yet seen me. Two of the men who faced the stairs spotted me as I came carefully down. They stopped talking immediately, their full attention now focused on me. I felt unusually self-conscious at the speculative look in their eyes, their openly admiring gazes. Nicholas, seeing their faces, turned slowly toward me, and the welcoming look of pride that crossed his face warmed me and set me adrift in a world where only the two of us existed. I could not believe that look was just for me; it did not seem possible.

With two long strides he came up the stairs to me and captured my hand, placing it in the crook of his arm possessively. His eyes took in the sparkling gown and traveled admiringly to my face and the tumble of hair about my shoulders. If this were his response, then I was glad I had let Denise convince me to wear the gown. And happy I had dressed my hair to please him.

"You are so beautiful." His voice was low, rumbling with an intimacy that sent chills along my spine.

"And you are more handsome than ever," I replied. The dark blue of his evening coat was a perfect match for his deep blue eyes. His white silk shirt front and brocaded waistcoat gleamed underneath the flickering gaslights. I thought he had never looked more exciting and confident. How had he chosen me for a wife? I wondered again. A young inexperienced schoolgirl who had never traveled far beyond the realm of home. And now I was here with this dashing man in a mansion by the sea.

I let him lead me to his friends, both of whom appeared to be near Nicholas's age, somewhere in their late twenties.

"This is James McClellan and David Murrell. We were all school chums. Gentlemen, this is Victoria Ancona, my fiancée."

The tall dark-haired one, who he had introduced as James, stepped forward. He took my hand, bowing formally as he bent to place a kiss there.

His brown eyes sparkled merrily and I guessed he would have been the prankster in his schooldays, the one who did anything on a dare.

"Nicky, you sly dog," he murmured. "Where on earth have you kept this lovely creature hidden?"

David stepped forward and took my hand from James's grasp. "Pay him no mind, Miss Ancona. James was obviously absent when we learned the basics of gentlemanly behavior."

We all laughed. David was as fair as James was dark. His hair was very blond as were his pale eyebrows and eyelashes above brilliant blue eyes. He was not as classically handsome as the darker James, but there was a boyish sweetness to his face and I liked him immediately.

I smiled, enjoying the mock rivalry between them for it was one of the things I had never had the pleasure of experiencing. In fact, I had never even attended such a party as this.

Nicholas moved closer, pulling me subtly to his side as he grinned wryly at his two friends. "I presume neither of you has a lady friend with you this evening?"

James and David looked at each other innocently and shrugged their shoulders. Nicholas only laughed and shook his head at their nonsensical behavior.

"Shall we go in to dinner?" Nicholas asked, gazing down at me. I nodded dumbly, for I found it difficult to breath when he looked at me in such a way.

"It was very nice to meet you, David . . . James." I spoke to them as if in a daze and hardly even looked at them.

But they were not about to be ignored, neither of them. "Well, since we *are* unattached for the evening, we would be happy to accompany you. It would be a pleasure indeed to dine with the loveliest lady in all of North Carolina." James's words were smoothly practiced.

I laughed aloud at Nicholas's good-natured wince. But he allowed both of them to accompany us into the dining room.

We seemed to be the last ones to enter the room. I immediately spotted Mrs. Hayne at the far end, seated like a queen holding court. Several guests were gathered about her, talking and laughing. She was in her element and I had never seen her looking as happy and carefree.

Ona stood near Mrs. Hayne. He was clad in his usual colorful garb and looked decidedly out of place amongst all the elegantly dressed people.

When Mrs. Hayne saw us enter, she beckoned us to her and introduced several of the people to me. There were so many people coming and going and being introduced that after awhile the names and faces began to merge together. James and David began to seem like old and dear friends to me, for they did not leave us for an instant and were very kind to point out people to me or whisper forgotten names in my ear.

The elegantly appointed buffet table was filled with polished silver and sparkling china. It was heavily laden with food and drink of every kind imaginable. The guests were able to fill their plates at leisure, then drift to the other table to eat, or stand about chatting with friends they had not seen in awhile. For all the formal beauty and elegance of the room and the food, it was a cordial night and I enjoyed it more than I'd have thought possible. I was very pleased and relieved at the gracious way Nicholas's friends welcomed me.

Later the four of us strolled to the buffet to sample the delicately seasoned sea pie, a favorite dish at Moonwatch, one we'd been served before. There were many other seafood dishes, as well as huge, thinly sliced smoked hams and turkeys, several chicken dishes, along with various salads and vegetables. There were silver baskets brimming with freshly baked bread. At the end of the table were dozens of desserts from which we could choose: simple custards, citron tarts, strudel, elegant French pastries, and lavishly decorated cakes.

There was music and dancing and I enjoyed myself immensely, as everyone seemed to be doing. I saw Frances across the room and noted with surprise that she wore a flattering and colorful gown. I excused myself and walked to her. The deep rose color of her taffeta dress was becoming to her silver-streaked hair and dark eyes. She looked pretty as she stood talking beneath the flattering light of the candelabra.

I thought seriously of persuading David or James to dance with her, but then I supposed that was being interfering, so I said nothing.

"You look lovely, Frances," I said. I did not know how she would react to my compliment, but I did hope that we could make an attempt at civility, if not friendship.

Frances was friendly and charming, although there was still a certain restraint about her when she spoke to me. I was sure that her friendlier tone was only an outward appearance for our guests.

When I spotted Lesley and Eric dancing, she raised her hand from his arm in a friendly little salute. I still didn't know quite what to make of her.

During the evening the wind had risen outside until

now it was a loud roar, but it went practically unnoticed by most of the genial crowd until a very strange and disruptive thing happened.

We had begun to see the flash of lightning outside the long windows and through the double French doors. Suddenly, there was a loud crash of thunder nearby and the doors flew open, rattling loudly in the music-filled room. Guests stopped where they were and turned to see what had happened. The musicians stopped playing mid-note.

As the doors swung wide and the curtains fluttered wildly in the howling wind, I felt a chill down my spine. Candles and gaslights flickered, some of them extinguished by the wind. Rain scattered across the floor as we all stood momentarily stunned. Then as one of the servants stepped forward to close the door, another flash of light streaked across the sky and there in its brilliance we could see the cloaked figure of a man standing on the balcony, directly outside the open doors.

Somewhere in the room a woman screamed and there were audible gasps as Nicholas and a number of men ran forward out into the darkness. The crowd murmured excitedly until a few moments later when the men returned.

"It must only have been an illusion caused by the lightning," James said to the quiet guests. "There is no sign of anyone, either on the balcony or around the house."

We only looked at one another, mystified by what had just happened and unable to explain it. Then one of the servants stepped forward rather reluctantly.

"It was no illusion, Mr. McClellan. There was someone out there, all right." He walked over to Nicholas and placed a small object into his hand.

Nicholas held it out into the light. I could see a flash of gold as he turned it about between his fingers. "It's a gold button," he said thoughtfully, "from a captain's uniform."

"Let me see it." Denise Hayne was there before us and her delicate skin had turned ghostly white. As Nicholas handed the button to her, she gasped and clutched the button to her breast.

"Oh, this cannot be!" she whispered. Lifting her pallid blue eyes to Nicholas she murmured. "It's from your father's uniform!"

"Mother," he said gently, "this could be from anyone's uniform." He took the shiny button from her trembling fingers and studied it more closely.

"No, Nicholas, look at it!" she said. "Your father had those buttons custom-made for himself. Those are his initials in the center!"

The button that Nicholas held did indeed have letters in the middle, intertwined with decorative swirls. Looking more closely I saw that the initials were J.H.—John Hayne.

No one spoke a word in the large room. No doubt many had heard the rumor about the captain's ghost in the lighthouse, or wandering the halls of Moonwatch.

"There must be some logical explanation for this, Mother," Nicholas insisted.

"No, it's true, son. It's true. . . ." She gasped. "Your father was here!" Her voice rose shrilly, hysterically as Nicholas stepped toward her.

Her skin was bloodless. Just as Nicholas reached her, she slumped forward in her chair.

He bent swiftly and scooped the tiny woman up into his strong arms. "Ona!" he said sharply.

The large black man was already there, hovering just behind Nicholas and following him as he carried the still body of Mrs. Hayne from the room. I saw the flash of rose-colored skirts as Frances also ran after them.

It was all I could do not to run after them. I wanted to be with Nicholas in case anything happened, but the room had suddenly burst into a near-hysterical frenzy of talk. I did not want the evening to end on such a disturbing note.

I walked to the front of the room as calmly as I could and stood on the music platform. "I'm sure Mrs. Hayne will be fine. Please, everyone, have more wine and food." I then directed the musicians to play a lilting Irish folk song which soon had the couples tapping their feet to its rhythm. Before long the floor was once again crowded with dancers. I could only hope it would be a memorable and unusual evening that most could laugh about later.

"Miss Ancona, I believe you have not danced all evening." It was Eric Roberts who stood before me, his hand outstretched in an invitation.

His dark eyes sparkled as he watched me and his stocky, muscular presence suddenly made me feel secure and safe again. As we began to dance, I breathed a quiet sigh of relief.

"Are you all right?" he asked as he guided me about the floor. He was an agile dancer, much more so than I would have thought.

"Yes, I will be fine. I'm just concerned about Mrs. Hayne, but I didn't feel I should leave the guests down here alone."

"You did exactly the proper thing and very gracefully too, I might add." His look was warm and admiring as he gazed at me, our eyes almost on the same level.

"Thank you," I said gratefully, letting his words reassure me.

We danced silently for awhile. It was nearly midnight and some of the guests had begun to leave.

"I should thank them for coming," I said, looking toward the hallway.

Eric went with me to the entryway and stood nearby as I bid our guests good-night. Through the open door we could see that the storm had passed quickly, allowing the stars to twinkle brightly between the wisps of fast-moving clouds.

Most of the guests expressed how much they sincerely enjoyed the evening. Some even laughed about the ghostly appearance as if it had only enhanced their enjoyment of the party, though it were part of the entertainment. I looked at Eric and shrugged my shoulders. He smiled.

James, David, and some of the close family friends would be staying the night and on through to the wedding, if indeed there was now to be one. I only knew it had been a long evening and was thankful when Vickers and the staff had everyone attended to and in their rooms.

Then there was only Eric Roberts and myself left downstairs, except for the few servants who were briskly carrying food back to the kitchen.

"Thank you, Mr. Roberts," I said, "for staying with me and for being so kind."

"Call me Eric, please," he said. "And believe me, it is very easy being kind to you, Victoria." He bowed stiffly and left to go to his room.

I wondered if my first impression of him had been so wrong, for he seemed genial enough now. Still, there was something about him that left me with a vague, uncomfortable feeling. Dismissing him from my thoughts, I went hurriedly up the stairs and to the landing outside Mrs. Hayne's room.

Before I could go in, I met Frances. Through the open door I caught a glimpse of Nicholas, his dark head bent as he sat by his mother's bed. The room was very quiet and the silent figure of the woman on the bed very still. I looked at Frances sharply.

"She's—she's not . . . ?"

"No, no. She's going to be all right, I'm sure." But Frances was clearly troubled and for the first time she seemed to be distracted from her usual self-indulgent rhetoric.

"It was such a shock for her . . . the horror of it all," she said.

"Yes. It was bizarre, to say the least. Who could have done such a thing?" I asked.

"I have no earthly idea. But at least Mother is going to recover," she repeated as if to reassure herself. "Nicholas and Ona will stay with her the rest of the night. It's probably best if we just go on to bed and try to get as much rest as possible."

I wanted to go to Nicholas, to sit beside him and comfort him. For as eccentric as his mother was, I did not doubt his love for her. Frances was right, though, all of us were not needed in the room.

I told her good-night and we went quickly to our rooms. Once I was inside mine I locked the door behind me and glanced uneasily about.

I was now more anxious than ever for the wedding and our trip to Charleston, if for no other reason than to be away from the continual disruption of this house. There was something frightening about the strange, somber Moonwatch with its mysterious and unsettling events.

Chapter XVI

Early the next morning Millie came hurrying into my room. Her eyes were wide and shining; her cheeks flushed a deep rose color.

"Miss Ancona," she said breathlessly. "The mistress is much better this morning and she's given orders that nothing shall interfere with the wedding tomorrow."

"Are you sure?" I asked. "She's so anxious for this marriage to take place that she would never admit she's too ill."

"Yes, miss. I was just in to take her tea and she's as feisty as ever!"

"Well, I'm not doubting your word, Millie, but I think I shall go see for myself." I took one last look in the mirror, pushing my hair back from my face. "Is Nicholas still with her?"

"No, miss. He stayed with her all the night, but now he's gone to his room for a bit of a rest."

"Thank you, Millie. I left her in the hallway outside my room and walked toward Mrs. Hayne's suite.

I tapped lightly on the door, almost afraid I would disturb her, but the voice from within that bade me enter was strong and vital.

The room which usually smelled like Oriental spices

was cooler now and the scent of fresh air and sea salt wafted in through an open window. She sat in one of the chairs near the window, a pot of tea on the pedestal table beside her.

"Ah, Victoria. I'm so glad you've come. Sit here and have tea with me, my dear." She acted as if nothing were amiss, as if last night's bizarre event had not taken place.

I sat in the chair opposite her and poured myself a cup of tea as I looked closely at her face. She was still quite pale, but her eyes were bright and clear, her movements quick and vigorous.

"You're not too cold are you?" I asked. "Shall I close your window?"

"No, the breeze smells lovely. I can tolerate the cool air for a few moments, at least. Nicholas sometimes insists that I have a bit of fresh air."

"I'm really surprised to see you up, Mrs. Hayne. Are you sure you're all right?"

"I'm fine! I don't know what came over me last night. Why, twenty years ago I would have searched the balcony myself for the intruder!" Her blue eyes snapped as she spoke.

I smiled, for that was not hard to imagine.

"Millie says we're to go on with the wedding. Are you sure—"

"Of course I'm sure," she answered before I could finish the question. "Nothing must stop this wedding!" Her adamant words were spoken almost frantically.

I watched her carefully. Her breathing seemed a bit fast. I certainly did not want her to become ill again as she had the first time we met.

"It's all right. Nothing will stop the wedding, I promise." I tried to keep my voice as quiet and soothing as possible. I wished again that she were not quite so obsessed with this marriage.

"And you, Victoria . . ." she said. "How are you feeling? Are you happy . . . nervous?" Her keen eyes searched mine as if she could somehow delve into my subconscious.

I took a deep breath and smiled, for now that I knew the ceremony could go on, I felt a great flood of relief. I could allow myself to feel the happiness that I had pushed aside till now. It was as if I had been afraid to feel the delight I should, afraid something would happen to whisk it all away.

"Both," I replied.

"You will be beautiful. I can't wait until the moment Nicholas sees you in your wedding dress. You shall look like an angel." Her soft words held a hint of wistfulness.

"I should like to thank you, Mrs. Hayne, for all you've done for me." I spoke impulsively, feeling the rapport of the moment, and forgetting the anger I'd felt with her.

"Oh, my dear," she said, the wistful look still on her face. "It is I who should thank you. This marriage between you and my son is something I've dreamed of even before you came. I'm sure your father did too. I hope you will remember that later, when the furor of the excitement has died away. It's what Anthony wanted. He loved Nicholas like a son, you know."

What a strange thing for her to say, as if she thought something would happen later to change my mind. She turned her head then to look out the window. Suddenly it was as if a door had been closed to me.

Seeing her withdrawal I decided I should go. "You must be tired now," I said. "I'll leave you alone so you might rest. Shall I close the window before I go?"

She did not answer me, but continued gazing out at the wind-swept dunes that surrounded the house. She was somewhere else now, lost in her memories of another time and other people.

Ona opened the door as I left, his dark eyes following me solemnly. On a whim I stopped before him and spoke. "Watch after her, Ona."

He nodded, his movement slow and graceful. "Ona always watches," he said.

I could not suppress the shiver that traveled down my neck as I walked past him into the shadowy hallway. I was almost counting the hours until my wedding and the trip that would take me away from the oppressiveness of this place.

My wedding day would remain in my memory forever. I awoke to a clear cerulean sky that ran together with the sea until the whole world seemed covered in blue. I threw open my window and let the cool crisp salt air waft into the room.

Soon the sound of arriving carriages could be heard. They were bringing guests who would breakfast at Moonwatch. It was to be a festive day.

The house came alive with people and the unfamiliar sounds of their activities could be heard reverberating through the mansion.

I was too anxious to eat and had Millie bring a light breakfast of tea and toast to my room. As I began to eat, the door opened and Tad entered slowly.

In his hand he carried a small gift-wrapped package which he handed to me. He watched rather shyly as I opened it.

"Oh, Tad," I said. "This is so beautiful." In the box lay a perfectly formed conch shell, the inside glistening pearly pink as I turned it about in the light.

"I found it myself," he said proudly, "and cleaned it to make it shine. It's for good luck."

Impulsively I reached forward and hugged him. He

did not resist, but smiled widely when I released him.

"How long will you be gone?" he asked, referring to the honeymoon.

"Only a few days I think."

"Uncle Nicholas says one day soon he will let me sail the *Galatea*."

"Did he now? I know you love ships as much as your uncle."

"I'm going to be a captain too," he declared. "Well, my mother says not to pester you, so I guess I'll be going."

"Then I'll see you after the wedding," I said.

I continued to smile after he'd gone as I turned the conch shell about in the light, admiring its perfect beauty. It made me so happy that Tad seemed to be accepting me, for more than anyone in the house, his sweet and innocent friendship meant the most to me.

When the door opened again I looked up expectantly, thinking it was Tad returning to tell me something else. Instead Nicholas stood in the doorway, his face thoughtful as he looked at me.

"What do you have there?" he asked, pointing at the shell.

"Tad gave it to me just a little while ago. Wasn't that sweet of him?"

"Tad is a fine lad. He needs some attention and a lot of love." He studied me and a light gleamed deep in his eyes. "You're good for him."

He walked across the room and sat in a chair on the opposite side of the teacart.

"I think it is Tad who's been good for me," I said.

"You'll be a wonderful mother someday," he said. He looked at me steadily until a blush crept across my skin. Then he smiled. He knew exactly why I had suddenly become so self-conscious. He rose and I looked up at his tall figure.

"I know you have things to do," he said. "So I'll leave you to do them. I wanted to see you for only a moment to give you a small wedding day gift." He pulled something from his pocket; the rich gleam of gold and jewels sparkled in the morning light.

I rose quickly to him. He held the earrings out and placed them in the palm of my hand.

The small wreaths of gold were encrusted with pearls and set in the middle with a small square emerald.

"Oh," I murmured, "they are so beautiful."

"They were my grandmother's," he said. "She gave them to me when I was only a boy. For my wife, she said. At the time I thought it was the most foolish thing I'd ever heard because I certainly never intended to be married." He grinned wryly. "But you've changed all that." He hesitated a moment almost shyly I thought, and it was the only time I'd ever seen him when I thought he was unguarded and unsure of himself. "I hoped you would wear them today . . . for me?"

"Yes, of course I will," I whispered. His tenderness moved me more than I could say and I was pleased that he had allowed me to see a more vulnerable side of him.

He stepped forward and took my face in his hand. Slowly he kissed my cheeks and my eyelids, then softly my lips until all I could do was lean breathlessly against him.

His smile told me how pleased he was about my response. Then suddenly he left me, pausing at the door to smile back at me, a warm promise deep within his eyes.

I was so stunned by the pleasure I felt that I could only stare after him, unable to speak. I could hardly believe that a man like Nicholas, who was so physically perfect, could also be kind and tender. Could I finally be so lucky?

With the earrings clasped tightly in my hand I

danced merrily about the room before collapsing on the bed giggling like a young girl. I held the gold wreaths up above my head and watched them sparkle as I moved them between my fingers.

When Mrs. Dalton arrived with my gown I was as excited as a child. I found it difficult to keep still.

She took the dress carefully from its wrappings and laid it on the bed. It was the first time I had seen it since the overskirt with its beaded design had been added. It was the most exquisite gown I'd ever seen, making even the star-sprinkled dress I'd worn two nights previously pale by comparison.

Almost before I knew it the time had come to dress and I was lost in a happy daydream as Mrs. Dalton and Millie buttoned and smoothed and turned me about to make sure every small detail was complete. Millie cooed and aahed almost as much as Mrs. Dalton.

Impulsively, I turned to Millie and hugged her.

"Good luck, Miss Ancona," she said with tears glistening in her eyes.

"Oh, Millie," I said. "Thank you for all you've done . . . for always being so kind to me. Thank you for being a friend."

Mrs. Dalton cleared her throat and looked at me oddly. I knew it wasn't proper to become so familiar with the servants, but I *did* consider Millie a friend.

We all three wiped tears from our eyes as I left them. When I turned to go toward the stairs I felt almost numb, as if I were in a strange dreamlike world where nothing was real. I did not stop to think on that glorious morning that I had been in the house less than a month and already I was accepting it as my home. That was only because of Nicholas and my intense love for him. It had changed my perspective about everything, including Moonwatch.

Nicholas had asked David to escort me into the

parlor for the ceremony. He stood waiting for me at the top of the stairs. I welcomed his familiar smiling face as he clasped my cold hand warmly in his and placed it in the crook of his arm.

"Nervous?" he asked. His pale eyes were kind as he smiled down at me. Gone was the mischievous fun I'd seen the night of our party.

"Very," I answered, feeling a tremble ripple through my stomach.

"You've no need to be," he said. "Nicholas will be spellbound when you enter the room in that dress. You are the most beautiful bride I've ever seen." His words made me feel reassured, comforted and I held onto him even tighter.

I reached up and readjusted the flowers that formed a crown upon my hair, then the delicate collar about my neck. For luck I touched the pearl and emerald earrings at my ears and said a silent little prayer that I would not make a complete fool of myself. I then nodded to David and we began our slow descent of the stairs. The iridescent gold-shot material attached at the shoulders of the gown whispered quietly behind me as it floated like delicate wings.

When we entered the parlor to the sounds of violins, I was momentarily stunned by the large number of guests seated there. They soon were lost, becoming only a blur in the background as my eyes found Nicholas and I saw the look of pleased astonishment on his face.

Before I knew it I had reached his side and David placed my hand in Nicholas's. My grip must have surprised him for quickly his blue eyes looked troubled and he looked down into my face. I smiled at him, reassuring him that I was only a bit nervous.

The ceremony passed in a hazy cloud. I hardly was aware of the words I spoke or of anything else around us. It was only myself and Nicholas, the man I loved desperately, alone, it seemed, in our own small world.

It was over then. I was Mrs. Nicholas Hayne, the wife of one of the most powerful men on the East Coast. I was only aware of feeling proud and relieved and a bit enchanted.

The reception was to be held in the dining room, using the same long tables we had on Friday night. Today, though, the room was filled with sunshine and music, the sound of laughter occasionally rising above it. The food, as always, looked wonderful, but I could hardly force myself to eat. I spoke with Mrs. Hayne and was happy to see her looking so well. Frances and Tad were there. He was excited at being a part of the festivities. Frances seemed strangely quiet, although not in a sullen way as she was when I first met her. I wondered if there was something on her mind.

I still had not seen Lesley, but as Nicholas and I stood talking to some of the guests I felt someone watching me. When I turned it was Lesley's dark eyes that rested upon me. There was something in her look I could not quite understand—resentment, perhaps. I wished now that I had asked Nicholas about Lesley and their relationship, if indeed there had been one. I'd wanted to several times, but I was never sure if it were something I really wanted to know or if he would be willing to tell me.

"Lesley," I said, acknowledging her look.

"You look quite lovely, Victoria," she said. She said it as if she were surprised. Her smile was friendly enough, her words sincere, yet I was sure displeasure framed her eyes. Perhaps, I told myself, I was only being foolish, imagining every woman I met was in love with Nicholas. He was my husband now. I hoped that would make me feel more secure.

"Thank you," I murmured.

She held a wine glass, and when she moved the dark red liquid sloshed almost over the crystal rim.

"Lovely and virginal," she said. "Ain't that right?" Her voice had grown louder and I detected a slurring of her words. "But that's the way Nicky likes 'em, I understand." Then she laughed loudly, and she sounded different than I'd ever heard her. Her voice had lost some of its cultured tone and I could hear the slight accent which I had caught only once before.

I frowned, realizing she was slightly drunk, and afraid of what she might say next.

"Ain't that right, Nicky darlin'," she continued. "The challenge is in the conquest. After that they all become boring."

Nicholas turned and looked at her sharply, anger glinting in his eyes. Quickly his gaze flicked toward James and before Lesley would utter another sound, he had stepped forward and clasped her arm in his hand. Consequently, only a few people nearby realized what was happening as he lead her hastily from the room. I could hear her slurred angry words even after they had gone out into the hallway.

When I turned to look at Nicholas, I was shocked at the fury I saw on his face. His skin had darkened and his jaw was clenched so tightly that a muscle twitched at the corner of his mouth. His dark blue eyes stormed. I had only seen him this way once before, the night I came to Moonwatch, the night his mother became so upset with me because I was not the pliant, obedient girl she would have liked.

With a start I realized I had become just as she had wished. When I'd fallen in love with her son I became caught up in a need to please him, perhaps in gratitude that he actually wanted me. How very easily I had fallen into her web. And I was now stunned at the rage I saw on my husband's face. I didn't seem to know him at all.

"Nicholas?" I said, placing my hand lightly on his arm.

He had to make quite an effort to appear calm when he turned to face me, but I was not so easily fooled.

"Pay her no mind, darling," he said smoothly. "She's had too much to drink. I apologize if she's upset you." Then he looked away from me and I was struck by his coolness.

When James returned a few moments later he whispered to Nicholas, but nothing else about Lesley was said and I did not pursue it.

I talked with many of our guests, all the while trying to pretend that nothing was wrong. I only prayed that Nicholas's anger would soon dissipate and would not spoil our trip.

Soon he came to me. "I think it's time to be on our way." His words were quiet and calm, but I could see he was still upset. "We need to be at the harbor before dark."

"I'll go up and change right away," I said.

"Good," he replied amicably, taking me by the arm. "Our bags have already been put in the carriage. I'll come for you in a few minutes."

Mrs. Dalton and Millie had my traveling dress ready when I returned to my room. It was a beautifully simple dove gray velvet with a skirt that tapered to a slight train in back.

I left my lovely wedding gown on the bed for Mrs. Dalton to attend to. "It seems such a shame to be able to wear it only once and for such a short time," I told her.

She laughed. "Ah, my dear. I can see you are a bit more practical than the world of wealth and society which surrounds you."

When Nicholas came for me, Millie's eyes seemed to

fill with a dreamy romantic look as she watched the two of us together. On impulse I turned and kissed her lightly on the cheek. I had grown quite fond of her in the short time we'd been acquainted.

"Look after Tad for us, Millie," I said.

"I will, ma'am," she said tremulously.

Back downstairs we were met by the throng of happily celebrating guests who followed us outside and to the waiting brougham. Nicholas turned back to kiss his mother good-bye and then we ran to the carriage.

The road leading to the inlet had been built on higher ground which afforded a perfect view of the boundless Atlantic on the east and the wide stretch of dunes to the west. It was the first time I had traveled from Moonwatch to the shipyard. I watched across the marshland as the low-lying afternoon sun dropped slowly toward the horizon. The autumn weather had been perfect for the wedding, but now we could feel a touch of coolness in the air. The wind whipped the sand about, blowing it against the windows, making tiny scratching noises as we drove.

I looked at Nicholas, noting how quiet he still was. He made no effort to touch me or talk to me, but instead sat looking steadily out the window toward the sea. His jaw was clenched and his sensual lower lip was held between his teeth.

"Nicholas," I said. "Is anything wrong?"

Quickly he turned to me, almost as if he had forgotten I was there. He closed his eyes for a moment and shook his head. "I'm sorry, darling," he said. "No, of course nothing is wrong. What could be wrong on a day such as this?"

I returned his smile as he took my hand, but within seconds he had once again turned his thoughts inward and sat gazing out to the sea. Even though his shoulder was pressed firmly against mine in the intimacy of the closed cab and his strong hand still held mine, I felt him growing further and further away from me.

I did not want to believe that this incident with Lesley had caused him to become lost in this brooding quietude. I could not bear to think that any other woman would cause this look of worry on his face. I did not like the feeling of helplessness it gave me or the burning possessiveness I felt on the evening of my wedding, so I tried to push aside the niggling doubts I had about my husband's strange mood, telling myself that he would soon come to love me as desperately as I loved him.

But I could not banish the thoughts that crept again and again into my mind, the thought of how very little I really knew about Nicholas Hayne.

Chapter XVII

I watched as the stunted scrub pine gradually gave way to waving acres of marsh grass as we neared the Southport inlet.

Soon the tall masts of the ships loomed before us, their sails cast in the soft golden light of sunset. The low-lying sun across the sandy dunes turned the calm waters of the inlet into liquid gold.

I must have made a slight sound as my breath caught in my throat at the beauty before me. Nicholas turned and smiled at me, pleasure in his eyes as I viewed what was considered his territory. It was one of the most magnificent sights I'd ever seen and caused tears of emotion to well in my eyes. I tried to tell myself it was a happy omen that this sight should greet us at the end of our wedding day.

Nicholas gently wiped away the tears as I smiled at him. "So, you cry at sunsets?" he teased.

"I cry easily," I confessed.

"I've never met anyone quite like you, Victoria," he said. "So sweet . . . and different." He turned his head to one side as he studied my face.

"Is that good?" I whispered tentatively.

"Yes," he replied softly. "Very good."

His fingers lingered warmly on my face, now brushing across my cheek and down to my lips. My heart caught in my chest at the look of intensity he leveled at me. I felt joyously relieved that he seemed to be himself again.

Slowly he bent and kissed my lips, his fingers still lingering at the corner of my mouth, caressing and teasing me. It was an unfamiliar gesture, yet intensely pleasurable.

When he lifted his head I felt myself begin to tremble with emotions I had never experienced before. Any fear I'd had earlier was slowly being replaced by an exciting feeling of anticipation.

Nicholas felt my tremble and laughed softly, his low voice sending waves of elation coursing through me. "Let me show you the *Galatea*," he said.

The crew had obviously been waiting for us, for as soon as we stepped from the coach three of them came forward to lift down our trunks and carry them across the wooden dock and up the gangplank of the ship.

I paused for a moment and looked up the dock toward the row of buildings—the warehouses and sheds, the larger ones where the ships were actually built, and the neatly painted office with its row of shining windows. I breathed in the tangy salt air of the sea which mingled with the scent of sun-warmed wood and wind-beaten grasses. I sighed happily at the familiarity of it all, which brought back poignant memories of my father and our trip that summer day from this very dock.

Nicholas took my arm and led me toward the gangplank as he gazed down at me. "I'm glad you like it here," he said.

"I love it. Oh, Nicholas, I'm so happy you brought me here." I hugged his arm lightly as we walked onto the deck of the ship.

I noticed one of the sailors, a dark muscular man, watching us with a sly, knowing smile on his face and I looked away from him. Most of the crew seemed infinitely polite to me and respectful toward Nicholas. It was obvious that the respect they gave him was genuine and not just a result of his being the master of the ship. I was surprised as he spoke to each of them, calling them by name and giving quick orders in his quiet authoritative voice, for our evening meal and the time of departure.

As we walked across the neatly scrubbed wooden deck I realized we had not yet met the captain.

"Where is the captain?" I whispered to Nicholas.

"Taking a well-deserved shore leave for a few days." The look he gave me was odd, with just a hint of mystery in his eyes as he spoke.

"But, who—?"

"Capt'n Hayne, ma'am," he said, bowing in a mock salute before me. "At your service."

"You . . . ? Nicholas, you will sail the *Galatea*?" I stuttered, unable to keep the surprise and awe from my voice.

"Only if you will agree to assist me," he said.

With a flash of intuition I knew he was doing this for me. I stepped forward and put my arms about his waist, uncaring that the crew was watching. His show of affection caused me to be almost overcome with emotion again as the tears threatened once more. My voice was muffled against his chest as I answered him. "Nicholas, you are so good to me."

When I looked up at him, there was a small frown between his eyes. "Your sweetness always touches me, Victoria." His hands held my arms tightly and his words were said with a tender fierceness. "I want so much to make you happy."

"You *do* make me happy," I replied. "I've never been

so blissfully happy as since I met you."

Without another word he guided me toward midship and down a short flight of stairs to a small, gas-lit hallway. He opened the door of what was obviously the captain's quarters. I saw a large comfortable room gleaming with polished wood paneling. Underneath a small porthole was a desk covered with ledgers and maps and lit by a green-shaded lamp. It was an austere room with not much space for anything other than necessities. A large brass bed occupied one side of the room and a round table was set on the opposite side, beneath a square sky light in the sloping ceiling.

It was only then that I noticed the dishes and candles on the linen-covered table. There was also a silver bucket containing a frosty green bottle and nearby two fragile, stemmed crystal glasses.

Nicholas had been watching me as I surveyed the room and I looked self-consciously at him. He put me at ease immediately.

"Shall we have dinner now?" he asked.

I removed my dove gray hat and gloves as Nicholas stepped forward to take my cloak. He then poured a pitcher of water into the porcelain bowl on a table beside the bed and handed me a small towel.

I was surprised when we sat down to eat that the food was so well prepared. I found, though, that I still had no appetite and was only able to eat a few bites of the succulent baked sea bass. The cold champagne tasted wonderful to me though and I quickly drank a glass of the bubbling golden liquid.

Through the skylight and porthole I saw that the sky had now darkened and a sprinkle of stars gleamed against the heavens. It felt warm and cozy inside our small room and I was only aware of the rhythmic lapping of the waves against the ship and my husband's deep blue eyes that watched me. I drank another glass of champagne for we both had given up the pretense of conversation.

"Don't be nervous," Nicholas said. He smiled at me and his eyes in the glow of the candles, took on an intensity and sparkle that caused my heart to flutter crazily at my throat. He reached across to take my hand, pulling me to my feet.

The effects of the champagne on an empty stomach set my head reeling and I stumbled slightly. Quickly Nicholas pulled me to him and picked me up in his arms. His dark head bent toward me and in the shadows of the darkened cabin I could not see his face clearly. I laid my head against his chest where I could hear and feel the steady beating of his heart as he carried me to bed.

I was surprised at my own boldness as my fingers went to the buttons of his shirt. His eyes held mine all the while even as a sound of pleasure escaped his lips.

Any inhibitions I'd felt earlier vanished, chased away by the cold champagne and the overwhelming longing that had been building up within me for weeks. I could not seem to get close enough to him, could not satisfy the feeling within me. Even as he began to slowly, expertly undress me, I pulled his shirt from his shoulders and ran my hands across the hard muscles of his chest, closing my eyes and breathing in the spicy masculine scent of him.

If I had thought before that I loved him, nothing could have prepared me for the emotions I would feel that night. He deliberately and skillfully caressed me and guided me until I thought I would die from the sheer pleasure of being in his arms, of being loved by him.

When he held me later, kissing my hair and whispering my name softly I was aware only of the beauty he had shown me and of how right it was . . . our being together.

As the gentle splashing of the waves drifted into our room and the ship rocked serenely beneath us, I was blissfully happy. I was so thankful that we had come here instead of remaining in the strange and sometimes disturbing atmosphere of Moonwatch.

I awoke once in the night, feeling slightly chilled, until I realized that the warmth of Nicholas's body was no longer beside me. I was frightened at first and sat up in bed. Then I saw him, standing silently beneath the skylight, looking up into the star-scattered darkness.

"Nicholas?"

He turned then and the soft gleam of light reflected upon the skin of his broad shoulders. "I'm here, angel," he said, his deep voice reassuring me in the darkness.

He came swiftly to the bed and sat beside me, taking me immediately, almost desperately into his arms. His kisses were full of hunger and a forcefulness as if he too could not get enough, as if we had never held each other. His desire was intoxicating, making me feel loved and wanted as I'd never felt before, sweeping me away so that I wanted only to lose myself in the urgency of the moment.

Early the next morning I opened my eyes languidly to find him propped beside me, watching me, with his chin resting upon his hand. I felt my face grow warm at his intimate, searching look.

"You are so beautiful." He brushed my hair back from my face and kissed me lightly on the lips.

When I put my arms about his neck and snuggled closer to him, he laughed, a husky, warm, delightful sound that made my skin ripple with pleasure.

"As much as I hate to say this, we must be up if we're to sail with the morning tide." His blue eyes told me just how reluctant he was to leave our room and I smiled in agreement with him.

"What would your crew say if we did not appear, Captain Hayne?" I teased.

"After seeing you? I'm sure they'd not be at all surprised." He leaned forward and kissed me again, then he groaned. "You should not tempt me so, my darling Victoria." He smiled and pushed himself from the bed, grabbing a nearby robe which he draped about himself.

"Billy has left hot water outside for our baths," he said walking to the door and bringing in a large copper tub and two buckets of water. "I'll go to the galley and bring our breakfast while you bathe."

By the time he returned I had just finished dressing in a plain skirt of kelly green and a soft white silk blouse. It felt good to be able to dress casually and comfortably.

"Are you hungry?" he asked, setting down a tray which contained fluffy omelets and hot buttered bread.

"I was so nervous yesterday I hardly ate anything," I said.

"And now?" he asked, grinning mischievously.

"I'm starving!"

He laughed, aware I was certain, of every emotion that ran through me.

I found I was not at all embarrassed by the intimacy we shared as he bathed and I ate the breakfast he had brought. Indeed I relished it for it seemed the most natural thing in the world and I had never been happier. All the horror of the events at Moonwatch with its petty mysteries, all the doubts seemed insignificant and far away. Even his mother's strange obsession with our marriage meant nothing that morning. I had not thought of the pagoda and had completely forgotten my desire to read Father's journal.

As we sailed out of the bay the sun was spreading its rose-colored wings across the ocean, its light catching in the top of the billowing sails as Nicholas took the wheel and shouted orders to his crew. I watched him seeing an entirely different man than the one I knew at Moonwatch. Here, at the helm of the big ship, he was truly in his element. The muscles beneath his billowing white shirt flexed and rippled as he moved the wheel; his thighs were tense as he stood firmly balancing himself against the waves beneath us. The sight of him there thrilled me and I stood aside, silently admiring his appearance and his skill at the wheel.

As the ship's bow plowed through the shadows and out into the deep green water beyond, we rode more smoothly. The sails were full and there was only the sound of the rushing wind and flapping canvas to be heard.

Nicholas turned to me and pulled me close, his arms about my waist. The salt-filled mist sprayed upon our faces causing Nicholas to tilt his head back, his laughter ringing delightfully across the deck. It was an entirely masculine gesture of triumph and pleasure at doing what he loved best. It was evident how much he loved the ocean and the feel of the ship beneath his feet.

In the joy of the moment and my delight at being there with my hands upon the wheel of Father's great ship, I had completely forgotten my fear of the sea and my usual trepidation toward sailing.

"Nicholas!" I shouted. "I'm not afraid!"

"I see you're not," he said. His faced looked young and carefree as he smiled down at me, the two of us sharing an experience which I would never forget. I could not imagine I would ever be happier in my life.

The ocean was calm that day and the prevailing winds gentle as we sailed into Charleston. The city was much different than I remembered. Many damaged buildings still stood, a silent reminder of the war and the Union's revenge for Fort Sumter. But the spirit and the hospitality still remained. There were new stores and shops opening every day we were told, and many citizens expressed the hope that the city would soon be even greater than before.

Those few days we spent in Charleston were as happy as any I'd ever known. Our days were busily filled with sightseeing and shopping, eating in quaint cozy inns. And the nights, with the sea winds whispering about our room at the inn, were filled with love and magic, making me wish we could stay forever, just Nicholas and I, alone together.

But all dreams must end and I knew reality would again prevail. Even though both of us were quiet on the sail back to Southport Inlet, there was no sadness or apprehension. Only a happy reflection of the days we had spent and the hope that all our married years could always be this way.

We sailed safely into the inlet, told the crew goodbye and thanked them for their expert help. We left the ship then, and climbed into the waiting coach. I sat close to Nicholas, my arm entwined with his and my head resting on his shoulder. He wore a dark suit, the stiff white collar against his tanned neck making me long to kiss the place below his jaw where the pulse beat.

"You look very different today, my captain," I said.

He looked down at me and I thought he had changed since we left—his smile more sincere, his look more surely only for me. Soon, I was certain, I would hear him whisper the words I'd longed for.

"Is that so bad?" he asked.

"No," I whispered. "You're perfect to me no matter where you are or what you wear."

"I hope you'll always feel that way," he said.

A little pang of fear shot through me which I quickly dismissed.

"Of course I shall," I said quickly.

"I'm glad you enjoyed the sail," he said. "Soon you must come with me to the office. Perhaps we might even build the *Victoria* together."

I had never felt closer to anyone than I did him at that moment. Perhaps that feeling was what prompted me to ask the question that had been burning in my mind since we left home. Where I had not been confident enough before to ask about Lesley, our days together had given me the courage to do so.

"Nicholas," I began slowly. "Before we go home, there's something I've wondered about. I hope you won't mind my asking."

He looked at me in surprise, his blue eyes widening at my words. There was only the slightest clenching of his jaw before he spoke. "Ask me anything you wish."

"Were you ever in love with Lesley?"

He frowned slightly, even though he seemed not to be surprised at my question. But to my relief, he did not seem angry. "No, I was never in love with her."

"You never cared for her, never had . . ."

"Whatever is in the past is best forgotten now," he said. "And whatever was between Lesley and myself no longer exists. It has nothing to do with you."

"Oh," I whispered, wishing now that I had never asked. I don't think I really believed it until then. I had only been asking for reassurance. I knew Nicholas was not the kind of man to disclose any of his past alliances and I should have simply left it at that.

He reached down and placed his fingers under my chin, tilting my head back so he could look into my eyes.

"If you were wondering about her comments at the dinner . . . ?"

"Yes, I was." I looked steadily into his eyes.

"Pure jealousy, nothing else. She had no right to say

such a thing to you and it angered me very much."

I turned away from him and looked out the windows, concentrating on the passing landscape.

"Darling, Lesley and I were, at one time, close. . . ." He paused as if to search for just the right words.

"She resents me very much, Nicholas—I can see that now. So I think it must have been more than *close.*"

"Angel . . ." he sighed in exasperation.

"Just tell me it's in the past and I won't say another word about it." I turned to him, hoping he would say what I wanted to hear.

"It is in the past—of course it is. You're my wife!" He took a deep breath and slowly breathed out. "I'm sorry if some mistake I've made in the past causes you to be hurt. Believe me, if I could change it, I would!" There was a sadness in his eyes and I knew he meant what he'd said. But there was also a kind of warning there, as if he had said all he wanted to about the subject.

With an ache in my chest I realized now the reasons for some of his intimate conversations with Lesley, the times I thought I saw them on the beach. I didn't want to know any more, but Nicholas continued.

"First of all, there was never anything serious between us, at least as far as I was concerned. And when I discovered, long before you came, sweetheart, that she was involved with a friend, I broke it off. And that, my dearest, is all I intend to say on the subject." He tried to speak lightly, but neither of us laughed, for I could not speak, did not know what to say. I felt ashamed that I had made him confess; he should never have had to do that for me.

"Victoria, have I failed, in the last few days, to show you just how much I love you?"

My eyes filled with tears at finally hearing him say those words, for not even during our lovemaking had he said them to me. And I had wondered why.

"You love me?" I asked.

He stopped any other words as his mouth covered mine, searching and warm, as he held me there in the dimness of the coach. "I have never loved a woman as I love you. I don't want you to ever doubt that, Victoria." His eyes searched mine, yet there was something more in that look than tenderness, something he was not saying. Whatever it was I brushed it aside, no longer willing to question and probe. I only knew that he loved me.

I wished at the moment that questions did not still crowd my mind, even as he kissed me. I wished I could take his words of love at face value and cherish them. Now that I heard the precious words, though, I wondered why he could not have told me before we married. Could it be he had only fallen in love with me *since* his proposal, and if that were the truth, why did he marry me? I wanted to stop thinking, stop doubting, and just accept it. I would ask him nothing else for I had already learned more than I really wanted to know.

Soon the gray outline of Moonwatch appeared in the distance, its shape stark in the gathering darkness as we approached. The tower light shone out in great widening beams which we drove through as we grew nearer.

I felt a growing reluctance to return to the house and I moved closer to my husband. I shivered as the driver pulled the coach up to the bleak, mist-covered gray stone house.

We had hardly alighted from the coach when the large doors were thrown wide and Vickers came quickly forward. He looked at Nicholas with eyes that were large and frightened.

"Capt'n Hayne, sir. Thank goodness you're home!"

Nicholas turned immediately to the man as a look of alarm crossed his handsome face.

"What is it, Vickers—is it Mother?"

Before the man could answer we heard Frances's voice from inside the house. Through the open doorway I could see her coming hurriedly down the stairs.

"Nicholas! Oh, Nicholas, thank God!" she shouted.

He went quickly to her and took her arms in his hands, looking down with concern into her face.

"It's Tad, Nicholas. He's terribly ill. The doctor says he may not live!" Her voice broke and she slumped into Nicholas's arms at hearing her own terrible words. "There was an accident—it was so horrible. Oh, Nicky, what am I to do if something happens to my boy!"

He gathered her into his arms, letting her weep against his shoulder. He did not press her with questions, but waited until she was more able to speak.

I came to stand beside him and touched her shoulder. The words she had spoken tore at my heart. I could not believe anything had happened to Tad. He was so vibrant, so full of life. I could do nothing to help; I could only wait powerlessly to hear what had happened.

Vickers closed the door and directed that our trunks be taken upstairs. He stood patiently waiting as Nicholas comforted his sister.

"Your things have been moved to the south suite, Capt'n Hayne . . . Mrs. Hayne."

"Thank you, Vickers," Nicholas replied.

"Frances, where is Tad? Take me to him, then you can tell me what happened."

Nicholas turned to me and held out his hand to include me. There was such pain in his eyes that I could hardly bear it. I knew he needed me to be with him.

Obediently, Frances quieted and led us upstairs and along the corridor to where her suite was. She did not speak again until we reached Tad's room.

The room was filled with several oil lamps which blazed brightly, causing the room to be overly warm. The strong scent of illness lingered in the air. For a moment my stomach surged at the heat and the smell, but it was forgotten as I gazed down at the small still figure on the bed.

Frances began to cry again and Nicholas pulled her to one side where two chairs had been placed near the windows.

"Tell me what happened, Franny." His voice was quiet and patient, full of concern as he called his sister by her childhood name.

"Millie's dead," she said bluntly.

My heart skipped a beat at her words. "My God," I whispered. Wordlessly I took off my hat and gloves and removed the cape. I sat down heavily in a chair beside Tad's bed. At Frances's shocking words I found that my legs trembled so badly I could no longer stand.

Nicholas looked toward me and I saw the disbelief on his face, but there was also concern for me. I smiled and nodded, needing to reassure him that I was all right. He did not need to worry about me now with all the others burdens he must shoulder.

"We don't know exactly what happened. Tad has been unconscious since yesterday and Millie . . . They went for an early morning walk during low tide—to look for shells, Tad said. When they didn't come back, I sent Ona to look for them. I didn't think anything of it; you know how Tad is." She clutched at Nicholas's jacket, her dark eyes seeming to plead for his understanding.

"I know, Franny. You must not blame yourself." He held her fluttering hand as he spoke.

"Ona found Tad trapped in the cave up the beach, the one he calls the Whale Cave. When the tide trapped them inside they must have tried to escape through the hole in the top, but somehow a rock had become lodged there and—" Her voice broke as she began to sob.

The thought of Tad and Millie trapped inside that dark cave with the ocean rushing in upon them was heartbreaking and I had to fight to control my own tears.

"Go on," Nicholas urged gently.

"Millie must have pushed Tad up against the rock as far as she could. He was wedged in with his little face . . . with his face near a crack around the rock. It was what saved him, but he still could not have gotten enough air and the water washed up over him. Later in the day they found Millie down the beach about a mile. Oh, Nicholas, please help my little boy. I've been so cold to him, so lacking in my duties to him and now . . . now I'm afraid it's too late!"

"No, sweetheart, it's not too late. Do you hear me? Now I want you to go and wash your face. Have you eaten anything today?"

"I . . . no, I don't think I have," she mumbled.

"What about Mother? Is she all right?" he asked.

"She's terribly upset of course, and I thought it best if she does not see him just yet."

"I think you're right. Now, do as I say. We're all going to go downstairs and eat. One of the maids can stay here with Tad."

"I'll stay with him, Nicholas," I said. I wanted to stay, could not bear to leave him alone. He looked so small and helpless.

Nicholas looked toward me as if he had almost forgotten me, but his eyes were grateful, and he did not urge me to go with them.

"Are you sure?"

"Yes, I'm sure. You go with Frances and I know you're anxious to see your mother as well."

As they left he touched my hair and smiled, before looking down at Tad. "I'll be back soon," he promised.

Tad's face was pale, but his breathing was slow and steady and did not seem to be labored. I could only hope that the shock had caused this coma and not a lack of oxygen. I picked up his small, lifeless hand and it felt warm and normal.

I poured cool water in a wash basin and proceeded to turn back some of the quilts upon his bed. Then I turned down the lamps to a less blinding glare and raised the window sash so that the cool sea air might permeate the corners of the musty room.

I sat beside his bed and bathed first his arms and hands in the cool water and then his small, pale face. I talked to him all the while, telling him of our trip and the great ship we had sailed on.

"I can't wait for you to see it, Tad," I said. "Your Uncle Nicholas is such a wonderful sailor. He knows all about the ocean, the winds, the currents—just as you said. He's a fine captain, just as you will be one day."

Tad did not move, my words had not made any difference . . . could not penetrate the deep, shadowy world where he lay.

"Oh, Tad," I whispered. "My little friend, please come back to us." Then as I sat in the quiet little room alone I allowed myself to weep for him and for Millie, the sweet-faced girl who had been so kind and friendly to me since I came. The vision of her on the day of my wedding flashed into my mind: her sweet starry-eyed tears as she helped me with my gown; when I told her to look after Tad.

"Oh, Millie," I groaned. My throat burned painfully. I could not believe this had happened.

I did not like the persistent feeling that kept nagging

at me, the voice that whispered over and over in my mind. Something was not right; there had been no large rocks at the cave that day. There was nothing for several yards except sand and a few windblown pieces of grass. Surely no one here would try to block the exit or harm Tad and Millie. Would they?

Chapter XVIII

Later when Nicholas returned alone I was still talking to Tad, rubbing my hand lightly over his arms, trying somehow to stimulate him into an awareness of his surroundings.

Without speaking, Nicholas placed his hands on my shoulders for a moment, then pulled a chair near the bed to sit beside me.

"How is he?" he asked.

"Still the same. Oh, Nicholas, this is all so terrible."

"I know," he whispered, pulling me to him. We sat for awhile, silently watching the boy for any sign of movement.

Finally Nicholas said, "Why don't you go down and eat something? I'll stay with him awhile."

I turned at the door to look back into the room at the small boy and the man who sat watching him as if he could will him to open his eyes. Nicholas's shoulders slumped forward and he bent to take Tad's hand in both his large fists. When he lowered his head to Tad's palms, I thought my heart would break. There was so much pain in his actions. It didn't seem possible that the strong, vigorous man who had just captained the *Galatea* should be so helpless now, but I loved him all the more for his compassion and his sweet tenderness.

After I had eaten a cold supper, Nicholas said he wanted to stay with Tad a while longer. I went up alone to our new suite. I walked past my old room, not bothering to look in, even though I felt a momentary twinge of homesickness. I reminded myself then that the new room would belong to Nicholas and me; it was where we would begin our life together here. I only wished it could be under happier circumstances. Nevertheless, I was suddenly anxious to see it and for Nicholas to join me.

That small bit of optimism died as I walked into the room, for the first thing my eyes rested upon was the conch shell that Tad had given me before the wedding.

I picked it up from the mantel, turning it in my hands, feeling its contrasting textures.

"Tad . . . you must get well," I said, whispering into the shell as if it were a magical instrument. I knew, though, it would take more than magic to bring Tad back. Dejectedly, I placed the shell back on the mantelpiece.

I looked about the room. A lamp had been lit and a small fire was burning in the hearth. The bedroom was spacious and more elegantly appointed than the one I'd been given before. The expanse of windows that looked out to the sea was wider and would drench the room with light during the day. Past the windows was the door to a dressing room. I opened the door curiously and saw a large, comfortable sitting room with a maroon velvet sofa and chairs arranged near another fireplace. The room was dark and I shivered unconsciously, trying hard not to think of Millie.

When I had closed and locked the door to the sitting room, however, I was reminded again of the girl. One of the maids had fluffed the pillows and turned back the elegant gold satin coverlet on the bed to reveal the sparkling white linens. Millie had always done such things to make me comfortable, even though I protested that I could certainly manage to turn down my own. She would smile and tease me about getting used to being a great lady in the old tradition of Moonwatch.

"Millie," I whispered. "How very much I shall miss your smiling face and your sweetness."

I seemed to be drowning in a swell of pain and sorrow that would not let me go. I needed a distraction and thought it a good time to read more of Father's journals. After I dressed for bed I removed one from my valise and settled myself in the large comfortable fourposter to read.

I winced as I read more about Father's gambling debts and his mistaken notion that he could stop if only he could have one more lucky game. How sure he was that he could gamble away all his problems, and that one more game would fix everything. He wrote often of Nicholas and it was obvious how much he cared for him. I was surprised that he mentioned Lesley even more often, sometimes referring to her only as "L."

My eyes had grown tired and sleepy when suddenly some of the words seemed to leap from the pages. Father wrote, *I fear I have fallen deeply in love with L., a foolish notion, I realize, for a man of my age. She makes me feel young again and positive I can do anything.*

Although I had begun to suspect as much, I still found it difficult to imagine my father and Lesley together. I read on.

I would do anything for her. I am a man obsessed with everything about her. Nicholas has warned me, but he does not understand and even though I love and respect him as my own son, we exchanged angry words.

Had my husband warned Father because he was

genuinely concerned for his welfare, or because he was jealous? Was this the *friend* for whom he relinquished Lesley? What kind of game had Lesley been playing? Was she involved with both of them at the same time? The thought sickened me.

I heard Nicholas in the hallway outside our door and quickly placed the journal in the drawer of the table beside our bed.

When he came in I could see his fatigue in the set of his shoulders and the drawn lines about his mouth.

"Still awake?" he asked.

"I wanted to wait for you. How is he?"

"The same," he murmured, throwing his jacket onto a chair and pulling the bottom of his shirt from the waist of his trousers.

"Nicholas," I sighed. "How could this have happened? It's so horrible. I just can't believe it."

"Neither can I. Not a very happy homecoming I'm afraid." He turned back the sheet and got into bed beside me.

He pulled me to him and we lay silently, holding each other as if we could somehow chase away the sadness that had greeted us on our return home. Nicholas sighed heavily and closed his eyes, his arm flung across his forehead. "God," he murmured in exasperation.

"He'll be all right, Nicholas," I said, trying to believe it myself. "He has to be."

"Yes," he whispered. "He has to be."

Almost instantly I felt his body begin to relax and soon he was in a deep sleep. I envied him his ability to shut out everything and sleep so quickly while I lay awake in the unfamiliar room thinking. I could not stop myself from musing on all the terrible events that had occurred on this deserted stretch of beach where Moonwatch stood. I could not stop the whirl of questions that my father's diary had brought, could not banish the picture from my mind of Lesley in Nicholas's arms, his head bent to—

"No!" I whispered fiercely.

I reached out and turned down the lamp by the bed, careful not to disturb Nicholas. I moved myself close to him, to the warmth of his body, listening to his quiet rhythmic breathing and praying that sleep would soon come.

Next morning Nicholas was gone when I woke, even though it was still quite early. I was just beginning to hear the sounds of the household stirring into life, people going about their chores. Today the voices seemed to have the somber, muted tones of grief as they spoke, passing in the hallway outside our room.

Breakfast that first morning back was a solemn, quiet affair. Mrs. Hayne was not there and I had not expected her to be. Evidently Frances was still with Tad. I was alone with Eric Roberts and Lesley.

Eric looked up at me kindly as I sat across from him. I thought I saw in his dark eyes a hint of sympathy, perhaps because my marriage was beginning with such a sad note.

It was Lesley, though, that caught my attention. I saw her in a different light now, taking in every detail of her, trying to see the attraction that Nicholas had felt and wondering with agony if he had kissed her, caressed her the same way he did me. I wanted so desperately to believe he had never touched anyone as he had me.

If I had expected her to be contrite after her scene at our reception I was mistaken. Her eyes assessed me boldly as she spoke in a short, abrupt manner, the kindness she'd shown me before gone. There was no longer any need for pretense as far as I was concerned, and she was openly antagonistic.

"Ah, the blushing bride," she said, smiling across at me. "And where is the handsome bridegroom . . . still abed?" I knew she meant to mock me with her words and I had to remind myself that Nicholas had chosen me for his wife, not Lesley. I was trying hard not to let her cause me any more insecurity than I already felt.

"Good morning to you too, Lesley," I said, deliberately keeping my voice sweet and friendly. "I believe Nicholas has gone to the mainland to bring back Millie's parents and to make arrangements for her funeral."

"My, hasn't he become the ever-dutiful son of Moonwatch?" She laughed disdainfully. "Believe me, he was not always so sedate and boring."

I turned to her, angered by her words, and smiled pointedly. "Nicholas is many things, Lesley, but boring certainly is not one of them."

I began to eat without waiting to see her reaction, but I could sense by her silence that she had not expected any resistance from me for her obviously ridiculing remarks.

One thing was clear to me now. There was absolutely no chance that Lesley and I would ever be friends. Strange that she had been the one person here whom I thought I could trust. After reading further revelations about her in the diary last night I found I did not even want to talk to her.

"It's been a sad homecoming for you and Nicholas, I'm afraid." I knew Eric's words were an attempt to clear the air.

"Yes," I replied. "Very sad indeed. I only hope Tad will recover."

"If there is anything I can do, Victoria, I hope you know you've only to ask." His look was warm and intent, it seemed, on putting me at ease.

"Thank you, Eric. I do appreciate it."

"I think you know, Victoria," Lesley said, her voice more chastened, "that I feel the same way. I'm indeed fond of little Tad and was horrified by the accident."

"Yes, thank you. If you'll both excuse me, I think I'll go up now and check on him."

Lesley continued with her meal, but Eric's dark eyes followed me, never seeming to leave me until I had walked through the door. Something was different about him. He was not as distant as he had been and I found it made me ill at ease.

I was lost in thought as I walked down the corridor toward Tad's room. Suddenly the door of the room burst open and Frances stepped quickly into the hallway, her eyes large and expressive. She seemed slightly breathless.

"Oh, Victoria, thank goodness, it's you! Tad is all right! He's awake and he's going to be all right!" She came forward impulsively and clasped me to her. A brilliant smile of happiness lit her face.

She took my hands in hers. "I was just going to find someone to stay with him. I must have someone go for the doctor. Would you mind staying? I should go right away and tell Mother."

"Of course I'll stay." But Frances was rushing down the hallway even as I spoke.

I opened the door slowly, but Tad heard me and turned his head to look at me as I came in. His face was still a bit wan, but he seemed almost normal as the pale November sunlight poured into the small room.

"Tad," I said, going directly to him. I sat on his bed and took his small hand. He smiled at me weakly, but there was definitely the old sparkle of mischief in his eyes.

"How do you feel?" I asked.

"Tired," he answered, "and hungry." His voice sounded hoarse and a bit weary, but I was overjoyed just to hear him.

"I'll have something sent up right away," I said,

standing to leave.

"Wait, Victoria," he said, reaching out toward me.

His look had grown more serious and I knew he wanted to ask about Millie.

"Yes, Tad," I said, sitting back down. "What is it?"

"Millie," he said. "I was wondering about Millie. She . . . she tried to help me. . . ." His voice trailed away and he seemed not to have enough strength to finish.

"Yes, she did, Tad. Millie did a very brave thing."

"But she's . . . she's dead, isn't she?"

"Tad . . ." I did not know what to say, did not know how his mother would wish him to be told. I couldn't take the chance that he would become ill again because of something I might say.

"I know she is," he said, tears filling his luminous eyes. "I felt the water pull her away." His words, childlike, were blunt and honest, with no attempt at pretense. He was still too young to know that adult characteristic.

"I . . . I closed my eyes and when I looked she was gone. I should have helped her!" he cried. "If I had been stronger I could have kept her from being washed away!"

I gathered him into my arms, holding him against me as I attempted to quiet his sobs. "No, Tad. No one could have held her. The tides here are too strong. You know how often Nicholas has warned you about the tides. You must not blame yourself. You did everything you could do." I held him away from me and looked into his eyes. "It was an accident, sweetheart, and there was nothing you or anyone could have done. Millie tried to save you and she tried to save herself, but she couldn't. It was just a terrible accident."

He lowered his eyes, looking away from me and I thought there was something else he wanted to say, but at that moment the door opened and his mother came back into the room. She held the door open as Ona pushed Mrs. Hayne in to see her grandson.

"Oh, sonny," Mrs. Hayne cried, reaching out to take Tad into her arms. "Thank goodness you're all right."

Tad squirmed a bit self-consciously at all the attention. I was sure it was one of the few times he'd ever received such loving consideration and I found myself wondering cynically how long it would last.

"You must be more careful, Tad," Mrs. Hayne warned. "I shudder to think what would have happened to you if Ona had not found you when he did. You should thank him for saving your life."

Tad looked shyly around his grandmother to the huge man standing silently by the doorway. "Thank you, Ona," he said, smiling sweetly at the dark-skinned man.

To my surprise, a wide grin lit the man's face and he nodded happily at the little boy in bed. "You are most welcome, little one," he said in his deep resonate voice.

It was the first time I'd ever seen Ona smile and it positively transformed him until I found myself smiling too. He and Tad grinned at one another as if they were two schoolmates. Ona looked at Tad with such affection that I became certain he could not have possibly been involved with Tad's accident or Millie's death.

"Well, I shan't stay longer and tire you, sweetheart," Mrs. Hayne said. Looking toward me, she added, "Victoria, I'm sorry we have not had time to talk since your return. Perhaps you'll visit me later today."

I nodded that I would.

"Are you hungry, son?" Frances asked Tad after her mother had left.

"I was just on my way to the kitchen when you came in," I told her.

"Oh, I'll do that. You stay and chat with Tad. He was so anxious for you to come home, I know he wants to talk to you."

Frances's change in attitude toward her son was almost amusing, but I was happy for Tad's sake that she had changed. I was also happy that this change seemed to include me, at least for the time being. Perhaps now she would be able to lose the apathy and selfishness that had consumed her since her husband's death.

Tad's eyes followed her from the room before he turned to me quickly as if to reveal a secret.

"What is it, Tad? I have a feeling that something still troubles you about the accident."

"Millie told me a secret that day. That's why we went for a walk to the cave. She didn't want anyone to hear.

"I see." I did not want to push him to tell me the secret; I knew he must do that in his own time. "But when the tide started to come into the cave, why didn't you and Millie leave?" I asked.

"'Cause Millie was afraid. She thought someone had followed us and she didn't want them to see us. So we hid. She knew about the whale spout, but after we got there someone put the rock over it and we couldn't get out!" There was stark terror in his eyes at remembering the horrible moment of entrapment.

My heart lurched sickeningly. "Tad, now think carefully before you answer me. You're sure someone put the rock there?"

"I saw them!"

"Who did you see?"

"I . . . I don't know. I couldn't even tell if it was a man or a woman. Someone rolled the rock across the hole, but through the crack I could only see a cloak. The bottom of it was wet and had sand all over it. I yelled for them to stop. I know they heard me."

I reached out and took his hand. "It's all right now, Tad," I said. "Rest awhile. You can tell me everything later."

"No!" he said. "I'm afraid they'll come back. They'll kill me and then they'll kill you!" His eyes were panic-stricken and he clutched my hand so tightly it ached.

"Kill us? Why should anyone kill you, Tad . . . or me?"

"It has something to do with you, but Millie didn't have time to tell me who—"

"Wait, sweetheart, just slow down. We are going to tell your uncle everything. He won't let anyone harm you, darling. You do believe that, don't you?"

He took a deep breath and closed his eyes tiredly before nodding his head. There were tears on his cheeks and I was virtually helpless to console him, but I knew he must finish what he had to tell me, or he would never be able to rest.

"Tad, can you tell me the secret Millie told you?" I asked.

He began more slowly this time and I knew that my mention of Nicholas had reassured him somewhat.

"She told me she was afraid . . . that she was walking by your room that morning and heard a noise inside. When she went in someone had gone through all your things. She said there were clothes on the floor and the linens were pulled from the bed. Your trunk was open and someone was there rummaging through it. They threatened Millie and I think they fought because she had a bruise on her cheek. She must have run away then, and that's when she found me."

"And she never told you who it was in my room?" I asked.

"She was going to, that's why she asked me to go with her. But then she thought someone was coming across the dunes so we ran into the cave to hide." He was silent then, as if he were totally exhausted.

"Rest now, Tad, until your mother brings you some food. I'll be right here and I'll tell Nicholas what you've told me just as soon as I see him."

By the time Frances came with a tray of food, Tad was asleep again. She smiled at me as if all the resentment she'd directed at me before was completely forgotten. I was so confused and worried about what Tad had told me, though, that I could think of little else.

"I'll stay with him until he wakes," she said. "Nicholas is home and I'm sure you're anxious to see him." Her smile was warm and open, causing me to stare at her dumbly.

"Yes," I answered. "And Frances, don't leave him. He's afraid of being left alone."

"Oh, of course I shan't leave him alone for an instant," she said in her new breezy tone.

All I wanted now was to find Nicholas, to feel the security of his arms about me and tell him what Tad had so painfully related about Millie's death. There was a chill within me that would not be banished until I could see the one who made me feel so secure and so loved.

Chapter XIX

After I left Tad I went directly to my old room. I walked hurriedly along the halls, being careful not to let anyone see me as I slipped quietly into the room.

I shivered in the dark stillness of the chamber. I halfway expected to find the disarray which Tad had mentioned, but everything seemed to be in order.

The curtains at the windows had been pulled together leaving the corners shadowy and gray. At the foot of the bed sat the trunk, one I had not needed on our trip. As I opened the case I caught my breath, for whoever Millie had surprised that day had forgotten to put this back in order. The clothes had been hastily pushed and pulled aside until all the items lay in a tangled heap. I slid my hand beneath the clothes to the bottom of the trunk. Father's other journal was gone! But who would even know about the journals and why would anyone want them? And had this person killed Millie?

Quickly I closed the trunk and left the room. I ran to mine and Nicholas's room. I only hoped that whoever had searched my room did now know about the other diary. Going to the table beside the bed I breathed a sigh of relief when I saw it was still in the drawer. I looked about the room, searching for a place to hide the book in case someone came to look here as well. I wished I could sit down at that moment to finish the journal, to find a clue as to why anyone would want it so desperately. With the upheaval caused by the accident and Millie's funeral, though, I didn't know when I would be able to finish it.

Finally I reached under the bed to where the edge of the Aubusson carpet lay. Curling back the border I quickly tucked the journal underneath, out of sight. Someone would have to tear the room upside down to find it and that would take a good deal of time. I didn't believe whoever it was would risk that with Nicholas here.

I wanted to see Mrs. Hayne. Perhaps she could tell me something about Lesley and my father, or give me some insight as to why anyone would be interested in what he had written.

It was growing late, well past lunch, but I felt no need for food. It was my curiosity that needed to be satisfied now and I could only hope Nicholas would not be too upset when I did not appear.

As I left our room I took notice of the sunlight that streamed through the curtains. It was unseasonably warm for this time of year. Perhaps at least the weather was in our favor, hopefully until tomorrow's funeral.

When I reached Mrs. Hayne's room, Ona opened the door for me as if he had been expecting me. Today he appeared more colorful than ever, with beribboned bands around his muscular upper arms. From the ribbons hung tiny brass bells that chimed faintly as he moved. It was a pleasant, melodious sound that I liked very much. Remembering his earlier grin at Tad, I smiled up at the quiet man. He looked at me oddly for a moment, but did not return my smile. What a strange man he was and one I did not quite know how to communicate with yet.

Mrs. Hayne was also waiting for me and had witnessed my brief encounter with Ona with some amusement. Nevertheless she greeted me very warmly and bade me sit opposite her.

"I must say your honeymoon certainly seems to have agreed with you dear. You've never looked lovelier. Your complexion is positively aglow." Her eyes assessed slyly as if she thought she would embarrass me, but I was determined that she would not cause me to lose my composure.

"Thank you," I said, smiling sweetly. I would take her words as a compliment even though she probably had not meant them. I would not be the stammering, blushing bride she wanted me to be. I wanted to tell the world of my love for Nicholas and how he made me feel and I would not be ashamed or embarrassed about that.

She read me very well and threw back her head, laughing. She made a throaty, earthy sound that surprised me. It was so odd coming from such a tiny and seemingly fragile lady. I had seen from the beginning, however, that her delicate looks were only a facade that covered a highly passionate nature.

"So, can I expect you to present me with a grandchild within the year?" she asked. Her abrasive words grated on my nerves and I fervently hoped I would not have to endure this line of questioning every few months of my marriage.

"Who can say?" I answered coolly, "but personally I'd like for Nicholas and myself to have more time alone before we begin a family."

"So, you have fallen even more deeply in love with my handsome son? That's good, yes, that's very good."

"Why is it so important to you that we have a child?" I asked. "Is it because of my father?"

"Did he ever speak of me?" she asked bluntly.

"No, not that I recall, but then, as you know, I did not see much of him the last few years. And, after all, it is not something a father would discuss with his child."

"No, no, of course, you're right." But she was disappointed and seemed to daydream for a moment. "I loved him, you know. I never loved a man the way I loved Anthony Ancona. But he was weak, too weak to fight for anything. He was just content to let life drag him around, allowing fate to make his choices."

Her bitter words about my father angered me, but I could not deny there was some truth to what she said. I was beginning to see evidence of it in his writings.

"But what about your husband?" I asked, growing more curious by the minute.

"I cared for John, but our marriage was arranged for the mutual benefit of our families. It was a good one. After all, it produced my wonderful Nicholas."

I looked at her strangely for a moment. "And Frances."

"Yes, of course. I was just going to add . . . dear Frances."

Her eyes seemed glazed for a moment before she continued. "John was very jealous of your father. I suppose he always knew how much I loved him, but Anthony never gave me a serious look. He had eyes for no one, except her. Even after she was dead, he loved her memory much more than he could ever love a flesh and blood woman." Her unkind words were said bitterly as if the pain were still fresh.

I did not reply for I was fascinated by the play of emotion across her face. The hurt and humiliation was still there when she spoke of him. I began to understand a little why she so obstinately wanted my marriage to Nicholas and an heir with Ancona blood. Perhaps it was part of a revenge that had played again and again in her mind over the years until it had become an obsession.

"There," she said, turning sharply to me. "I've shocked you, haven't I, speaking in such a manner about your own father?"

"No, not at all. Actually when you speak of him, it is as though you're talking of another person, someone I never knew," I replied.

We sat for a moment, both of us silent, I not knowing what to say to her. Through the window I caught the flash of movement on the sand dunes beyond the house. Mrs. Hayne spotted the two people at almost the same instant.

I frowned slightly as I recognized them. There was no doubt this time. It was Nicholas and Lesley.

Mrs. Hayne looked at me, her eyes cool and mocking. "Nicholas is a handsome man, desired by many women. I hope there is widsom enough in that pretty young head of yours to handle that well."

"So do I," I murmured, taking a long, slow breath. I could not drag my eyes away from them.

He walked slowly beside the petite woman, his head lowered to catch her words above the roar of the pounding surf. She was looking up at him, smiling. Nicholas carried himself proudly, his muscular body erect, and my heart fluttered at seeing him there with her.

Mrs. Hayne continued to watch me, a tiny smile playing upon her lips. She was as pleased as a pampered cat by what I had allowed her to see on my face. I knew then she hoped I would be vulnerable and weak where my husband was concerned. But why? Did she somehow think to exact her revenge on Anthony Ancona through me, his daughter?

Suddenly I only wanted to be away from her scrutiny, her ever-changing moods and away from the oppressiveness of the dark, brooding house.

I got up with no explanation and blundered from the spice-scented room. I could not seem to erase the picture of Lesley with my husband as they talked so privately. Crazy suspicions ran through my mind. I wondered if Nicholas had told her about me, if he compared Lesley and me in any way. Not for the first time since my marriage did I feel totally vulnerable and insecure. Had they been laughing together about me and my lack of experience, my total naive absorption in Nicholas for the past few weeks, my eagerness to marry him?

"No!" I whispered aloud. "I could not bear that."

I went to our room and stood gazing down at the beach and the fingers of water that washed upon the shore. The late afternoon sun marked its path across the glittering water in streaks of gold and pink. I stood for a long while, mesmerized by the endless waves. I allowed the scene to hypnotize me, blotting out all my worries about Nicholas or Tad. I did not hear the sound of the door open behind me.

"Victoria, what are you doing here in the dark?" I jumped at the sound of Nicholas's deep voice and turned to face him.

I could see his face in the flare of the match as he lit one of the lamps. I had never noticed before how his eyebrows curved downward between his eyes when he had a question, or how cool his dark blue eyes could be.

"Nicholas," I said. "I . . . I was just watching the evening sun on the ocean. Look, you can already see the dim outline of the moon. It's going to be full tonight." I walked past him to the bed and began to smooth imaginary wrinkles.

He walked slowly to me, looking all the while into my face as if he were puzzled about something.

"Sweet, what's wrong. What's bothering you?"

"Nothing," I lied. "Really. I'm just a little nervous I suppose, with all that's happened in this house."

He pulled me around so that I had to face him. He turned his head in a curious gesture and studied my eyes. "Little liar," he whispered. There was just a flicker of a smile around his lips.

At his words, my eyes flew upward to meet his and I saw the familiar spark of desire deep within their depths. No matter how hurt and angry, no matter how puzzled I was by his behavior, I felt the warmth of that look race through me. My limbs grew weak and I leaned toward him.

"You saw us, didn't you, walking on the beach?" he asked.

It angered me that he seemed amused somehow by that.

"No, I don't know what you mean." I could not bear to admit that I had seen them, for I knew my fear of losing him would be plainly visible. I was afraid he would laugh at me.

Lesley was worldly, experienced, and I had seen for myself the voluptuous figure she tried to disguise. I knew in my heart that a man like Nicholas could never really prefer someone like me to her. That was what Lesley had been trying to tell me all along but I was too blind to see.

I pulled away from him, not wanting to look into his eyes.

"I was walking with Lesley," he said, his voice now more serious. He made no further attempt to touch me. "She wanted to apologize for her behavior at our wedding reception."

I whirled to face him then, furious that he could shrug off her remarks to me so easily with a friendly walk on the beach and an apology. He seemed so willing to accommodate her.

"That's odd," I said as I felt my face growing warm

with resentment. "At breakfast this morning Lesley gave no indication of being sorry at all!"

One eyebrow quirked in surprise, then a slow smile moved across his features. "You know I'm very flattered," he murmured, "but I assure you, darling, you have no reason to be jealous of Lesley. Or any other woman for that matter."

"I'm not jealous," I said coolly, shrugging my shoulders. "It's just—"

"Yes," he grinned. "You are."

He pulled me slowly into his arms, his cobalt eyes holding mine with their magnetic gaze, stopping any protest I might have.

"Nicholas, don't—"

My words were stopped by his mouth that teased lightly and brushed across my ear, lingering just below where my pulse beat wildly at my neck. My hands reached up to touch his face and his thick black hair. I loved his hair and the clean scent of him, a blending of sunshine and sea wind.

"Your cat eyes can never lie," he insisted gently, pulling me toward the bed. "How can I convince you there's no need for jealousy?" He laughed softly, the sound warm in my ears and filling my heart with gladness, for I could not yet believe that this beautiful man actually wanted me, had even fallen in love with me.

There in the growing darkness of the room, the golden dusk of light filtered through the windows. Nicholas began a slow and pleasurable campaign to convince me he meant what he said.

Much later as we drifted off to sleep I forgot everything . . . the only conscious thought I had was of him and our future here together.

When I woke, the sky outside was completely dark

and our room was dim except for the oil lamp Nicholas had lit earlier.

Nicholas was beside the bed watching me.

"Oh," I said, sitting up abruptly. "We must have missed dinner. What will the others think?"

He laughed. "I don't care what they think."

"You're terrible," I said, smiling up at him.

"Yes, and you love me." Again he laughed, his confidence in himself obvious in a teasing and endearing way.

"Now, put on your robe and I'll have our dinner brought up." He kissed me lightly on the lips, then headed briskly for the door.

"Nicholas, you're coming right back, aren't you?" I asked.

"Yes, why?" He stopped and looked at me.

"I have something important to tell you, something Tad told me. I should already have done so, but—" I stopped, not able to put into words the interlude that had kept me from telling him.

"I won't be long," he said.

Soon after he left, a young girl of about seventeen knocked on the door, bringing into the room two pails of steaming water.

"I'm Amy, ma'am," she said, rather shyly. "I was workin' in the kitchen and now I'll be takin' Millie's place."

"I'm glad to meet you, Amy," I said. "Here, let me help you with those." I took one of the heavy buckets and poured it into the copper tub that had been placed before the fireplace.

The girl was plump and petite with fine wispy curls of reddish gold hair about her face. Large green eyes looked guilelessly at me from her round pale face.

As I poured the water into the tub, she watched me uneasily for a moment, as if she were uncertain about something. Then she turned and began to stoke the fire and add more coals into the grate.

After she had done that, she turned and curtsied slightly to me. "Will there be anything else, ma'am?" she asked.

"No, Amy. Thank you very much. I'm happy you shall be working upstairs now."

"Oh, me too, ma'am, and, if I may say so, I'm happy to have a lady as nice as you to work for." Her eyes were bright and expressive as she spoke, quickly warming to me. "Never knew a lady to carry her own bathwater," she added shyly.

"No?" I said, smiling at her expression. "Then I suppose we have something in common, for I've never grown used to having all these things done for me. Perhaps we might do them together." I didn't tell her how awkward I felt having a girl not much younger than I address me as ma'am and treat me as if I were a matron.

"Yes, ma'am, I'd like that. Thank you, ma'am."

I laughed aloud as Amy left. There was a grin on her face and she fairly danced out the door. I knew I had made an ally. Having Amy was going to prove to be a delight.

By the time I bathed, luxuriating in the warm water and the glow from the fire, Nicholas was at the door. He looked to make sure I was dressed before motioning a servant behind him into the room. The servant carried a silver tray which he placed on our table before the fire. Without speaking, he then carried the tub from the room and left us alone.

Nicholas reached out and fingered the lace at the neck of my deep blue velvet dressing gown. "You are too beautiful for words," he whispered, bending to again kiss my lips tenderly.

He pulled away and grinned wryly at me, amused, no

doubt, by my total absorption in him.

"If you continue to look at me that way, our dinner shall go begging once again."

I returned his smile, feeling so at ease and comfortable in his presence. I liked being alone with him here in our room, with dinner before the fireplace rather than under the eyes of everyone downstairs.

"Now, tell me about Tad."

"Have you been to see him this afternoon?" I asked.

"Only briefly, but he was eating and I told him I'd come back later."

As I began to relate Tad's words to Nicholas, he put down his fork and looked at me. He frowned worriedly and shook his head slightly. Then he rose from the table and stood looking down into the fireplace as he rested his hand on the mantel.

"What in God's name is happening here?" he said, as if to himself. "First those two attacks on you and now this." He shook his head again in consternation and I could sense the turmoil within him. It was plain to see in the set of his jaw and the tense muscles in his thigh as he placed a foot onto the tiled hearth.

I told him all of it: my room being searched, the threat of danger I sometimes felt. For some reason I could not explain even to myself, though, I did not tell him of Father's journal which I'd hidden under our bed.

"I'm going to stay with Tad tonight—all night. I don't like leaving you alone, but I hope you understand. If he's afraid and depending on me, I can't leave him alone."

"Of course I understand," I said firmly.

"I want you to lock your door as soon as I leave. I'll have someone posted outside the room if you'd feel better."

"No, that's not necessary," I insisted.

"After Millie's funeral tomorrow I shall question every servant in this house and if there is an answer to be found I promise you I will find it!" His eyes had darkened to a determined cold blue-gray and I knew how much it angered him that someone had attempted to harm his nephew.

So why didn't I tell him then about Father's journal? What kept me from trusting him completely? It was a question I could not answer.

After he had kissed me good-night and locked the door, I wanted nothing more than to be alone. I wanted to climb back into bed and finish the journal. If there was any clue there about what had happened to the Ching tê chên pagoda, I wanted to find it, for I could not help wondering if the bizarre and frightening events in this house were related to its disappearance.

After retrieving the journal and turning out all the lamps except one beside my bed, I got into bed, settling down comfortably to read.

Father's reference to Lesley, or "L" became more and more frequent. He was becoming obsessed with her, falling more and more in love. How very outré that seemed to me, for what woman who had Nicholas for a lover could turn to someone else—especially an older man like my father? I could only surmise that there was another reason entirely for her relationship with Anthony Ancona.

I began to notice a different tone to the writing, clearly one of anxiety. I gasped aloud when I read the next lines: *I know now for certain that Lesley has another lover; I found them together in the study, hours after she thought I had gone to bed. I am shocked that this man who I trusted has betrayed me. He even became belligerent and threatening to me in my own home, mocking me and calling me an "old man." He taunted that I could not satisfy such a woman as Les-*

ley. I do not know what to do about this now.

I read on quickly. In the next few entries Lesley seemed to have convinced him that she cared only for him. I could see he wanted to believe her. He did not mention her lover by name, but I knew with a sinking, leaden feeling, that the man who had betrayed my father and threatened him was my husband.

Father seemed to despair between believing Lesley and being afraid of losing her. My heart ached for him as I read his pathetic words.

I know I haven't much to offer a woman like Lesley, not even Ashford Place. Since I have lost that to Nicholas, and even though he has graciously allowed me to continue living here, I do not want that for Lesley. There is no way out for me now. If only I had the pagoda, Lesley and I could go away. Let Denise and her son have everything—my home, my ships. She had even planned for Nicholas to marry my daughter one day. But I will never allow that to happen now. I don't care about any of it as long as I am with the woman I love.

So it seemed Lesley had replaced me in my father's heart. Had he planned to go away with no word to me and leave me to face Denise Hayne's wrath alone?

The next day's entry had grown even more frantic. I noted that the entry date was only two days before his death. I read on, oblivious to anything around me, aware of nothing except his words and their prophetic meaning.

He was with Lesley again in the garden, and I overheard their conversation. He wants her to go away with him. I was so furious I wanted to confront him right then and there, but I heard him tell her he would kill me if I tried to interfere. I know he is capable of it, so I stood back and listened. What I saw makes me certain now that L. is entranced with him, for they embraced passionately and she responded as she never has for me. I am certain it is only the aura of danger that attracts her to him. I know that once I take her away she will forget him.

I put the book down and closed my eyes, leaning back against the pillows. "Oh, Father," I whispered. Tears filled my eyes and I could not see to read any more. How could Nicholas treat me as if this had never happened? How could he say he never loved Lesley when this intense passion existed between them and he had even begged her to run away with him? He and Lesley had betrayed my father and broken his heart. A terrible sick feeling washed over me knowing that I was married to the man my father had come to despise, a man who had even threatened to kill him. All because of Lesley. Was it any wonder her looks at me were so smug and self-confident?

Finally I read on. I could not stop until I knew everything—all the secrets that Lesley and my husband had kept from me. God! How they both must have laughed when I agreed so readily to marry Nicholas. For now he had everything: Ashford Place, my father's share of the business, and his ships. Had that plan of destruction also included me?

Father's words continued: *There is nothing to do now except go to Moonwatch and take the pagoda. When it is sold I shall have enough to take Lesley away for good. I know where John once kept it hidden before he had the case made. Once I take it from its case I shall hide it there once more until Lesley and I make plans to leave. When they discover it is gone, they will not suspect it is hidden in their own house, right under their noses. The riddle shall help me once I get the pagoda.*

And now I shall have my sweet revenge. I will never forgive Denise for what she did those many years ago. After we're far away, I shall delight in sending word to her that her precious pagoda was right beneath her nose and she could not find it.

If only it had never happened. But I was young and foolish and drank too much wine. If only I had known then what a deceitful schemer she is. Denise planned it all along and little Franny was the unfortunate result of that night of madness. Denise is still using it against me after all these years!

With my heart beating loudly I reread the words. Franny? Was he saying Frances was my sister? The daughter of Denise and my father? No, I could not believe it! Suddenly the whole world seemed to be spinning, just as my life had been turned upside down by the revelations written in my father's own hand. Quickly I turned the page and read on.

I am a coward, the lowest of men, for I never acknowledged to anyone that Frances is my daughter. I could not. Once Anna and I married, I intended to tell her, for I never doubted Denise's ability to ruin our happy life. I think that infuriated her more than anything, the fact that she could not do it. But she managed to turn my best friend against me. God knows how John must have hated me . . . went to his grave hating me and I'll never forgive Denise that! And poor little Frances, what a living hell her mother has made her life because she reminds her of me. The one thing I fear is that Franny will become a sick, bitter old woman just as her mother has. In truth Denise has made her pay for my sins. That is why I will never allow my sweet, innocent Victoria to become involved with them, why she must never know. I fear what Denise, in her madness, might do.

"Oh, my God," I murmured, disbelief coursing through me.

I turned the page and it was blank. That ominous passage had been the last entry before my father's accident. My heart was still pounding furiously with shock.

A small slip of paper, folded in half, fell from between the pages. I opened it to find a riddle, evidently the one Father had written of.

I read the riddle aloud.

"Between the hours of dark and dawn
When Moonwatch tower glows,
And on the night that shadows fall
From a moon's full halo
Upon the face of the lovely nymph,
Her eyes shall hold the key
And once unlocked you'll find within
The Emperor's treasure be."

This must be a clue to where the pagoda had originally been hidden. And where it was now? My hands were trembling as I folded the paper and returned it to the book.

If he did as he planned, he had taken the pagoda from its case and hidden it somewhere in the tower, but he had died before he could return to claim it. I knew exactly where it would be found.

I could no longer deny my father was a thief. It hurt to know what kind of man he had really been. But this man, the one who had written in the journal, was not the father I knew as a child.

I had to find out what had happened the night he came here and hid the pagoda. Had he and Nicholas fought over Lesley? Had my father died that night, perhaps even here at Moonwatch? And now I was more frightened than ever, for I knew whatever had happened that night, the man I had married was more deeply involved than I had ever dreamed.

Chapter XX

I hardly slept that night. Images of Nicholas and Lesley together swirled about inside my head. Whenever I closed my eyes I could see them laughing, mocking me. They had managed to dupe both my father and me. I could not let them get away with it and yet . . . I could not seem to completely banish Nicholas from my heart.

I threw back the covers and walked to the windows. The full moon's halo bathed the crashing waves and the beach below with a shimmering silver glow.

A full moon! Suddenly it dawned on me. According to the riddle there had to be a full moon to find the pagoda's hiding place. I had been so preoccupied with Nicholas that I completely dismissed the search for the treasure.

I threw a robe about my shoulders and started to the door, then I stopped. Perhaps I should not go searching, not yet. I needed time to think, to plan exactly what I would do if I did find the pagoda. I wanted to have it in my hand when I confronted Nicholas and Lesley—confronted them all! Then I would leave this wretched, cold house. And if I had not been able to prove my father innocent, at least I could return the treasure to the Haynes and put an end to it all.

Tomorrow, with the distraction of the funeral, I could pack my clothes and make arrangements for a coach. I wanted to be ready when the time was right. I could only pray that the clear weather pattern would hold, at least until tomorrow night.

I did not know how I was to avoid Nicholas until then, but I knew I must, for he was often able to read my thoughts, had been long before I knew him as I did now.

I paced the floor, concentrating on each detail of what I wanted to accomplish. Finally I heard the mantel clock chime four. I felt exhausted, but finally I knew exactly how I would carry out my plans.

I got into bed and was asleep within minutes. When Nicholas came in sometime near daybreak I pretended to be sleeping too soundly to hear him as he whispered my name softly.

But then, even knowing what I did about him, I still felt that familiar stirring within me at his touch. I wanted to turn and lie in his arms. I had to force myself to be still for I knew I could not contend with the touch of his hands or his searching lips.

He murmured softly under his breath some whispered endearment before he turned over and slept. After I heard his steady breathing, I quickly slipped from bed and reached underneath for the journal. I tiptoed to the dressing room and filled a small traveling bag with a few necessities. I would send for the rest once I was safely away from here.

I cracked the door and looked back toward the bed. Nicholas was still sleeping quietly. Hastily I carried the bag to the door and slipped out into the hallway. There was no one about although I could hear the clinking of dishes down in the dining room.

I placed the bag in my old room knowing it was unlikely anyone would be in there.

Later I would tell Amy to retrieve the bag and place it downstairs out of sight, somewhere near the entryway. It was a fortunate coincidence that the girl had come to me and expressed such willingness to help.

I thought of Tad and felt the guilt rush through me. He needed me, of that I was certain, but I had no rights where he was concerned, none at all.

I walked softly back into the bedroom I shared with Nicholas. I wanted to be dressed and away before he woke. If he asked later, I would simply say I had not wished to disturb him. With luck I would be able to successfully avoid him until after the funeral later in the day.

That last long look at Nicholas almost proved to be my destruction. He looked so peaceful, so vulnerable in sleep that I began to doubt he could have done anything wrong. Against my will I found myself wanting to reach out and touch him, trace the outline of his chin and his lips with my fingers. I had to force myself to turn away, berating myself for my weakness where this man was concerned. I had been a fool, but I would be one no longer!

I dressed in a black bombazine gown with large puffed sleeves and a row of pleats about the bottom of the full skirt. I had worn it before in honor of my father and now it was Millie, poor sweet Millie, whom I would mourn. The dress would probably be hot and uncomfortable in the oddly warm November weather, but it could not be helped.

It was still too early to visit Tad and I didn't want to wake him. My stomach was churning uneasily and I knew I could not eat a morsel of breakfast, but after missing dinner last night I felt I should make an appearance for the family.

Unbidden, the remembrance of last night came flooding into my mind, causing a sharp ache in my chest.

"Oh, Nicholas," I whispered. "Why couldn't you only have loved me as I love you?"

I could not look at him again, lest I give in to the longing within me that made me want to throw myself on the bed, waken him, and demand an explanation. For a moment, I was filled with optimism and hope. Perhaps he *could* explain, perhaps Father had lied.

"No," I said, backing away from the bed and the man who tempted me. He would only lie even if I did confront him. "No," I repeated. "I have to go!"

I ran quickly down the hall, pausing at the top of the stairs to catch my breath. I looked toward the corridor leading to the lighthouse. Soon I would go there and find the pagoda, but as for now I must do everything according to the plan I'd already made. I didn't want anything to keep me from leaving, and when I did, the pagoda would once again be in the case downstairs.

When I walked into the dining room I was sure no one could see by my expression that anything was wrong. Frances, evidently was still with Tad. So there was only Lesley and Eric.

I felt a momentary tug of regret about Frances. My sister, my own flesh and blood. I could still hardly believe it. I had always wanted a sister. Frances and I were so different—and yet, I remembered the first night here, when I'd glimpsed the red underskirts and felt surprise at my swift feeling of comradeship.

Now I would be forced to leave Frances and Tad, never be able to know her as I wanted to. Would my father's shame haunt me the rest of my life?

Lesley watched me as I seated myself slowly and tried to smile graciously. I wanted no quarrel with her this morning. Eric glanced up at me, his eyes warm and friendly as he drank from his coffee cup.

"Well," Lesley said. "'Tis so kind of you to grace us with your presence this morning. We missed you and Nicholas at dinner last night. Were you ill?"

I smiled faintly. I would offer no explanation to this woman.

"Hardly," I said.

I could not miss the venom in her eyes. How very much she had changed from that first meeting in her elegant office when she said she wanted to help me. Of course that had been a lie, for I knew now she had probably hated me from the beginning, knowing I'd been chosen as Nicholas's bride. I had to admit the woman was an accomplished actress.

Suddenly something clicked in my mind. Of course, could that be the reason for her lapses into another accent, for her flair for the dramatics, and her knack for making one believe everything she said?

"Well?" she demanded. "Are you not going to speak to us this morning? Too good for us, eh?" By her expression I could see she had not meant this time to drop her cultured tones.

I stared at her, clearly surprised by her lack of composure. It was not like her to let anyone see past her carefully applied veneer.

"Lesley," I sighed. "I'm sure a woman with your intelligence and abilities must have more interesting things with which to occupy herself. So, why not do so? In the meantime, allow my husband and I to attend to our interests on our own."

Her eyes opened wide and her face flushed with fury. She rose jerkily and threw her napkin onto the table. "You shall regret your impudence, Victoria. I am not a servant in this household to be addressed by you in such a manner!" Her eyes were cold and threatening, never leaving my face until she turned and marched away from the table.

Eric sat watching the whole scene, his mouth quirked in an odd smile. "Why is it you two seem suddenly to grate on each other's nerves?" he asked.

My look toward him was cool and I did not attempt to answer him for I thought he knew very well why. I made a pretense at eating.

"Victoria," he said with an exasperated sigh. "Don't shut me out. I'm not the enemy here."

His words made me feel slightly ashamed of my behavior. But I had had simply enough of the place and everyone in it. "I know," I whispered, finding it difficult to meet his eyes. "It's just . . ."

"What? You can tell me."

"Everything!" I said. "This house, the accidents, and now Millie's death. I'm sure you've heard all about my father and how he is regarded in this household."

"The accusation, you mean, that he took the pagoda?"

"Yes," I answered, toying with one of the silver forks. "But if it's the last thing I do, I shall see it returned to the Hayne family before—" I stopped, looking up into his inquisitive eyes. I had already said too much.

"Before what?"

"Nothing, never mind. I have to go."

But Eric was persistent. He rose quickly from the table and walked around, blocking my way. He stood close to me, his hand only lightly touching my arm.

"Victoria, let me help you. I'm not blind you know." Fleetingly my eyes looked into his dark gaze and for a moment I was tempted to let him hold me, to pour out all the anger and pain to someone who might care. I had thought with Nicholas that my days of being alone were over. Only for an instant did I sway toward Eric, but it was long enough for him to see my weakness and to know that he had been right in his assessment of my mood.

"I can't," I whispered. "Please, let me go."

After the slightest hesitation he moved aside allowing me to pass. "If . . . *when* you need me, Victoria, you've only to come to me. I hope you know that."

I paused, but did not turn to look at his face for I was afraid of what I might see there. "Yes," I answered. "I do." Then I fled from the room and his too intimate looks.

I went directly to the servants' quarters and asked for Amy. When she came to me, the look of surprise turned quickly into a warm smile. "Mrs. Hayne," she exclaimed. "Is anything wrong? Something I can do for you, ma'am?" she asked.

"As a matter of fact, Amy, there is," I whispered, pulling her out into the hallway behind the laundry room where no one could hear.

I told her about the traveling bag and where I wanted her to take it. "Be sure no one sees you, Amy," I said.

"But, ma'am," she said, her plump face looking worried. "You're not thinking of leaving without telling anyone, even Captain Hayne? He seems ever so wonderful!" At my look she timidly placed her hand over her lips as if she had spoken out of turn. "But, of course, 'tis not for me to say, if it be what you want, ma'am."

"It is, Amy. I have no choice."

She still looked doubtful, but agreed to help me. She also promised to mention it to no one, not even any of the other servants.

I wanted to go upstairs and see Tad before the depressing service in the parlor got underway. It might be the last chance I'd have to see him.

As I approached Tad's room I could hear his laughter. How good it was to hear that musical sound in this house. If there had been more of it perhaps it would not always seem so depressing.

I was smiling as I opened the door, but the smile faded when I saw the person who'd been so successfully entertaining Tad.

"Nicholas," I said. "I . . . I thought you would still be sleeping."

He looked at me strangely, reminding me I was not very good at hiding my feelings from him.

"I don't require much sleep," he said. He rose and came to take my hands in his, pulling me to a chair beside him.

"Darling, is anything wrong? Your hands are freezing. You're not sick, are you?" When he looked at me that way, with such tenderness in his eyes and his brow wrinkled with concern, I could hardly remain cool. Whatever was wrong with me? I was having a very difficult time remaining undetached when I should feel only anger toward him, even hatred.

"No," I said, forcing a smile. "I'm fine, Nicholas. Really." I pulled my hand from his and turned to Tad who lay patiently watching us.

"Tad," I said. "You look so well I think you'll soon be up to your old tricks again."

He smiled at me. "And school," he reminded me.

"Yes . . . and school." My voice grew weak and I could not meet his eyes. It was even harder lying to him than to Nicholas, for he was a complete innocent in all of this. Children always seemed to have a way of getting straight to the heart of a matter.

"Maybe tomorrow! Mother says it will be fine with her if it is with you." His face was full of eagerness as he waited for my answer.

"Well, let's . . . let's just wait and see how you're feeling tomorrow." I hated this, hated deceiving this boy who had been so starved for affection. I had encouraged him, convinced him he could trust in me, and now I too would desert him. I was afraid this would devastate the boy, but there was nothing else I could do and it broke my heart.

I could feel Nicholas's steady gaze upon me as I talked with Tad. He could see my hesitation, my nervousness. He knew something was wrong, for he, more than anyone I'd ever met, was a man of instinct. He seemed to know my every emotion just by looking into my eyes. I felt my face grow warm with the memory of what his looks could do to me. And how well he knew it. I looked quickly over at him as he sat watching me and it proved to be an almost fatal mistake.

His eyes caught mine and there was a surge of feeling between us such that I felt my breath leave my lungs. I could see everything there in those fiery blue depths—sadness, regret . . . and love, most of all I hoped that I saw love. It stunned me for a moment, for I knew it could not be true, not after all that I'd discovered about him. But then he, it seemed, as well as Lesley, was a convincing actor.

"I suppose we should go downstairs for the service," I said.

He seemed to shake himself back to reality, then he nodded and rose to take my hand, pulling me from the chair, very close to him. I felt strongly then that he did not want me out of his sight.

"I'll send Ona to stay with you, son, until after the funeral."

"But can't I go to the funeral? I'm well enough, really I am," he said. "Millie was my friend too."

"I know she was, Tad, but I don't think it would be a very good idea." Nicholas's words were gently spoken, and filled with compassion as he touched the boy's dark hair.

Tad made no more protest. As we both kissed him good-bye I tried not to let myself think it would be the last time.

Walking down the hall, Nicholas put his hand possessively to my waist and pulled me close. Without thinking, I drew away from him causing him to look at me oddly.

"Victoria, what is it?" he asked. "You're as jumpy as a cat. And don't bother lying to me, I know something's troubling you."

"It—it's nothing. Just the funeral . . ." I kept my eyes upon the front of his shirt.

"Look at me," he demanded. "Why can't you even look at me?"

He pulled me up to face him and I was surprised at the pain I saw in his eyes. How did he do it? I wondered. How did he manage to look so serious and so loving?

"Is it me? Have I done something to hurt you?"

"No, of course not. Why would you ask such a thing?" I said, my voice sounding like someone else.

"Angel, I can see it in your eyes—they never hide anything! I had hoped for awhile that I had banished that look from you forever, but now it's back and I'd like to know why."

He was not going to let me get away with the lie. Why couldn't he just leave me alone. The longer I was with him the more I longed to ask him the one question I was burning to know. And so in that volatile moment as he held me and demanded an explanation, I blurted it out. "Did you love me, Nicholas, when you first asked me to marry you? Or was it because your mother wanted it? Tell the truth—love has never really entered into this union as far as you're concerned!" My voice sounded hard, but I didn't care. It was the only way I could keep from crying.

He looked stunned. "You asked me that once

before," he said quietly, "but evidently you still do not believe me." Now there was a glint of resentment in his eyes.

"Not if you loved me . . . I never asked if you loved me," I insisted.

"What is this all about?" he asked, refusing to let go of my arm.

"I think you know," I replied. I was finding it more and more difficult to still the trembling of my lips and to keep the tears from falling from my eyes.

"No, dammit, I don't know! And I don't have the time or patience for games. So why don't you tell me, Victoria, what it is that has you so upset. Can't you at least give me the chance to explain whatever it is you think I've done?"

"Excuse me, sir." It was Vickers who walked up behind us.

Nicholas turned to him impatiently. "Yes, what is it, Vickers?" he said curtly.

"Mrs. Hayne sent me to find you, sir. 'Tis almost time for the service to begin.

I turned as if to follow Vickers, taking the opportunity to get away from Nicholas while I could. I had already said too much. But as Vickers walked on, Nicholas caught me from behind and whirled me about to face him. His hands on my shoulders dug into my flesh as he pulled me to him.

"The service be damned!" His voice was harsh and demanding. "You're not going until you tell me what's wrong!"

Suddenly the tears I'd been holding back could no longer be contained as they filled my eyes and spilled down my cheeks. I hated myself because I could not accuse him of all the things Father had written.

"I . . . I can't now, Nicholas. I can't talk right now."

Just as suddenly as it had come, the anger in his eyes

was gone. He sighed heavily and placed his hand behind my neck, pulling me to him until my cheek rested against his chest. I could feel his chin moving against my hair as he spoke. "All right, angel. Don't cry. I can't stand to see you cry."

"We . . . should go," I said, pulling away from him.

His look was frustrated as he tilted my face upward. He took a handkerchief from his pocket and wiped my tears away. His eyes searched mine as if he could find the answer on his own. I pulled away from him then and it was the hardest thing I'd ever had to do in my life.

Chapter XXI

The servants had already gathered in the parlor. Mrs. Hayne was sitting quietly with her hands folded demurely in her lap. There was relief in her look as she smiled and motioned for us to sit beside her. I had not noticed Frances until we were seated and she stepped from behind a large flower arrangement to sit next to me. I smiled at her, searching her face from the corner of my eyes. She did not look like Father . . . much more than I did.

As I glanced about the room I saw an elderly couple, both of them dressed in black and wearing mourning bands on their arms. It was obvious by their grief-stricken faces that they were Millie's parents. They clung together, gazing toward the closed wooden coffin at the front of the room as the pastor began the solemn ceremony. I could not tear my eyes away from them, so poignant was their mutual grief.

Suddenly I could not help myself. The tears I'd shed for Nicholas now returned with a force that jarred me. All the pain, all the horror of Millie's death became real to me. And so was the fact that I was losing the only man I thought I would ever love. I had once pictured us as the couple before me—growing old together, sharing the joys of life as well as the sorrow, but always together. The thought of never having Nicholas's beautiful children tore painfully at my heart and I had to clamp my teeth tightly together to keep from crying out. I should have hated him. Why couldn't I, instead of feeling this sadness, this great well of sadness?

Nicholas bent his dark head toward me to look down into my face. He said nothing, but reached to take my hand, gripping it tightly. I clung to him. For this one brief moment of sorrow, I told myself, I could surely be allowed the luxury of doing that. Perhaps the years ahead would bring forgetfulness and ease the ache, but for now I felt as if I were dying. I only wanted to be close to him this one last time.

Thankfully the ceremony was brief. We expressed our sympathies to Millie's parents before Mrs. Hayne drew them aside. She looked intently into their faces as she spoke, and I suppose she too was expressing her sympathy. Perhaps there was also a bit of guilt on her part since Millie was in her employ and her care when she died.

"Victoria, will you be all right while I'm gone?" Nicholas spoke close beside me.

"Gone?" I said blankly.

"I'm going back across the ferry with Millie's mother and father. It might be late when I return. I thought you knew that."

"Oh, yes . . . yes, I suppose I did."

"I want to talk to you when I get back," he said, looking at me pointedly.

"Yes," I murmured, afraid to meet his eyes.

"Would you be happier if we moved to Wilmington, to Ashford Place perhaps? Away from the isolation of Moonwatch, and the distractions of others?"

I looked up at him in surprise. His eyes looked almost black in the dimly lit parlor.

"You mean you would leave here? Leave your home and the shipping company?"

He pulled me not too gently over to the side of the room, away from the others. Almost angrily he forced me to look at him. "Don't you know yet that I would do anything for you? Do you think I want to see you worried and afraid every day, or harassed by anyone in this house? What must I do, Victoria, to prove to you how very much I love you? *You* are my life, not Moonwatch, not the ships!" He turned from me then, his hands on narrow hips as he took a deep breath, trying to quell his impatience with me.

"Not even the sea?" I whispered, knowing I was pursuing an impossible course. Whatever he said could make no difference to me, but I wanted so much to hear it, even if it were a lie.

"No, dammit! Not even the sea!" He turned back to me and his face was angry and full of frustration. I could feel the glances of others in the room as he raised his voice. "If we were not in this room with all these people . . . What's happened, Victoria, since that night on the *Galatea*? What's happened to change you so?"

I did not know what to say. I found myself wanting to believe him, wishing against hope that what he said was true, but I knew I could not.

As Millie's coffin was being carried out, Nicholas kissed me swiftly and hard upon the lips, whispering fiercely, "Wait up for me, we'll talk about this tonight."

I watched his tall form as he moved gracefully from the parlor. His shoulders moved easily beneath the smooth fit of his dark jacket, only hinting at the powerful ripple of muscles.

I felt a deep ache of loss within my chest, realizing this was the last time I would ever see him. But it did not matter. For after I found the pagoda and gave it to Mrs. Hayne I had no other choice except to leave here.

For a fraction of a second I hesitated. My heart told me to wait, to at least tell him what I knew and to see his eyes when I told him about the journal and Lesley. I knew even as I hesitated, though, that that was not the real reason I wanted to stay. I wanted to stay because I loved him and at that moment I hated myself for it. Hated myself for being so weak that I found it difficult to turn my back on the man who had betrayed my father, and who, God help me, might even have been responsible for his death.

I whirled about, quickly leaving the room as I wiped the tears from my cheeks.

"Victoria, wait!" It was Denise who called to me from inside the parlor where she sat. Reluctantly I turned back, hoping my tremulous smile did not betray me.

One of the servants pushed her toward me. "Dear, we're having tea in the dining room. Please join us. I've seen so little of you lately."

I did not want tea, did not wish to be in the same room with these people. Did they all know about Lesley's affair with Nicholas, know all along what a fool I'd made of myself? The strange events of my life here at Moonwatch seemed to be accumulating, one upon the other, until my nerves were frayed. I took a deep breath and smiled at her, determining that I could hold on for a few hours more. Only a few hours and I would be away from here forever. I would need to play my role for just a bit longer.

"Of course," I murmured. "I would like that very much."

I followed the girl as she pushed Mrs. Hayne's chair across the hallway and into the dining room.

Frances was already there, briskly showing the servants where to place the food and china service.

I watched her more carefully now, aware of the

similarities between us. My half sister. I knew now why her face had seemed so hauntingly familiar to me. Her dark eyes were so much like Father's that I was surprised I had not recognized it before.

"Frances," her mother said tersely. "Come sit down. Let the girls do their job. I'm sure they know more about it than you."

I never had seen her behave in such a manner with Nicholas. Of course I knew now why she resented Frances, crazy though it was. The daughter of Anthony Ancona had not given Mrs. Hayne the leverage she counted upon. And he became only the man who used her, then tossed her aside. I'm sure she resented me in much the same way. But Frances was her own daughter. Had her bitterness blinded her to that over the years? What a sad, pathetic way to end one's days.

Frances did as her mother asked, but there was a spark of defiance in her brown eyes which I had not noticed before. I knew well from my own experience that that did not lessen the pain any. But anger and defiance made good substitutes, I knew that well.

I saw Frances differently that afternoon, with more empathy than before and even with a touch of affection. Both of us had suffered because of two people . . . her blatantly partial mother and our cold, indifferent father. How ironic. By all standards we should have been friends; perhaps still could have been if circumstances were different. I only regretted that I had not known about Frances when I came. It might have made no difference to her or her feelings toward me, but it certainly would have made a difference in mine.

I moved over on the sofa to make room for Frances. "Sit here," I said.

Perhaps my feelings were expressed on my face, for when she sat beside me and looked into my eyes I knew she felt it too. That bond that should have been between us all along.

She smiled and impulsively I reached forward and covered her hand with mine. If only we could have come to this sooner! How good it would have been having someone to talk with, to share with.

I took the cup of tea that one of the maids handed me. Just then Lesley and Eric came into the room and Eric's eyes immediately sought mine. I looked away from his direct gaze, but not before the woman beside him caught that silent exchange. Her dark eyes flew to Eric's face and I saw anger in her quick glance.

"Tad is so looking forward to continuing his lessons, Victoria." Frances voice was low, meant only for me.

"Tad is a delight to teach. He is a very intelligent little boy," I said, noticing the new, softer look on France's face.

"Yes, he is," she agreed. There was a slight, but wistful smile about her lips. "Like his father."

"And a blessing that is," Mrs. Hayne interrupted rudely. "I'm afraid the boy would never survive if he were like his mother."

Her blunt sarcastic remark angered me when I saw the look of pain that crossed Frances's face. Did Frances know, I wondered, why her mother treated her this way? No, I was sure she did not.

"I never knew Tad's father, but the boy could hardly do better than to take after his mother," I said, looking straight into Mrs. Hayne's pale blue eyes. "Perhaps you underestimate your daughter, Mrs. Hayne. She is a strong person in her own, very special way." I knew my words sounded impertinent, but I was far from caring now what I said. "After all," I continued, disregarding her blazing eyes, "look at her strong mother . . . and father." I took pleasure in her flashing eyes . . . in her knowing that I had discovered her secret. It struck me then that Mrs. Hayne could have been the one to search my room for the journal, knowing I would learn this very thing. But if I believed that could I also believe that she had deliberately trapped her own grandson in the Whale Cave? As I met her steely gaze I felt a shiver crawl across my flesh.

"I think it is hardly your place to tell me about my own daughter, Victoria," she replied. She was obviously angry, causing the others in the room to watch her with curiosity. "I'm sure I know her good qualities as well as anyone!"

"Oh, I hope you do, Mrs. Hayne," I answered, taking a sip of tea to hide the smile that came unbidden to my lips. As I looked across the table I once again caught Eric's gaze upon me and he was smiling as well. Did he understand what our sparring was about?

"And you, Victoria," Lesley said rather loudly, "are you a strong person as well; one who fights for what she wants—a survivor?"

I looked at her then, this woman whom I'd first hoped to befriend. She had so easily fooled me, but she could no longer hide her animosity. As I met her look I felt her rancor like a lash across my face. She hated me; I could feel it. I did not look away from her though. It was almost like looking at a deadly snake . . . being frightened and yet fascinated at the same time. I wasn't afraid of her for I knew I'd soon be free of this place and the undercurrent of seething emotions, as deadly as the riptide around Cape Fear.

Seconds passed as we watched each other. Lesley's question hung in the air as everyone seemed to wait breathlessly for my reply.

I became bold, hungry for a confrontation with this woman I had grown to despise.

"Why do you ask, Lesley?" I said slowly. "Do you have reason to hope I am not?"

Frances gasped beside me. "Victoria!" she warned quietly.

"No, Franny," Mrs. Hayne said. "Leave her alone." Her eyes were glowing now as she watched us, hoping all along, perhaps, for such a confrontation.

"Oh, I'm not so foolish as to underestimate someone like you." Her soft words were deceptive, I knew. "And I must admit, you're much stronger than I expected."

"Unlike my father, you mean?" I taunted.

Lesley laughed. "Yes, that's exactly what I mean. I had thought you would be more . . . indecisive, more easily frightened, perhaps." Her brown eyes mocked me.

"Oh? And why would you want to frighten me, Lesley?" I asked, not looking away from her gaze.

This time it was she who flushed beneath my angry, accusing look. She recovered quickly, covering her nervousness with another trill of laughter.

"Oh, I don't, of course. You're being foolish. I only meant you've experienced a good deal of anxiety since coming to Moonwatch and I must say you handled it extremely well for one so young and . . . inexperienced."

"Youth and inexperience have little bearing on intelligence. I'm sure you'll agree, Lesley. Why, I'm sure when you were young you were every bit as clever as you are now."

Her eyes glittered dangerously and I'm sure her failure to find a quick response piqued her even more.

Mrs. Hayne frowned at me, not at all happy I was sure with how the exchange had gone. But I felt giddy with my victory. I smiled broadly as I rose, scanning briefly their surprised faces. I wanted to remember this moment after I was safely ensconced at Ashford Place. I had no doubt Nicholas would allow me to have my childhood home in exchange for his freedom.

"If you will all excuse me, I think I will go to bed

early. It's been a very tiring day."

When I was away from them I breathed a sigh of relief for now all that awaited me was the discovery of the pagoda, followed by my exit from this dark and unwelcoming place which was as stormy and frightening as the Atlantic on which it sat.

Perhaps I had overrated my brief surge of optimism, for as soon as I entered our bedroom my senses were assailed by memories of Nicholas. The scent of his shaving balm filled the air and a shirt lay across one of the chairs. I was completely unprepared for the sense of melancholy and longing that stabbed through me. I picked up the shirt and held it to me as his fragrance drifted to my nose. For a moment, I was totally engulfed in my forbidden feelings, remembering his voice so deep and warm in the darkness of the night, and the gentle touch of his hands.

I let myself remember then, gave in to it at last and just let myself feel all those moments that had meant so much to me. I still did not understand how I could love him so completely and feel the rightness of it all if he had not been sincere. How could I have been so wrong in my judgment of him?

I cried then . . . bitter, cruel tears that threatened to tear me apart as I sank to the floor. The shirt that I still held in my hands became damp and wrinkled. Yet, still I remembered the intensity of his blue eyes that could somehow look into my heart, his crisp black hair that I loved to touch, and his lips . . . so warm and sweetly persistent. His memory threatened to make me forget any sense of reason.

"No," I said, forcing myself to stop thinking. "It was all a lie. I must come to grips with that, I must."

I rose and folded the shirt back over the chair, then I checked about the room to make sure I had packed everything I would need.

There was nothing to do now except wait until the others had gone to their rooms for the night, then go to the lighthouse and search for the pagoda.

I sat near the window, trying to quell my rising nervousness. I hardly noticed the lovely evening sheen of the water or the seagulls that swooped and soared for each morsel of food before nightfall halted their flight.

I was lost in a world of thoughts and dreams, wishes and regrets, when I noticed with a start that the moon had risen high in the eastern sky. If I had correctly interpreted the riddle, the moon would have to be in a certain position to find the hiding place, so I made leave to go to make certain I did not miss the exact moment.

I turned at the door one last time and glanced at the room where I had come home as the bride of Nicholas Hayne. Quickly I closed it, just as I had to close that chapter of my life and go on somehow to a happier one.

Chapter XXII

I brought a lamp from my room which I lit as soon as I was safely away from the landing. When I reached the bottom of the stairway, I thought I heard a noise farther up in the tower. I stopped, unable to make my legs move. A stab of fear ran through me as I recalled the darkness there. I could almost feel the hands of the person in the cloak who had waited for me and pushed me down those stairs. I shivered, wanting more than anything to turn around and run from this place, from the thing that I must do.

But as I listened, I heard nothing else. Taking a deep breath, I forced myself to go on, proceeding slowly. I could see that Ona had already been there and lit the lamps at each landing. I watched as the heavy curtains at the windows moved eerily in the draft from the stairwell, and I told myself again and again that it was only the wind that moaned around the tall structure.

Finally I reached the top and breathed a sigh of relief as I stepped into the darkened study. Through the windows that encircled the room I could see the bright beams of light that reached out through the darkness from the lighthouse above me.

It would have to be dark within the study if I were to

see the moon's path clearly. Quickly I placed my lamp on a table and blew out its wavering flame. It took only a few seconds for my eyes to become adjusted to the night.

Soon I was able to see the flow of light through the windows as the moonlight cascaded into the room. To my disappointment, the stream of light fell far short of the sea nymph. I had no choice but to sit and wait . . . watching the moonlight as it inched across the floor toward the corner where the figurehead now stood in total darkness. If the riddle were correct, the figurehead of the "lovely nymph" was the key to finding the pagoda.

It seemed hours rather than minutes that I sat quietly in that darkened room. The hushed roar of the sea far below could be heard where I sat, and the odd creaks and groans of the old house sounded all around me. Sometimes it was almost like the sound of people talking, whispering. A quiver of anxiety ran up my spine, making the hair at the base of my neck tingle. I tried in vain to banish all thoughts of the Captain's ghost from my mind. After all, I was in his sanctuary and I certainly did not want to conjure up his image.

When I looked again, the moon splashed across the beautiful rich wood at the bottom of the figurehead, rising higher and higher. In only a few minutes it would reach the face, turning the eyes into some kind of signal which I hoped I would be able to interpret.

Quietly I repeated the words of the riddle as I watched the moon's beam inching upward.

"Between the hours of dark and dawn
When Moonwatch Tower glows,
And on the night that shadows fall
From a moon's full halo
Upon the face of the lovely nymph,

Her eyes shall hold the key. . . ."

That part seemed the easiest to understand. Somehow the light upon the eyes of the figurehead would tell me something.

"And once unlocked you'll find within
The Emperor's treasure be."

Within what? Within the nymph? As I watched, the moonlight was now upon the face of the figurehead. I held my breath as it crept slowly upward, eerily illuminating the face of the water spirit. Long shadows fell on the wall behind the nymph as if outlining a real person there. When the light reached her eyes I pressed my fingers upon them, hoping some secret door would snap open. Nothing happened; the nymph only stood watching blankly as I moved my hands across her face, pressing each eye, testing each part for movement.

"Nothing!" I whispered angrily. "Her eyes shall hold the key. . . . Her eyes . . ."

I stepped back and suddenly the moonlight reflected upon the eyes once again. The light was blinding as it hit upon my face. I moved aside, out of the stream of light and gave a small murmur of delight as I saw the eyes more clearly. I had assumed the eyes to be painted, but I quickly realized they were clear and only dotted with green paint to give the reality of an eye. They were actually large oval diamonds which glittered now in the moonlight like crystal prisms!

There in the darkened room, the moonlight transformed the nymph, giving her life as the eyes sparkled and glittered, ever changing as the light shifted and moved. But the moon had almost reached its zenith, and I knew in a few more seconds its light would be gone, passing away from the room to illuminate the rooftops of Moonwatch.

Turning to the opposite wall, I saw the rainbow colors where the diamond eyes reflected brightly. I walked to the spot and tapped on the paneling. It echoed hollowly in the room and I could not resist my laugh of jubilation. I knew the pagoda was there within. I could sense it.

I ran my hand across the small square of paneling. There was a minute crack all the way around it. Quickly I relit the lamp and placed it near the wall. Taking a letter opener from the desk I gently pried into the crevice, slowly inching the piece away from the wall.

Inside the opening was a small wooden box which I removed with trembling hands. Carefully I opened the box and took out a heavy object wrapped in silk.

As I spread the silken cloth on the table I could only stare soundlessly at the treasure before me. At last! The Ching tê chên pagoda!

"It's the most beautiful thing I've ever seen," I whispered, awed with its loveliness and unable to take my eyes from its glittering perfection. An Emperor's treasure, indeed!

It was nearly ten inches tall, the exquisite creamy porcelain glistening in the light of the lamp. There were various paintings on the walls of the pagoda—tiny, intricate pictures of dragons and birds in delicate hues—turquoise and coral, gold and fern green. Carefully I sat the pagoda upright and I could see that each level of the upward curving rooftops was green, covered with rows of small square emeralds. At the corners of the roofs hung tiny gold bells that jingled daintily with each movement. I held my breath as I reached out to touch the top of the pagoda where the roof swept upward to a delicate point. There atop the pagoda was a large, pear-shaped jewel. A rare, perfectly shaped blue diamond.

Lightly I touched the bells, enjoying their tiny pleasant sound in the stillness of the room, but as the golden bells swayed and then were still I realized with a start that I still heard the tinkle of bells in the tower! And they were right outside the study door!

"Ona!" I knew it had to be him with his armbands of jingling brass bells.

I took the pagoda and wrapped it back in its silk cloth and placed it inside one of the desk drawers, then quickly I blew out the lamp. I almost panicked as I realized he was coming into the room, for I had no place to hide.

I saw a door which I thought was a storage closet. Once inside, however, I saw it was the stairway up to the light room . . . probably where Ona was going. The stairs continued past the light room. I followed them upward, hoping to hide out of sight until he was gone.

There was a heavy metal door at the top of the stairs. I pushed against it and found myself on the roof of the tower. The bright moonlight spread across the roof illuminating the stone parapet around the edge of the building. The fierce wind blew against the door making it difficult to open. It whipped my hair wildly about my face and set my skirt flapping against my legs. The air was heavy with the smell of the sea that shimmered beyond the house. It was hard to distinguish the water from the white beach and sand dunes that surrounded the house.

As I stood against the door, my eyes came back to the rooftop again. My heart began to pound and my knees trembled uncontrollably. My palms grew moist with fear.

This was the place in my dream, the dream I'd had my first night here when I'd seen Nicholas beckoning to me. Ona was coming up the stairs but I was powerless to move. I could hear him there just beyond the door. I stepped away, watching the door and not knowing what to do or where I could go.

Without thinking I ran to the edge of the roof and

looked down. I closed my eyes as I felt my head spin dizzily from the height. There was nowhere to hide.

It was too late. Suddenly the door burst open and Ona stepped onto the roof. He was only a shadow standing ominously there in the darkness. I could feel his eyes upon me.

"You must come inside, Missy," his voice rumbled, carried to me by the wind.

"How did you know I was here?" I asked. My voice trembled as I spoke and I knew he was aware of my fear.

"I watched you. Mr. Nicholas told me to watch you."

"Nicholas? But why?" A sickening feeling invaded my whole being, a feeling of doom that set my limbs to shaking. Just as I suspected—Ona had been watching me all along but I had not dreamed it was on Nicholas's orders. A sense of danger and the reality of impending death surrounded me. That sense threatened to suffocate me just as it had in my dreams. The nightmare was coming true, except it was Ona who was here.

Suddenly there was someone else behind the big black man. He moved catlike in the darkness and I saw his arm raise, then crash down on Ona, who slumped with a moan onto the rooftop.

When the man stepped forward, I could see his face clearly in the moonlight.

"Eric!"

"It's all right now, Victoria. I'm going to take you away from here. Don't be afraid," his voice whispered gently to me as he stepped slowly toward me.

"Don't! Don't come any closer, Eric," I said. I was confused, trying to reason that if Nicholas had sent Ona, then who else could I trust but Eric?

He stopped. "All right. I don't want to frighten you. I only want to help you. You see, I know everything . . . about your father and Lesley. I know how hurt you are and I only want to take care of you . . . protect you."

"No," I said, taking another step backward. "I can't."

"Why not? You were planning to leave anyway. Let me go with you."

"How did you know that?" I asked.

"After what you said this morning, I began to check around. . . ."

"Amy!" I said beneath my breath.

He reached out to me, his eyes compelling and demanding. "Take my hand, darling. Trust me."

But I could not. Something kept me from going to him. I was more confused now than ever and wanted only to be away from here and the people who were trying to manipulate me—all of them! I could trust no one except myself.

"Victoria!" The deep voice that called to me from the doorway was unmistakable.

"Nicholas?" I felt a deep stab of pain as I saw the figure that moved beside him. He was with Lesley. He had returned to Moonwatch and gone straight to her arms.

He moved toward me, he on my left and Eric on my right.

It was just like the dream, with Nicholas beckoning to me, but in the dream I had reached out to him while he laughed and stepped aside, letting me fall crashing to the sea below. I could feel it now . . . the fear and a great crushing sense that this was the end.

"No, Nicholas. Don't come any closer," I warned.

I stepped backward. Without warning the corner of the roof crumbled beneath my feet and there was nothing except the deep empty space of the night below me!

Instinctively my arms flew outward as I grasped frantically for anything in my path. Suddenly I felt the rough stone wall of the parapet in my hands and I clung to it with every ounce of strength I had left.

I could see the moonlight shimmering on my hands and upon the rooftop where moments ago I had stood. The wind whistled keenly in my ears, blowing my hair into my face so that I could hardly see.

No one moved. All eyes were upon me and the night was silent except for the crash of the sea below, and the wind. I could see the horror on their faces, Eric and Nicholas as they both stood on the opposite side of the gaping hole.

I hung on desperately, my feet dangling in space and my heart pounding wildly with fear. I had grabbed onto one of the large granite gargoyles just below the edge of the roof. Its grotesque face, half man and half beast, grinned at me there in the moonlight. I closed my eyes and began to cry helplessly for I knew I had not the strength to hold on much longer.

"Victoria, angel. Hang on, please . . . don't let go!" Nicholas could not reach me across the hole in the roof, but he began to edge his way around to me.

"No!" I screamed. "Don't!"

He stopped, stunned by my words. "Trust me, darling," he pleaded. "You have to trust me." His voice was low and pleading, coaxing me like a child to believe him.

"Don't listen to him, Victoria. Can you really trust someone like Nicholas Hayne, the man who ruined your father? Take my hand, darling, and I'll take you away from here."

"I . . . I don't know . . ." I sobbed. My arms were trembling and I could feel my grip weakening with each second that passed.

"Shut up, Roberts!" Nicholas growled. "Or I'll kill you right where you stand!" He turned to me again.

"Please, darling. Give me your hand. Reach out as far as you can," Nicholas ordered.

"Think, Victoria," Eric said. "What do you really know about this man?"

Lesley's laughter rang through the night air, an almost hysterical sound. "Yes, choose, Victoria! And may God help you!" I knew then she wanted me to die . . . would enjoy watching me fall to the sand below. Eric's words ran through my mind. What *did* I know about Nicholas?

Instantly it all flashed before me. I knew he was a strong, powerful man, yet he had treated me as gently as a kitten. I knew eyes that could be hard and demanding, yet filled with warmth and love when he looked at me, lips that were insistent, yet tender. And I knew the time had come for me to finally trust my heart. Without another thought, I reached to my left . . . toward Nicholas.

I saw the light that leapt into his eyes and the small frown of worry upon his brow. As his strong hand took mine and pulled me up into his arms I knew I'd made the right choice. Perhaps I'd known it all along and that was why I agonized so over leaving him.

"Eric, you fool!" Lesley screamed.

"Shut up, Lesley," he growled between clenched teeth. "Just get the pagoda and let's go."

"You wanted her, damn you. I could see it in your eyes, you bastard! And after all I've done for you!"

Nicholas held me away from him and took a step toward the couple. "And exactly what have you done, Lesley?" His voice was a rumbling threat.

Suddenly as Eric's hand moved to his jacket I saw the dull gleam of a gun barrel. "Let's go, Lesley," he urged. "Get the damned pagoda and let's go. Don't make a mistake now!"

"It was you!" I said. "You were the one my father found with Lesley . . . the one who threatened to kill him!"

"That's right," he said, his smile a sickening grimace. How could I ever have thought I could trust him?

"But you're smarter than your old man. I thought I

might convince you to come away with me, but then again I think I knew all along how you felt about old Nicky there."

"Shoot them both, Eric!" Lesley demanded. "Now! Do it now!" Her voice had risen into a shriek completely devoid of any hint of refinement.

"Now, Lesley sweet," he said. "I think I'll just take her along. You won't mind, love. It's only temporary, you understand. I'd hate for a beauty like her to die without knowing what a *real* man is like." He laughed then, throwing his head back and enjoying his crudeness.

It was just long enough for Nicholas to spring at him. With a growl that emitted from deep within him, he knocked the gun from Eric's hand. Eric swung wildly at Nicholas, but was not as quick or agile. As he turned about grotesquely, he seemed to hang suspended in the air for a second. There was a look of utter surprise and horror upon his face. Then he was gone, over the gaping hole in the parapet, falling silently to the ground far below us.

"Eric!" Lesley screamed, running to the edge of the roof. "Eric, my love."

She turned from the rooftop and ran toward Nicholas. Her hair had come unpinned and her eyes were wild, crazed as she came at him, fists raised in the air.

"You've killed him!" she screamed.

Behind us, Ona had gotten to his feet and with a roar he went toward her. He lifted her easily in his hands, thrusting her high above his head. The sound emitting from his throat was frightening, a kind of primeval call to battle.

I knew then he intended to throw her from the roof. Unable to utter a word, I grabbed Nicholas's arm.

"Ona, no!" Nicholas cried.

Lesley, still suspended in the air, had begun to

scream and cry in terror. For a moment, Ona stood there at the edge of the roof, then slowly he lowered her to her feet.

He did not release her arm, unwilling to let her escape. He must have heard enough of Eric's words to realize what was happening.

"Are you all right?" Nicholas asked me.

I nodded, for I still could not find my voice. My throat felt dry and I was suddenly so exhausted I could barely stand.

Without a word he picked me up into his arms and carried me as easily as if I were a child. My long arms and legs which I had always felt to be awkward and ungainly did not seem to bother him at all.

He spoke quietly to Ona, telling him to take Lesley downstairs. Then he carried me down past the light room and into the study.

"Wait," I said as we reached the desk where I'd hidden the pagoda. I reached into the drawer and gathered the wooden box to me.

"The pagoda," I said.

It seemed unimportant to him. He was intent only with getting me downstairs safely. Never before had I felt such security and such a sense of being loved and cared for. And to think I almost threw it all away because I was afraid to trust him.

Even in my worn state of mind I realized briefly that my insecurities had always been in the way of my relationship with Nicholas. I had not been able to believe that anyone, certainly not a man like Nicholas, could ever love me. And so I'd thrown all the obstacles and doubts I could in our pathway, even imagining some that did not exist.

As Nicholas carried me to our bedroom, he whispered soft words to me all the while . . . comforting, soothing words. I could not understand exactly what he said, but the nuance was there so I had no doubt about his meaning.

"Nicholas, I'm fine," I told him as he placed me gently on the bed. "I don't need to go to bed. I'm not ill."

"I know," he whispered, his voice husky with emotions. He pushed my hair back from my forehead and searched my face as if he'd never seen me before. "But indulge me, won't you? I almost lost you tonight." His eyes were bright and I was stunned to see the glitter of tears hidden there.

"I'm going downstairs and see to Lesley, and find Eric's body," he added in a quiet tone.

"I'll be all right. You go," I insisted, reaching to touch his face. I could feel the roughness of a day's growth of beard and saw tiny lines of fatigue beside his mouth. He seemed always so strong and invincible that these small telltale signs of weariness tugged at my heart. My eyes shimmered with tears and I knew I could endure almost anything on earth except this man's destruction. I made a silent vow then that nothing would ever cause me to doubt him again.

Carefully I placed the pagoda in the drawer of the night table. Somehow its presence, as exquisite as it was, held little meaning now in relation to what I had gained this night.

I had not meant to sleep after he left, was certain, in fact, that I could not. But it must have been hours later when Nicholas returned and I was sleeping soundly. I felt him touch me softly before he turned off the light and came to bed. I wanted to talk, tried to protest that I was awake.

"Shhh," he said, holding me close as he quieted me. "Rest now. Tomorrow we'll talk."

Chapter XXIII

I don't think either of us stirred during the night and I was surprised when I woke feeling as well as I did.

The wind had risen while we slept and was now a constant roar about the windows and the walls of the house. It was not the sound of the wind that woke me, however.

Amy was busily placing covered dishes of food on the table before the fireplace. The fire burned high in the chimney, its crackling roar a pleasant sound in the room.

"Amy?" I said, sitting up in bed.

"Oh, I'm sorry, ma'am. I tried to be quiet. Mrs. Hayne just insisted that everything be perfect for you this morning. After last night . . ." She hesitated, and I knew what she was thinking.

"I'm sorry, ma'am, for telling Mr. Roberts . . . but he spoke as if he already knew."

"It's all right, Amy. I understand," I assured her. "I know how persuasive he could be. So, everyone has heard about last night?"

"Yes, ma'am," she said. "And 'tis hard to believe too!"

"Yes."

"I brought your bag back upstairs, ma'am," she said quietly. "Well, there's hot water in the pitcher and I'll be right outside if you need anything else. Then I imagine Mrs. Hayne will be in to see you. She's been most nearly worried out of her mind. Says she won't rest until she's seen the both of you for herself."

I smiled at Amy's chatter. It made me feel normal just hearing her again. I sighed and watched as she busied herself about putting everything in order.

"Thank you, Amy!" Nicholas's groaned words of dismissal were muffled against his pillow. I recognized the hint of amusement in his voice.

"Oh . . . yessir. I'm goin'!" she said, turning to leave.

"Nicholas," I scolded after she had gone, "she's just full of spirit."

"Yes, but I was afraid that 'spirit' might keep me in bed all day," he laughed.

He sat up, his hand reaching for me, caressing my arms. "How do you feel this morning?"

"Remarkably well," I answered. "And I'm ashamed to admit how happy I am."

"There's no need to be," he assured me. "It's time you realized that you deserve to be happy."

"I was so worried about you, Nicholas. The past few days have been terribly hard and last night you looked tired."

He took a long breath and his eyes darkened with some hidden pain.

"I'm sorry you had to find out about your father this way." He reached out to stroke my hair. "But you still haven't told me why you were so upset with me yesterday before the funeral."

"I . . . I wasn't. It was just Lesley and, of course, Millie's death. I was distracted."

He could not hide the disappointment that lingered in his eyes before he looked away from me. I couldn't hurt him again, couldn't let him know I had actually suspected him of having something to do with my father's death.

I knew my answer did not satisfy him, but he did not push me. Instead we both made a silent vow to dismiss the sadness for awhile.

We sat down at the table and tried to forget everything that had happened in the last few days. We laughed as we saw Amy's hearty breakfast. She had brought more food than four grown men could eat. Rich slabs of ham, scrambled eggs surrounded by rich buttery biscuits, crisp brown waffles and a pitcher of warm syrup. For the first time in days I was hungry.

"I don't think I've ever seen you eat so much, my darling wife," Nicholas teased.

"And I, dear husband, thought you disliked heavy meals."

We were still laughing when Mrs. Hayne was wheeled into the room by Ona. She sat looking at us, her face puzzled and confused that we could be laughing.

"You're both all right?" she said. Her pale hands shook as she reached for Nicholas and I was touched when he took her hand and kissed it. He smiled, reassuring her we were both fine.

"Don't be alarmed, Mother—it's all over now. All the accidents and the mysteries make sense now."

"Then it was Eric . . . and Lesley?" Her hand clutched at her silk robe. "Why, I just cannot believe such a horrible thing has happened, and right here in my own home!"

"Move here, Mother, closer to the fire. I'll tell you and Victoria everything I learned from Lesley last night."

Suddenly I was very alert. My curiosity had been eating away at me since we woke, but I had not wanted to push Nicholas if he were not ready to talk about it. There had been a certain look about him, a reluctance, perhaps, to admit how wrong he had been about Lesley.

Ona stood back by the door and this time when I smiled at him he returned the gesture. "Ona, would you like some breakfast?" I asked.

"No, Missy. Ona already had breakfast."

His face was so sweet and kind that I wondered how I could have mistaken his watchfulness as sinister or threatening. Nicholas had even told me what a gentle man Ona was. I had been so blind, so unable to trust anyone, that I could not see the truth.

When Mrs. Hayne was comfortably seated, I poured her a cup of tea. We both sat almost breathlessly waiting for Nicholas to begin.

"Last night, I sent Vickers and one of the men from the stables to the mainland for the sheriff and coroner. While they were gone I spoke with Lesley for a long while. She was strangely cooperative."

"And she confessed?" I asked. "To trapping Millie and Tad in the cave?"

"She claims it was Eric," he said. "And how can we disprove that now?"

"But why would anyone possibly want to harm Tad or Millie?" Mrs. Hayne asked.

"It was Millie they were after. Tad already told us that Millie had caught someone searching Victoria's room while we were away. It must have been Lesley or Eric. I think Millie suspected that it was also Lesley who attacked Victoria on the stairway and locked her out on the balcony during the storm. Perhaps she accused Lesley of as much that day. We probably will never know for certain. When I asked Lesley, she became vague about Millie. After all, it's one thing to be accused of attacking someone, or of thievery, but murder is something else. So, she was not about to confess that. As for Tad . . . I think he was just a victim of circumstances."

"But it certainly proves how far they were willing to go to recover the pagoda," I said.

"Yes, that's it exactly," Nicholas said. "Lesley told me she knew Anthony had hidden the pagoda, but she didn't know where. She'd known him for years, you know . . . met him in Charleston at Madam Polignac's."

"A theatre?" I asked.

He paused oddly and smiled rather crookedly at me. His mother answered the question.

"A bordello!" she scoffed, her eyebrows raised haughtily. "Go on."

"He visited her there for years and also gambled there. Much of the money he won was given to Lesley and it seemed she demanded more and more as time went on. Your father fancied himself in love with her and I suppose he thought he could buy her love in some way." He looked at me as if to make an apology for my father's behavior.

"I know," I said. "He wrote about Lesley in his journal. Not where he met her, just that he was in love with her. It was obvious how insecure he was about her."

"His journal?" Mrs. Hayne asked. "Did he say anything else . . . about anyone?" She had become very agitated and I knew she was wondering if he had written about Frances.

I didn't know what to say, or how much Nicholas knew. Hesitantly I looked at him. He seemed greatly disinterested, but his eyes were alert, waiting just as impatiently as Mrs. Hayne, I thought.

"Go ahead, Victoria," he said softly. "I think I already know what you're so reluctant to say. It's time it came out anyhow."

Mrs. Hayne stared at him, but she did not refute what he said; I took a deep breath and began.

"He said Frances was his daughter." I said the words quietly. "My half sister."

"Oh." Mrs. Hayne let out a sigh. "He finally acknowledged it." Her eyes filled with tears as she spoke, but there was a tremulous smile upon her lips.

As I watched Nicholas I could see plainly that he was not shocked. "You knew?" I asked.

"Yes. Your father told me last year when we made the transaction for Ashford Place. His world was falling apart and I suppose he needed someone to talk to. We were friends."

Mrs. Hayne seemed finally to realize the significance of our odd conversation.

"Oh, son, I'm sorry. I had not thought how you would feel. I know I've made such a terrible mess of our lives—all because of Anthony Ancona!" The bitterness was still there as she spoke his name.

"Mother, was it really because of him . . . or was it because you became obsessed with having your way?"

It was the only time I'd heard him speak so coolly or so critically to his mother. Mrs. Hayne was stunned by his words. She blinked, her mouth moving soundlessly. Then she shook her head slowly as she spoke his name, holding her hand toward him imploringly.

"I'm sorry, Mother. I know you're not well, but can't you see what you've done to Franny? Your own daughter? And what of Victoria? Was she just another pawn in your game of revenge?" His eyes were hard now and cold as he confronted her. "Can't you see how you've wasted so much of your life because of some injustice you thought was done you?"

But Denise Hayne was not one to be penitent, and if Nicholas's words penetrated, she gave no indication. Instead she sat thoughtfully as if trying to understand his meaning.

"I have the pagoda, Mrs. Hayne. I'd planned to return it to you. You were right, my father did take it. He mentioned in the journal where it was hidden." I wanted to change the subject, for it was too painful for all of us. I could not imagine how we would tell Frances.

Mrs. Hayne sighed rather heavily and looked at me with a mixture of sympathy and disbelief. "What else did he say in this . . . journal?"

"He knew Lesley was seeing someone else, evidently she was with him at Ashford Place then. Father seemed to be on the brink of a breakdown. I could see the desperation in every word he wrote." I looked away from Nicholas for I hoped he would never know the thing of which I suspected him. "He overhead Lesley and . . . and Eric once, only a few days before he died. He said the man, Lesley's . . . that is, Eric, threatened to kill him."

A light flickered in Nicholas's blue eyes and he reached forward, lifting my chin, looking searchingly into my eyes. It was as if something had suddenly become clear to him.

"But you only realized last night on the rooftop that it was Eric, didn't you?" he asked quietly.

"I . . . Yes, Father didn't say in the diary who the man was."

"So, that's it," he said beneath his breath. "And you . . . Who did you think this man was? This man who threatened to kill your father, the one you thought was Lesley's lover?" His words were gentle but insistent and I knew it was no use to lie to him. He was beginning to put together enough to understand why I had been so troubled.

"You, Nicholas. I'm sorry, but I thought it was you." My voice could barely be heard as I spoke, but I looked steadily into his eyes, wanting him to see how sorry I was that I had doubted him.

His breath seemed to leave him almost as if he'd been hit in the stomach. I could see the anger and the pain in his cobalt eyes. He frowned and gave his head a shake, looking at me as if I'd slapped him.

"Nicholas?" his mother cried. "Why on earth would you ever suspect Nicholas? I mean it was perfectly obvious how Lesley felt about him but—" She stopped then, seeing the closed look on her son's face. "Oh, I've done it again. Blundered into someone else's business as usual." For a moment she looked truly dejected. "I've hurt you both so much, and Frances. I'm sorry, truly I am. I don't mean to be such a crotchety old woman, bitter at everyone and everything."

"It's all right, Mrs. Hayne," I said.

"No, it's not! It's not all right! I've lived most of my life wanting something . . . someone I could not have. Someone of half my husband's worth—forgive me for saying so, dear. But never mind that, I've hurt my daughter terribly. Even when I realized years ago it was John I should have loved, it was too late, the pattern of hostility was already established between Anthony and myself and I could not let go of it. And you were right, I intended to use Victoria as well."

Neither Nicholas or I spoke as she seemed to need to confess, to vent her anger and frustration.

"But you two managed to turn the tide against me, didn't you? You actually fell in love!"

Nicholas and I only looked at each other, smiling, for she was right.

"So perhaps I did not do so badly, did I?"

"I hate to tell you this, Mother, but you had nothing to do with our falling in love. We did that very well on our own." Nicholas smiled crookedly at her.

She reached out and caressed his cheek. "Nicky, do

you think it's too late for a meddling old fool to change?" she asked, not solemn and contrite.

"And which old fool is that?" he said in a quiet, easy manner.

She smiled, tears again filling her blue eyes. "I *am* going to try, Nicky. It's not too late for me to change. You know very well I can do it!" She lifted her chin and threw back her shoulders with a gesture of pride.

Nicholas reached for her hand and regarded her seriously. "I know you can, Mother . . . and I hope for Franny's sake you will."

She drew herself up straighter in the chair and lifted her eyebrows with determination. She turned to me. "Now, my dear, tell me where the pagoda was hidden."

"There was a riddle in the journal. Father wrote in there that he planned to take it, just as you all thought." My voice faltered for it was still hard for me to acknowledge that. "Rather than take it with him, he hid it in the study where Captain Hayne once kept it. He intended to come back for it later. He was convinced he had to take Lesley away, out of Eric's reach. The pagoda, once it was sold, would afford him a way of doing that, but he died before—"

"Yes . . ." she said, looking at me with sympathy.

"What your father's journal did not tell you, darling, was that Lesley and Eric knew your father planned to take the pagoda. In fact, she urged Anthony to steal it. Anthony did not know that once he brought it to her, Eric planned to kill him. Then she and Eric would be free to leave, taking the treasure and no one would ever be the wiser. There would not even be a reason to suspect them."

"I felt all along his death was no accident," I said. I could not keep the tremor from my lips as I spoke.

"But if Anthony did not have the pagoda that night,

why did they kill him?" Mrs. Hayne asked.

"There was a confrontation that evening between Eric and Anthony. Lesley thought he was lying about the pagoda. There was a fight and suddenly your father was dead. They tried to make it look like an accident. I'm sorry, Victoria. I know it's upsetting to hear all the gruesome details."

"No, no. I realize now how very little I really knew about my father. He was not the man I thought he was."

"He was a desperate man, my dear," Mrs. Hayne said. "And desperate men sometimes do foolish things. And while we're on the subject, there is something else I want to tell you, something Nicholas would probably never confess to but I think you should know."

"Mother . . ." Nicholas cautioned.

"No, Nicholas. I'm going to tell her." She turned to me. "Your father lost so much. He became obsessed with the game, with recouping his losses, and it seemed he had time for nothing . . . or no one. So it was Nicholas who saw to your tuition and sent the beautiful clothes, the extra money."

I turned suddenly to Nicholas, my eyes wide with surprise.

"When your father gave Ashford Place to Nicholas for the money he had stolen from the company, Nicholas put the deed back in a trust for you until you came of age. Why, he even hired Lesley as a favor to Anthony. We were all fooled by that little minx."

"Nicholas . . ." I said, looking into his eyes. He smiled so sweetly at me that I wondered how I could ever have doubted his love. It was there to see each time I looked at him.

"Speaking of Lesley, what will happen to her now?" Mrs. Hayne asked.

"I can't really say," he replied. "It will depend on

whether or not the jury believes she was actually involved in the murders. I imagine she will try to persuade them that she was only an innocent victim, used by Roberts. And he cannot defend himself."

"We can only pray that the jurors will see through her act," Mrs. Hayne replied. "Well! I'm only thankful it's over and we can get back to normal . . . but better . . . I promise." She smiled at both of us. "But for now, I think I shall return to bed."

She was thoughtful for a moment, making no effort to leave. "Children, when we go down to lunch, I'm going to tell Frances everything. I'd like it if you could both be with me." For a moment I thought I actually saw a hint of fear in her eyes, and I felt sorry for her. She too had lost so much.

"Of course we will," I answered, looking at Nicholas as he nodded his approval.

"Ona," she said, beckoning him to her.

After she had gone we sat for a moment in silence.

"All those things, Nicholas: the Gullah doll, the ghost at our dinner party—that was Eric too?"

"I wondered about that, for I recall seeing Eric inside that night. According to Lesley, he hired one of the sailors from the docks to help search for the pagoda. If, in the process, he strengthened the rumors about a ghost, that was all the better. And, of course, Lesley hoped to frighten you away, especially when you determined to find the treasure on your own. She didn't count on your stubbornness," he said with affection.

Nicholas pulled me to my feet and to the windows that faced the sea. The fierce wind-tossed waves crashed heavily onto the shore. The morning sky had grown dark, heavy with clouds that were almost black. We could feel the cold air seeping through the glass panes.

"It's going to snow," Nicholas said quietly, looking

up to the sky.

"Really? I asked. "How do you know? Isn't that a rarity here?"

"Trust me," he said lightly.

As he searched my face I knew his words had a much deeper meaning.

"I do, my love. Oh, I do. How can I explain to you all the things I've been feeling? All the misunderstandings that have caused us both so much pain? I don't know why it was so hard for me to trust, but I want you to believe I never meant to hurt you."

"I want to know everything, Victoria. All your doubts, every question you have. I want to prove to you no matter how long it takes how very much I love you."

"I know you love me, Nicholas. I know that now. But there are emotions, from long ago . . . things I need to sort out in my own mind. I need some time . . . just awhile, before I can talk about everything." I had to look away from his eyes and the pain I saw there.

"I understand," he said quietly, turning to look out to sea.

"Don't give up on me, Nicholas," I said. I could not bear to see him that way, hurt and alone. It was not what I had intended. And his patience moved me, made me want more than ever to trust him completely and trust in our love. And I would. I knew without a doubt that one day soon it would happen. First, though, I needed to forget and forgive my father for the hurt his rejection had caused.

I put my arms about Nicholas's waist, resting my head against his broad back.

"I love you so much, Nicholas . . . loved you the first moment I saw you here at Moonwatch. But that love is nothing compared to what I feel for you now. I have never met a man like you—so gentle and kind, and yet so strong. Be patient with me, my darling. You are everything to me."

He turned then into my arms and I saw the light returning to his eyes. "Forever, if you need me to be," he replied.

Then he looked at me oddly. "When you thought I had betrayed Anthony, did you still love me?"

"Yes," I whispered. "I was so ashamed, so confused that I could love you believing what I did, and it tore me apart. I was convinced there was nothing for me to do except leave, but I could not do it. I should have listened to my heart all along."

He pulled me fiercely to him as if he would never let me go. Then he took my face gently between his hands.

"Marry, me, Victoria," he said.

I laughed and looked at him oddly. "But . . . we are married."

"Marry me again . . . in the spring aboard the *Galatea.* We'll take Tad with us, and Ona if he wishes. We'll cruise to the sunny islands. I'll show you exotic flowers and beautiful wild birds—places where life is bright and carefree!" He hugged me tightly, smiling down at my surprised expression. I'd never seen him this way and it delighted me.

"Yes, Nicholas," I said. "I will marry you again. Over and over . . . a hundred times!" I laughed.

He kissed me then, his lips sweet and warm with the promise of springtime. And when we looked back out toward the stormy waters of the Atlantic, the snow had begun to fall—large snowy flakes that descended upon the house at Cape Fear, covering its dark exterior with a soft, cleansing blanket of white.

Epilogue

December 25, 1871

I loved this time of year, when the chill of winter could be felt in the sea breeze. I loved the way the winds whipped across the sand and tossed the waves into a misty spray. It was early morning and I wanted to be alone to think before our hetic Christmas day began.

I reflected upon those early days at Moonwatch and my burgeoning love for Nicholas. I smiled as I recalled my feelings, so uncertain, so desperate, so afraid of losing the man who was growing more precious to me each day.

I stopped and looked out to sea, at the deep blue water, so much like his eyes, so ever-changing. They could be sometimes calm and serene, and the next moment stormy . . . dangerous. I felt a tingle move over me and I laughed. "Oh, Nicholas, my love," I whispered to the water, "will you always do this to me, I wonder?"

It was Nicholas who had eased tensions at Moonwatch those first days after Eric Robert's death and the revelations that followed. And it was Nicholas who had tried to comfort Frances.

I'll never forget the hurt in Frances's eyes the day her mother told her the truth, for she had adored John Hayne, the man she thought was her father. She could not have despised anyone more than she did Anthony Ancona. And to hear that he was her real father was a terrible blow. My heart went out to her, but I dared not touch her, or offer her comfort. She had looked at me then with a sense of wonder, but she said nothing.

I could see in the following days and weeks that she was trying hard to come to grips with this new situation in a calm and reasonable manner. On that first Christmas, her gift to me was a small gold ring with two entwined hearts, and a card that read: "To my dear sister Victoria."

Of course we'd always had one thing in common, our love for Nicholas and Tad. Now there was another, even more binding reason for us to become friends . . . and we did.

Just as Nicholas wished, we repeated our wedding vows in the spring of '71 aboard the *Galatea*. It was a glorious trip to the south Atlantic and the islands where Ona was born. Tad had loved every moment of it, and grew into quite an accomplished sailor.

It was on our trip that Ona met Melina, a beautiful dark-haired native of the islands. I think they fell in love as swiftly as Nicholas and I had, but it was a bittersweet meeting for all of us at Moonwatch, for while we were happy for Ona, we were also saddened when he decided later to return to Jamaica and marry the lovely Melina. It wasn't the same without him.

Our friend David Murrell graciously agreed to look after the household while we were gone. In him, Frances found a kind and sympathetic listener, and one who helped her to forget the past and try to forgive her mother. Before long, she had overcome almost completely the distance between them.

Although Denise Hayne has tried hard, there are still times when she is obstinate and overbearing, times when she tries desperately to run all our lives in the way that would most suit her. But she is Nicholas's mother and I know he loves her. And that love does not threaten in any way what we have together. So, I've made my peace with Mrs. Hayne.

Lesley was convicted as an accessory in the murder of my father and of Millie. Had she been a man she would no doubt have been hanged. As it is, she is in prison where she will spend the remainder of her life.

"Victoria!" I could see Tad running toward me from the house. How tall he had grown. He was becoming as handsome as his uncle.

"Yes, Tad," I answered. "What is it?"

"Guess what? Mother and David are to be married—he gave her a ring for Christmas! They want you to come right away!"

I smiled, although it was no real surprise to me. I told Frances long ago what a wonderful husband he would be. And when we had come home from our trip last spring I did not miss the warm looks and smiles they exchanged.

"Well, it's about time!" I laughed. But I knew, even if Tad did not, that David had waited until he was sure that Frances's son would welcome him. And the light that shone in Tad's eyes left little doubt about that decision.

"Tell them I'll be right in, Tad." As he ran back to the house I thought again of how very much I loved him. He would always have a special place in my life.

When I turned back toward the ocean for one last look before going inside, I saw a tall, familiar figure walking toward me. His confident stride and athletic grace still had the power to make my heart flutter crazily in my throat. Nicholas, who had taught me with sweet patience and understanding what love really was.

"Nicholas," I said, running happily to meet him.

He took me in his arms and kissed me slowly, sweetly as if we had not just breakfasted together moments ago.

"I wondered where you had run to. Are you cold?"

"No," I said, looking into his dark blue eyes. "Not anymore."

"What was it you wanted to tell me earlier?" he asked.

"I have an early Christmas gift for you," I answered.

I took a deep breath and smiled, watching his eyes carefully. I did not want to miss the spark of happiness I knew I would see there when I told him. It was the final affirmation of our mutual love—this child that I carried.

I looked at Moonwatch, the house I'd once thought so ominous. It seemed to glow now in the early morning light and there was no longer any fear within me.

It was our home, Nicholas's and mine, and now when summer came our dreams would be complete. The next generation of Moonwatch was beginning.